MIDNIGHT
CHAMPAGNE

MIDNIGHT CHAMPAGNE

A. Manette Ansay

ORION

First published in Great Britain in 2001 by Orion,
an imprint of the Orion Publishing Group Ltd

A CIP catalogue record for this book is available
from the British Library.

'Too Fat Polka'. Words and music by Ross MacLean and Arthur Richardson.
Copyright 1947 Shapiro, Burnstein and Company, Inc., New York.
Copyright renewed. International copyright secured.
All rights reserved. Used by permission.

Printed in Great Britain by
Clays Ltd, St Ives plc

The Orion Publishing Group Ltd
Orion House
5 Upper Saint Martin's Lane
London, WC2H 9EA

for Diane Northam
for Amanda Rauth Haar

Contents

If you fear loneliness, then marriage is not for you.

—ANTON CHEKHOV

CEREMONY

VALENTINE'S Day. Mid-afternoon. A crossroads thirty miles north of the Illinois line, each highway straight as a stickpin holding fast a tidy seam. Who can't describe the American heartland, those glorious patchwork quilts of corn and wheat? But this is deep winter, the sun pale as ice. The fields are the featureless white of amnesia. Fence posts and windbreaks divide them like the clean lines of desire. And right smack in the middle of it all sits the Great Lakes Chapel and Hideaway Lodge, mired in a pool of plowed asphalt.

At a glance, the Chapel doesn't look so bad: big-shouldered old house with twin dormers overlooking the parking lot, red-brick chimney, lace curtains thick as cobwebs in the windows. After checking in at the lobby, guests zig and zag along an asphalt path until they reach the Hideaway Lodge, a long, low structure housing thirty-six suites—some with peekaboo views of Lake Michigan—divided by a shotgun hall. All are decorated according to theme: Caribbean Holiday, Night in Tunisia, Mountain Vista, Paradise. But locals still remember the Chapel and Lodge as the notorious dance hall and roadhouse it once was, operating without censure until 1959 when its proprietress, a woman named Gretel Fame, was murdered by a jealous lover. People who spend the night here are usually from Milwaukee and Chicago: tourists looking for a little local flavor, adulterers with prerehearsed alibis, couples lugging the weight of their marriages between them like so many stickered steamer trunks. Couples who get married here are generally those (so the saying goes) too young to know or old enough to know better: the brides' beauty spelled out in eyeliner and whipped-topping hair; the grooms sporting ruddy, alcoholic noses and flashing too much cash.

What else about this crossroads catches the eye? Not much. A stretch of struggling businesses known as Bittner's Plaza: a discount liquor store, a minimart, a pizza parlor run by two elderly German sisters. A few houses, no more than a dozen, spaced as neatly as buttons. A billboard advertising the Great Lakes Chapel and Hideaway Lodge's Fabulous Hot Tub Suites: a handsome man and woman smile in a lazy, self-satisfied way, the woman's breasts caressed by a burst of steam. Every few years, crossroads residents join forces with various church groups, perhaps an aspiring politician or two, and present Ralph Bamberger—owner of the Chapel—with a petition regarding that billboard. Bamberger files these and other petitions in the circular file. Opposition is the nature of business; he doesn't let it bother him too much. A man can't expect that everybody will throw flowers at his feet all the time.

What yanks his bobber is how often bullet holes have scarred the billboard couple's complexions like a rash. Each time, he pays good money to have everything repaired. What else can he do? Bullet holes don't make the right impression on potential clients. Bullet holes don't fit with the storybook wedding Bamberger helps them imagine when they all sit down together in his posh planning parlor off the lobby: the bride- and groom-to-be, sometimes their parents, more likely their grown children, and all of their wallets fat as plums.

His daughter, Emily—both caterer and consultant—takes notes as Bamberger explains the options. Marriage is a challenge, that's a fact, he'll say. So you might as well start things off on the right foot.

Don't I know it, the groom-to-be might say. *My first wife, she never forgave me that quick trip to the courthouse. Never mind we went to Hawaii afterward . . .*

I've been around the block a time or two, the bride might say, *I don't deny it. But I'm turning over this new leaf, see? This time I want everything traditional, I want the wedding June Cleaver dreamed about . . .*

I want to invite every one of my friends who said this would never work out . . .

I want to invite my ex, let him see what he's missing . . .

Bamberger has heard it all before, and it means pretty much the same thing. They are young and afraid; they are not so young and afraid. They've screwed up in the past, but damn it, they still have hope. And they'll pay whatever it might cost to set that hope, like the precious stone it is, into an appropriate 24k setting. So Bamberger shows them through the lobby and into the ballroom, where guests will first observe the ceremony and, later, dance to celebrate it. The ballroom is an airy restoration: Gothic windows, a stage for the house band, everything outlined in strings of crisp, white lights. Golden cherubs, the size of human infants, hang suspended around a massive chandelier. At the front of the room, an exposed stairway leads to a balcony; this is the spot where, during the dance hall's glory days, men stood to choose from the ladies dancing on the floor below. The hallway behind him led to small rooms available by the quarter hour. Now these same rooms are elegant dressing rooms: HIS to the left, HERS to the right. Rose-scented hand lotion in the dispensers. Padded toilet seats and potpourri. Full-length mirrors and plush red rugs, even a small TV.

And a secret—a narrow service elevator built into an expanded dumbwaiter shaft. Once, the shaft had been concealed, used only during police raids, when Gretel Fame and the luckier of her ladies lowered themselves into the basement, one by one, and escaped through the root-cellar door. Now the basement is a game room. Just before the ceremony, the bride takes the elevator down from her dressing room, weaves her way between the pool table and pin-ball machines, then climbs the public stairwell that returns her to the lobby. When the "Wedding March" begins to play, she enters at the back of the ballroom, surprising unsuspecting guests whose eyes are fixed on the balcony.

Is everybody happy so far? Does everybody like what they see? Then it's on to the dining room just beyond the ballroom, accessed through arched doorways, one on either side of the balcony stairs. Walk to the left or the right—take your pick! For here is yet another surprise: the original mahogany bar, its marble top intact. The groom imagines his aging buddies coveting the bride from the tall bar stools. The bride envisions the long tables filled with members of her family, and everyone getting along *so* beautifully: Mother speaking charitably with Father's new wife; Sister downplaying her own successful marriage; Brother, for once, laying off the politics. And no one making jokes about déjà vu, comparing this wedding to the last, now *he* was a dud, they all saw that one coming and if only she had listened—

Now, now. There will be none of that. For the room is softly lit, like a church. The windows look out upon a quiet patio and the shaggy windbreak of pines. Through the trees, the bride and groom can see the little path leading toward the Lodge, where they'll spend the first night of their married lives in a king-size, heart-shaped bed. There will be champagne in a small refrigerator, chocolates and hot-house strawberries in a basket, thick white terrycloth robes. Yes, this is the place, this is exactly what they've been looking for, the bride and groom are fully prepared to make a deposit right away!

Only let them snap a few more pictures. Let them ask Emily yet another question about the cake. Poor girl—she's clearly on the wrong side of thirty, and still no prospects. What a shame. The bride and groom clasp hands gratefully. It's a terrible thing, to be alone. They stand one last time beneath the balcony, imagine themselves mounting those winding stairs before most of the people they love and more than a few they don't. Before full-blown ghosts of past disasters and new ghosts clamoring to be born. Before the ancient flourishing grief between women and men. Still, they will promise, without hesitation, to love and honor and cherish in richness and poverty, sickness and health, speaking in time with the rhythm of their hearts: I do, I do, I do.

ELMER Liesgang usually wasn't inclined to cast stones. If a couple wanted to get married in an old whorehouse, well, let them. He didn't pretend to understand half of what went on in the world these days. But this wasn't just another Chapel wedding, unrecognized by any church. This was the wedding of his oldest child, April, just twenty-two years old, with a newly minted college degree and her whole life still ahead of her. It was unthinkable. It was unbearable. And it was happening, like any accident, in terrible slow motion. Angrily, he paced the length of the lobby, ignoring the attempts of the desk clerk to engage him in friendly conversation. Outside, a light snow had started to fall. Most of the guests had already been seated, but as the light dimmed to an uneasy twilight, those who had not secured reservations at the Lodge were slipping out of the ballroom, one by one, to phone the nearby Budgetel. The reception was scheduled for five o'clock, immediately after the ceremony. At six-thirty, there'd be a sit-down supper; at eight o'clock, a dance. Ten-thirty bouquet toss. Midnight champagne. Nobody wanted to get stuck driving home in a winter storm.

Elmer checked his watch: already ten past four. He opened the door leading to the game room, in case April was waiting downstairs. She wasn't. Perhaps she was having second thoughts. Perhaps she had realized she was making a mistake she'd regret for the rest of her life. Perhaps her mother had managed to talk some sense—but no. Through the ballroom doorway, he could see Mary Fran chattering amicably, even happily, with the groom. Caleb Shannon had grown up in Nashville: his father, a minister, had founded a church called the New Life Christian Joy Fellowship. Caleb was twenty-six years old. He had red, wiry hair and freckled skin, dimples so deep they looked as if they'd been made with a nail set. Other than these features, he seemed like any other young man you might see on the street and not particularly notice. There was, of course, his Southern accent, which Elmer understood was something women found attractive. It allowed him to say things like *Yes, ma'am* and *No, sir* without the slightest hint of condescension. He did not consider himself particularly religious. He liked to cook. He never watched TV. Sports? Well, he'd played some tennis as a kid. These were the facts, and the facts explained nothing. The couple had been dating for fourteen weeks, sharing Caleb's condo for ten.

There'd been only one bedroom in Caleb's condo. There'd been only one bed in the bedroom. Up until his surprise visit, Elmer had been willing to give April the benefit of the doubt. Had he seen a small cot, even a sleeping bag rolled up in a corner—but no. Just the bed, a *double* bed, with a masculine pine frame. It was nothing like the twin bed with the quilted white headboard that April had claimed, only months earlier, from her bedroom at home. *This* bed reclined massively beneath one of April's paintings—something new—which depicted the suggestive shapes of a man and woman ensnared within a purple web. Stepping closer, he squinted at the title.

Lovers.

There could be no doubt after that.

So what had gone wrong? Elmer didn't understand. After a protracted and theatrical adolescence, April had pulled herself hand over hand into adulthood, and he'd dared to hope that she'd really turned out okay. True, she'd broken off her long-standing engagement to Barney Lohr—a disappointment to everyone—but she'd redeemed herself by graduating from UW-Madison with highest honors (and the art department's annual prize) and moving to Minneapolis, where she'd landed a job at a cooperative gallery. She'd recently sold two of her own paintings to museums, each for a fair amount of cash; new work was on display in group exhibitions in Chicago, Indianapolis, and Louisville. She'd quit smoking. She'd even removed her nose ring and allowed that distressing little hole to close. She came home to visit less and less, though when she did, she spoke energetically about her responsibilities at the gallery, describing in bright, laborious detail the squabbles between the directors, the outrageous behavior of the other artists, the ways in which the "exposure" was helping her gain perspective on her own work.

Looking back, Elmer could only wish that he'd paid closer attention during those visits, rather than opening the *Journal-Sentinel* and leaving Mary Fran to supply the *uh-huhs* and *oh, reallys*. For the gallery was where she had met her new fiancé. He'd arrived in search of paintings to liven up the walls of Maple, Curry, Pederson and Tauschek, the law firm where he'd worked for the past five years. Not as a lawyer, either—now, *that* Elmer might have understood. But no, Caleb Shannon had majored in liberal arts at a small, experimental college outside Minneapolis. In fact, he was *considering* law school. He was also *considering* a master's degree in art history, and a welding apprenticeship. The Peace Corps had also occurred to him, but he wasn't sure, he just didn't know. For now, he was happy as a company gofer, an errand man, the one to whom the lawyers handed their keys when their BMWs needed an oil change; the one who picked up their shirts from the cleaners, their prescriptions from the pharmacy; the one who brewed their coffee, fetched their lunches, arranged the flowers in the lobby, and generally made certain the office atmosphere was, in every way, a pleasant one. And that day in the gallery, when his eye had swept over countless floral bouquets and pastoral landscapes to rest upon one of April's own bright, turbulent paintings, she had known—just like that—he was the one.

Just like that. Elmer sank into one of the twin leather couches, stared up at the head of an enormous moose, which was mounted above the fireplace. He tried to gauge the expression in the creature's glassy eyes. Embarrassment, he decided. Embarrassment flecked with dread. Life was never *just like that*. It was complicated, and painful, and never the way it seemed. *Just like that* he'd gotten engaged to Mary Fran. *Just like that* he'd become a father. *Just like that* he'd woken up to discover he was yet another middle-aged man. For twenty-five years he'd worked for the city of Holly's Field, trimming the grass in summer, plowing the streets in winter, and he ran a bicycle repair shop on the side. At night, he watched TV until long after Mary Fran had gone to bed. Then he eased himself gingerly between the sheets, as if sinking into an uncomfortably warm bath.

"Are we ready?" Ralph Bamberger ducked out of the back office, fixing Elmer with a polished smile.

"Not yet, no," Elmer said, but with that, the door to the game room opened, and April stepped up into the lobby, wearing her mother's wedding dress. Hastily altered, the dress was still too big, and her small, cropped head emerged from all that fabric like a child peering out of a snowbank. The sleeves and hem were tinged with yellow, and as she turned to untwist the train—nearly dropping her bouquet—a couple of fake pearls *pinged* from the beaded bodice, bounced across the parquet floor, and disappeared.

"Sorry I'm late," she said. Her face was flushed, nervous. Not pretty—to Elmer's regret, none of his children were particularly good-looking. But today, there was something appealing, attractive even, in her excitement. "Another button popped off and I had to find a safety pin—"

"Excellent," Bamberger said, and he pointed to the ballroom door. "As soon as you hear the music, start walking down the aisle." Then he hurried back into his office. Elmer studied his daughter, saw his own dark eyes staring back. She had his narrow chin, his slight build, his long hands and feet. For once, her hair was its natural color— a dusty shade of brown—instead of blond, or black, or streaked with pink.

"Well," he said.

"A deep subject," April said. It was Mary Fran's tired line, and Elmer hated it.

He said, "Maybe down the road you'll think about a church service."

The fire in the fireplace hissed and spat.

"Look," she finally said. Her voice was matter-of-fact, resigned. "I don't expect your blessing or anything like that. But you could, you know, say something nice."

From the ballroom came the sounds of a microphone, the scratch of a tape clicking into place.

"Well," he said again.

April sighed. "There's the music," she said, and now there was nothing he could do but take her arm, guide her into the ballroom. Together, they began the long walk down the aisle toward the base of the balcony stairs where Caleb stood waiting, those dimples deep as buckshot. Elmer tried not to think about the lovely church wedding she'd have had if she'd married Barney Lohr. He tried not to think about the Chapel photographer, who walked backward just ahead of them, the bright eye of a video camera balanced on one shoulder. He tried not to think about the cherubs, fat as buzzards, patiently circling the crystal chandelier. He tried not to think about the guests, who sat in crowded rows on metal folding chairs, or the noise those chairs made—a shrill symphonic lament—as people twisted in their seats to stare out the windows at the snow piling up on their cars. Pete Lapenska, justice of the peace, waited on the balcony with all the enthusiasm of a commuter waiting for a train. He and Elmer had gone to school together. Pete had been popular, good-looking, confident. Elmer had been none of these things, and neither man had forgotten. The sight of him made Elmer's jaw pop; he tightened his grip on April's arm.

"Dad," she whispered.

Startled, he let go. Something was wrong with Mendelssohn. The familiar melody modulated into a low, erotic moan before the tape died altogether in a thunderous roll of static. They walked on in silence. A few of the guests tittered. "Give it a minute," the photographer whispered. "They'll fix it, they always do." But to everyone's amazement, Caleb turned to face the crowd and, in tones clear as a mockingbird's, he started to whistle in tune. One after another, guests joined in. By the time Elmer ferried his daughter's hand into Caleb's, everyone in the ballroom had puckered up to complete a frail, fluttering round of "Here Comes the Bride." There was applause, general laughter. April was laughing, too; she threw her arms around Caleb, who kissed her long, hard, happily, until Pete Lapenska's voice boomed down upon them like the voice of God.

"None of that till you're legal."

Elmer sank into the reserved folding chair beside Mary Fran, who was snorting into her hand. Eight-year-old Margo was giggling, too, fingering the paper flower in her hair. Only Elmer's son seemed to share his humiliation, but Stanley was a pale, wizened thirteen, and nearly always humiliated, regardless of the circumstances. Still, Elmer tried to catch his eye.

Stan stared straight ahead.

"April and Caleb," Pete Lapenska intoned, deadpan. "Approach the nuptial canopy to be conjoined."

More laughter. The pump had been primed. Even Caleb's mother released a few small, unhappy chuckles—though she blotted her lips with a handkerchief, after, as if she had tasted something bitter. The rest of Caleb's family had remained in Nashville, offering vague last-minute regrets: the distance, the weather, a rash of sudden illnesses. Corrine Shannon's only companions were two half-grown grandchildren, a boy and a girl. Their mouths, too, were set in adult smirks.

But Elmer knew, without turning around, that *his* mother wouldn't be laughing. The odor of Hilda Liesgang's disapproval was as distinctive as the odor of her corsage, which was roughly the size of a popcorn ball, made up of red roses and pink lilies. ("Call 911," Mary Fran had said when she'd first seen it. "Your mother's just been shot.") Hilda had arrived at the Chapel an hour early, carrying a box filled with candles she'd purchased at Holy Hill retreat, crepe paper flowers blessed with holy water, and a two-foot-tall hand-carved crucifix which, according to family legend, had come over on the boat from Luxembourg. While she'd Scotch-taped the flowers to the top of archways—like Elmer, she was just over six feet tall—

he'd hung the crucifix behind the nuptial canopy in place of a large, heart-shaped mirror.

Pete Lapenska had taken one look and shaken his head. The crucifix, he said, violated the nondenominational spirit of the Great Lakes Chapel. "If you want a Catholic service, Elmo, take your girl over to Saint Michael's," he'd told Elmer, and the tips of Elmer's large ears pinked with rage, for Pete knew—everybody knew—that Father Bork had refused to marry April in the church after learning that she and Caleb were, in his words, *shacking up*. There was a way around that kind of thing: a couple could agree to live apart for a while, to attend prenuptial counseling sessions, to rededicate themselves to the teachings of the Church. Or, they could have done what most people did; they could have simply lied in the first place. But April had decided it was all *too much of a hassle*—that had been exactly how she'd put it—to marry in the church. She and Caleb would simply elope. Or else stop by the courthouse. It was no big deal.

And when, at Christmastime, Elmer had treated her to a nice dinner out in order to talk about her wedding plans, to let her know how much it meant to him that she have some kind of ceremony, something witnessed and shared by family and friends, what had she gone and done? She'd taken the check he'd given her and put down a nonrefundable deposit at the Great Lakes Chapel and Hideaway Lodge. A last-minute Valentine's Day cancellation! she'd told him, phoning with the happy news. Wasn't that the luckiest thing? The bride-to-be had discovered her intended, a long-distance trucker, had a wife in another state. And the Chapel was so retro, so totally kitsch! Those tacky theme suites! Their friends would die laughing! He'd been right to insist on a wedding! It was going to be a blast!

"No crucifix," Elmer had told Pete, smiling helplessly, "no check."

"No check," Pete said, smiling, too, "no ceremony."

Hilda had finally volunteered the compromise. She'd climbed the stairs in her grand, unhurried way and draped the crucifix with a pretty silk scarf. Now, as Caleb and April climbed the narrow stairs to the balcony, fighting the bulk of the wedding dress, Elmer saw Jesus' toes peeping out, looking every bit as cold as his own toes felt in his fancy wing tips. The blessed candles—which Pete had over-looked—had been snuffed by Bamberger, who claimed they were in violation of the fire code. The anointed paper flowers mutinied as soon as the guests arrived, drifting down from the archways. Children had scavenged for them, fought for them, carried them away like trophies. Elmer had watched unresisting as these last scraps of his hope were scattered, piece by piece. He'd wanted something better for April, something blessed, something of another world. Because this world, well, it could only disappoint you. Nothing was ever what you thought you'd been promised. Nothing was ever quite enough. Here he was, surrounded by relatives and friends, his wife, their children, and he'd never in his life felt so lonely.

He uncrossed his legs, crossed them again; his folding chair yipped twice. Mary Fran put a strong hand on his knee.

"Done is done," she told him. "So you might as well just relax."

MARGO Liesgang was small for a third grader, but she was strong, and quick to fight dirty. The other kids called her Jaws. Just before the ceremony, she'd managed to swipe a blessed flower from the Tennessee girl, who was foolish enough to try and snatch it back. So Margo bit her on the arm; the Wisconsin kids chanted the theme from *Jaws*—*DA-dum; da-dum DA-dum; Dum-dum-Dum-dum-Dum-dum-Dum-dum*—until adults swooped in to break things up. "I *warned* you she's an animal," Margo's cousin Mickey told the Tennessee girl, and Margo felt her face flush with pride. Under Mary Fran's stern gaze, she'd apologized—but indifferently. The girl's name was *Lacey,* which wasn't even a name. Her brother's name was *Anderson,* which was weird. Both of them talked funny, like the groom, like famous singers and people on TV. Margo would have no qualms about biting again, should the situation require it.

Now she felt like someone in a beauty magazine with Lacey's flower tucked behind her ear and April's sweet lipstick stiff on her lips. She was wearing her first pair of grown-up-style shoes: peach-colored, with a half-inch square-cut heel. Her curly hair had been combed, pinned, and sprayed into something Mary Fran called a *chignon.* Every now and then Margo shook her head hard to make sure it was still there. Poor April didn't have a chignon. Her hair looked the same as it had since she'd moved to Minneapolis— cropped short like a boy's—and her face had broken out, she said, from *the stress.* She didn't even have an engagement ring. Her dress, which had been stored in the basement for years, smelled like the sump pump, and fresh starch, and old newspapers.

"It doesn't matter," April had said. "I just wish we had eloped the way we wanted to." This was just before the ceremony, when she and Margo and Mary Fran were crowded into the little bathroom off the dressing room upstairs. "*Dad* was the one who wanted all this foolishness. *Dad* was the one who said any kind of ceremony would be better than nothing at all." April was running a brush through what was left of her hair—*snap, snap, snap.* "But no matter what I do, it *still* isn't good enough. I mean, where did he expect me to make reservations with just a few weeks' notice—the Taj fucking Mahal? Well, I'm sorry he's pissed. I'm sorry I don't feel like kissing the pope's wrinkled ass."

Then she said a few more things that Margo wished Mary Fran

would repeat, because Mary Fran had to pay Margo five dollars each time Margo heard her curse. But all Mary Fran said was, "Done is done," and April said, "Would you please stop saying that?" and Mary Fran said, "Well, honey, I just don't know what else to say."

The whole time they were arguing, Margo had been crawling around on the floor, collecting the pearls that were falling off April's dress. How proud she was to stand up and present her sister with a warm handful! But April accepted them indifferently, impatiently. "They're just beads, Margo," she said. "They're fake." And with that, she'd tossed them into the wastepaper basket.

Now, as a few more beads fell like raindrops from the balcony, Margo wondered how April could be *certain* that a couple of real pearls weren't mixed in. Each time Margo turned her head, the stolen paper flower shifted in her hair, as if it were trying to get her attention. As if it had something important to say. And with that, Margo realized that the paper flower's rustle was the voice of God whispering in her ear. Yes, there *were* pearls among the beads. And because she had taken the time to find them, she was to be rewarded. God would grant her anything she wished. In a flash, she was changed into a wild pony, red ribbons in her mane. She was cantering into the aisle! She was galloping out of the Chapel! She saw herself outside the window, kicking and snorting and rolling in the fresh-fallen snow!

"Look," Margo told Mary Fran, tossing her head the way ponies do, but her mother merely put one finger to her lips, so Margo turned to Stanley. Poor Stanley's flowers had been wrestled away by Anderson, who'd just turned fourteen and looked like he was sixteen. Stanley looked like a fifth grader. Margo could see that he was miserable, that he thought everybody was looking at him and thinking about how he was the same height as the last time that they'd seen him. His wrists were thin as a girl's, the tender insides lavished with veins. Sometimes, he'd let her press one with her thumb; she'd wait until it disappeared, then release it to see the blood spring back.

Abruptly, Margo was overwhelmed with love for her brother.

"Look." She danced up and down, shook her hips, shimmied her shoulders. But Stanley didn't look, didn't even flinch, his mouth held in the flat, straight line that meant he had made up his mind to ignore her.

Regretfully—what else could she do?—Margo ground her peach-colored half-inch square-cut heel into the yielding toe of his foot.

When Stanley's eyes brightened with tears, she felt the fierce white heat of his pain. The truth was that she loved him more than anyone in the world except her mother, more than her father or even April, and this ranking was a terrible secret that burned inside her always, like the Sacred Heart. Sometimes, Margo lay awake imagining that the house was on fire. At any moment the roof would collapse, but she could only save one person at a time. Night after night, she rescued her mother first and Stanley second. That was the easy part. But she never knew who to rescue next. Her father, she supposed. He'd taken her to work with him on Father-Daughter Day and let her climb up into the cab of his snowplow and showed her which levers did what. He gave her a dollar whenever she got Good Conduct marks at school. On weekends, he let her watch while he repaired other people's bicycles, provided she didn't touch anything. She'd even named her favorite doll Sprocket, after one of the words he'd taught her.

But April had taught her some good words, too: *triptych, monochromatic, pastiche.* And rescuing April would be like rescuing two people, because she was never just April, she was always April-and-Barney. April-and-Barney drove Margo to McDonald's whenever they came home from college for the weekend. April-and-Barney let her sit between them when they watched *Star Trek* and the new *Star Trek*. Summers, April-and-Barney had taken her to the beach, and taught her to swim, and helped her chase the swarms of swift little fish that nobody ever could catch.

But then, without warning, April was only April. And now she was marrying somebody else. Margo felt another wave of love for Stanley, who would never change, who stayed exactly the same, year after year. "Look, okay?" she said to him gently, an apology, and Stanley leaned down and whispered, "If you were a prostitute, you'd starve."

It took her a minute to fully understand. The thing dangled there, surprising as a spider, all those quick black legs opening and closing. Suddenly the paper flower's magical powers drained away. Like Margo, it knew about *prostitute*, the way it knew about *shit* and *damn* and even the F-word, the worst word of all, the word that Elmer said hurt Jesus most when someone used it. After April and Caleb moved in together, Elmer had started going to Mass on Sunday mornings—*every* Sunday, not just on Christmas and Easter and special occasions. He'd tried to get the rest of them to go, but Stanley liked to sleep in and Mary Fran said that until the American Catholic Church split off from Rome, she had no plans to contribute more soldiers to the machine.

"The Church will never split," Elmer said, and Mary Fran said, "Then it will die, and it will be a mercy killing," but before they could really start fighting, Margo volunteered to go along. She liked getting up early with Elmer on Sunday mornings, and fasting—even though he said she didn't have to—and bundling up to walk the three blocks to Saint Michael's. When they arrived, he held the door for her as if she was a lady, and when they reached their pew, he always stood aside so she could enter first. During the week he was tired, indifferent, or simply gone, but on these Sundays he wore a suit coat and tie and cleaned underneath his fingernails. He put on cologne that smelled faintly like Comet cleanser; he sang boomingly with the hymns. On the way home, he talked about olden times when the world was a better place, when men didn't want to be women and women didn't want to be men. He talked about the importance of family values, and a diverse stock portfolio. He warned Margo that she'd be growing up soon and, like people in the Bible, she, too, would be tested.

"How?" she asked, and he said he couldn't exactly say, but she would know when the time came and he had every confidence she would make the right choices. It reminded her of an episode of the new *Star Trek*, where Captain Picard warns the young cadet, Wesley Crusher, about the rigors of Starfleet Academy. Elmer didn't know about the new *Star Trek*, but he said it sounded like the same thing, only this was more important because Margo was real, and Wesley Crusher was just TV. Then he told her she shouldn't watch so much TV, that he and Mary Fran weren't being strict enough with her, that he was worried she was growing up wrong.

"Bullshit." Mary Fran had been tucking Margo into bed, fixing the blankets and pillow just right, when Margo repeated what her father had said.

"Five dollars," Margo said.

Mary Fran sighed. "You're growing up fine," she said. "It's your father who's having a difficult time."

"Why?"

"I wish I knew." Mary Fran nuzzled her nose into Margo's neck. "Don't worry about it, snicklebritches. It's just because of the wedding. Everything will be back to normal soon."

But Margo knew that the wedding wasn't going to solve anything, because it was nothing like the weddings people had in olden times with a real priest in a real church, with an organ, and lilies on the altar, ring bearers and flower girls and a wedding dress with pearls that stayed on. Elmer said in olden times, weddings were special because people hadn't lived intimately before marriage, and when Margo asked what that meant, he said, um, it meant all the little things you know about someone, like whether or not they squeeze the toothpaste from the bottom of the tube or the middle. He said that in olden times, there was respect for things like tradition, and honesty, and beauty, and faith. And whenever he talked that way, Margo found herself longing for olden times, too, because even she could see that the modern world in which she got up and went to school and came home and went to bed was nothing like the place her father said he remembered, a place where no one was ever bored or sad or lonely and everything was wonderful all the time.

Now, as April and Caleb chanted I do, Margo finally, fully understood what Stanley had said to her. He hadn't just called her a prostitute. He'd called her an *ugly* prostitute, right there at their sister's wedding, as she sat securely between him and Mary Fran, the two people she loved best. In a split second of clarity, she wanted nothing more than to kill Stanley, to bisect the veins in his wrists with her sharp, white teeth, to punt his head clean off his shoulders, to stomp on his chest with her sharp, strong heels until one plunged between his ribs and punctured his heart. But before she could do any of these things, a warm flush fell behind her eyes like a red velvet curtain at the end of a play. It was over. She was going to cry, no matter how hard she tried not to. Caleb, blushing furiously, was reciting a poem he'd composed especially for April; Margo tried to hang on by concentrating on the rhyming words:

shine . . .

mine;

love . . .

above;

luck . . .

amuck;

and for a moment, she thought she'd be all right, but the poem
ended with the word *April,* which didn't rhyme with anything, and
Margo gave a little sniffle, which was always a mistake, because
then she had to sniff harder and that knocked the tears out of her
eyes. Mary Fran handed her a tissue, and it smelled like the inside
of her purse—cough drops and breath mints, leather and gum, hand
lotion and lipstick and dull, greasy pennies—and it was this comforting odor, familiar as her mother's own skin, that shredded the
last remnant of Margo's restraint.

Outside, the snow fell hard and fast. Frost angels filled the windows, linking hands across the glass; beyond them, the cars were
soft white humps, like rows of coconut candy. The rest of the world
might as well not have existed. There was only the ballroom and its
long rows of chairs, the hovering cherubs, the small white lights that
winked and blinked with each strong blast of wind. Mary Fran put
an arm around Margo's shaking shoulders, leaned down and whispered that April would still be April and Margo would see her as
much as ever and maybe she'd like to spend a whole weekend in
Minneapolis after April and Caleb got back from their honeymoon,
but this only made Margo cry harder and Mary Fran knew enough
not to push it. Instead, she simply pressed her daughter's face into
her dress—a gesture of comfort, yes, but also a practical attempt to
stifle the rising siren of her grief. Sadness hit Margo like a tornado,
without any reason or warning that Mary Fran could see. It was best

not to fight it. It was best just to open the windows a crack and trundle down into the safety of the basement. Later, when things were calm again, the two of them could leisurely pick through the rubble for the intricacies of what had actually happened.

"Shh, baby," Mary Fran said, but then Elmer's mother—bless her pointed head—couldn't leave well enough alone. "What is it, pumpkin?" she asked, leaning across the back of Mary Fran's chair. "You can tell Grandma, can't you?"

"Hilda, she's fine, we're fine," Mary Fran said, but it was too late. As Pete Lapenska joined April and Caleb's hands to symbolize their eternal union, Margo exhaled in a voice that was anguish itself, "Stan-ley called-me-a-PROS-TI-TUTE!" The last word landed on the altar like a grenade. As April and Caleb turned to look, Margo flung herself at Stanley, nearly toppling him into the aisle before Mary Fran could scoop her up and pin her arms and legs.

"Get her out of here," Elmer spat, as if Margo were a problem Mary Fran had invented all by herself, and Mary Fran loosened her grip on Margo's leg just enough so she could land a wild kick on Elmer's shoulder. Then she set her down in the aisle and propelled her, still screaming, down the long, red carpet which seemed to keep unfolding like a magician's limitless scarf.

How far could it be from the front of the chapel to the gilded doors at the back? Everything seemed to be happening in slow motion. Mary Fran set her face in a smile as they passed Caleb's mother, his nephew and niece (thank heavens Margo's bite hadn't broken the girl's skin!). They passed Mary Fran's sister, Melissa, and her husband, Brian, who were childless (they preferred the term *child-free*) and self-appointed experts on the discipline of children. They passed Mary Fran's brother, Aaron, the golden boy who'd done everything right until last year, when he'd left his wife, Libby, and their three kids in order to marry the twenty-four-year-old office assistant of his Allstate branch. Sara had unnaturally white teeth and tinted contact lenses; she was sitting a little too close to Aaron, her pregnant belly gracefully draped in designer fabric. Mary Fran could tell she'd never suffered morning sickness, hemorrhoids, flatulence, or mood swings. For Sara, labor would be the sensual experience the New Age books all promised. Sara's child—they already knew it was a boy—would qualify for the Gifted and Talented program at school; he would say please and thank you without being prompted; he would never succumb to hysterics and have to be forcefully removed from a nondenominational chapel. Farther down the aisle, Libby had a righteous arm around her brood, even the notorious Mickey, airbrushed down to his apple cheeks, and while once Libby would have lifted her head to share with Mary Fran a look that said, *There but for the grace of God go I with one of mine*, she now stared straight ahead, and Mary Fran knew there'd be no point in trying to explain that Sara hadn't actually been invited, that Aaron had been asked to come alone to save everybody the embarrassment, but he'd said that if Sara wasn't invited, Mary Fran might as well never invite him to anything ever again, and while she was at it, she could forget about being his sister, too.

This no longer seemed like a significant problem to Mary Fran— Margo was trying to bite the hand Mary Fran had clamped over her mouth—but done was done and there was no choice now but to keep on down the endless aisle toward the temporary sanctuary of the lobby, where she'd try to calm her daughter before it was time to receive the guests, before it was time to eat chicken à la king and butter beans with garden salad and choice of dinner roll and, later, dance the bunny hop and the beer-barrel polka, drinking too much and laughing too loud so that no one would ever suspect this had been a long and miserable day. It was like going through the Spanking Machine— there was no backing up once you'd started through that terrible tunnel of legs, your butt tucked under and your head held high enough to accidentally-on-purpose knock a few crotches. The Spanking Machine! She hadn't thought of that for years. How she'd dreaded her birthdays when all of her friends, along with Melissa and Aaron, lined up and spread their legs. Sometimes her dad would tag on, too, calling himself the caboose. For the first time it occurred to her that she could have refused to participate. She could have let them stand there forever with their legs spread foolishly. Why hadn't she?

Ten more feet, five more feet, and now she had reached the end of the ballroom. The moment they passed through the doors into the lobby, Margo stopped crying. She swayed for a moment, blinking owlishly, then listed toward the warmth of the fieldstone fireplace. Mary Fran sighed. How many graduations, family dinners, parties, and Christmas pageants had she missed as a result of Margo's eruptions? And afterward she'd always swear that *next* time, she'd let Elmer take his turn at handling the situation. Now, once again, she'd leapt to the rescue: a reflex. A nervous tic.

"Trouble?" asked the boy behind the front desk.

"Excuse me?" Mary Fran said. She was not in the mood for conversation. She was going to miss the rest of the wedding, there was nothing she could do. At least she could see it on video.

But the boy persisted. He jerked his chin at Margo. "She's got a good set of lungs."

"She gets them from my mother-in-law."

He laughed and nodded pleasantly, as if he knew firsthand just how mothers-in-law could be, though he couldn't have been much more than eighteen. He looked a bit like a leprechaun in his tidy green uniform and matching round cap. Mary Fran gave him a cautious smile. She'd heard there were still certain rooms over at the Lodge which could be rented by the hour. You had to know the code phrase, something like, *Is the President available?* This boy certainly didn't look as if he knew anything about that. But looks were often deceiving. She thought of Stanley's slender frame, his sweet smooth face, trying to align these facts with the magazine she'd found beneath his mattress. Not a homey *Playboy*, either—some awful thing called *Ouch!* On the cover, a woman wearing pigtails and a very short dress sucked savagely on a lollipop, a Band-Aid wrapped around her finger, a white gauze X across one knee. Mary Fran had removed the magazine and replaced it with a Red Cross pamphlet on first aid. Neither she nor Stanley mentioned it, but the last time she'd checked, the pamphlet was gone.

"That her sister gettin' married in there?" the boy said.

Mary Fran nodded wearily.

"Here." He picked through the bowl of complimentary candies sitting on the counter and came up with a handful of peppermints. "I hate that taste you get in your mouth, you know, when you've been crying real hard?" He held them out to Mary Fran, and there was something so eager, so earnest about his expression that Mary Fran wished she had something to give him in return. Their hands touched. His fingers were cold. The peppermints filled her palm.

"I sure do hate that taste," the boy said again, and Mary Fran wondered how he knew so well what it tasted like to cry. It was barely half-past four, but the falling snow had swallowed the last murky dredges of light. Across the road, the neon sign for Bittner's Plaza had been reduced to a faint red smear. The one good thing about the weather was that it appeared to be keeping Barney Lohr at home. Over April's objections, Mary Fran had sent an invitation to his parents, hoping to show that there were no hard feelings on the Liesgang side of things. But there'd been no response from Larry and Alma, well-mannered soft-spoken people who read books together and went on vacations to historical sites, the sort of couple Mary Fran wished that she and Elmer could be.

It was Barney himself who had RSVP'd.

"I can't believe you'd do this to me, Ma," April had said, and Mary Fran said, "It'll be fine," and April said, "It will be really, really awkward, that's what it will be."

The thing was that Mary Fran sincerely *missed* Barney. For nearly five years he had been like family, a broad-shouldered, red-faced chatterbox of a guy, friendly as a golden retriever. He'd torn both Achilles playing varsity football—a freak accident; it had made the papers around the state—and the first time April brought him home, he'd told Mary Fran all about his physical therapy, detail by excruciating detail, and how depressed he'd been until his mom suggested he try something new, maybe try out for the school play. He hadn't even expected to get a part, much less the lead! And then he'd met April—she was in charge of set design—and everything that had happened to him had started to make sense.

"When God shuts a door," he'd told Mary Fran earnestly, "He opens a window, don't you think?"

He hadn't waited for her reply. He had a fluid way of talking, one sentence overlapping the next, so it was hard to get a word in edgewise. Mary Fran didn't mind. In the past, April's boyfriends had been sallow-skinned, monosyllabic creatures. They'd smelled of cigarettes and recklessness. They didn't so much make eye contact as size you up, like thieves assessing a lock. Barney, on the other hand, had greeted Mary Fran politely, deferentially. He kept his hair in a neat, military buzz. He wore button-down shirts and loafers. He was popular at school, got reasonably good grades, worked hard on weekends at the Lohrs' carpet store. He carried himself so well, and talked so easily, you didn't even suspect he was shy till after you'd known him for a while.

He and April had gone off to Madison together, kept on dating even after Barney took an academic leave and came back home to work full-time at the Magic Carpet. Nobody had ever believed he'd complete his drama degree. But what did that matter? He already did a great job in the summer musicals—one of the few young men in town who could act, sing, *and* dance a bit—and he stood to inherit the family business. The couple's sudden breakup in spring had left both families stunned. April's engagement in December was the echo after the gunshot, the tremor after the quake.

Mary Fran joined Margo at the fireplace, let the heat spread over her shoulders and back like a large, compassionate hand. "Feeling better?" she said. In response, Margo pulled the paper flower out of her hair and flung it into the fire. "Hey!" Mary Fran said, but it was too late. The flower bloomed brighter than it had ever been, a brief spectacular moment, then disintegrated into ash. Mary Fran sighed. Then she kissed Margo's forehead, which was hot and salty and damp. Her precarious chignon had finally tumbled down; bobby pins stuck out like cactus spines. Her braid was a rat's tail, gummy with hair spray. Her permanent teeth were enormous. This was the child they hadn't planned for, conceived at a time when they were *finally* getting financially on their feet, the semester Mary Fran had returned to school to complete the accounting degree which her first pregnancy (and subsequent marriage) had interrupted. This was the child Elmer had insisted he didn't want. The child Mary Fran had refused to terminate, and for reasons that had nothing to do with Rome. The child who reacted like a mood ring, or a lightning rod, absorbing the household's joys and sorrows and tensions.

The child they both loved best.

"Here." Mary Fran pressed the peppermints into Margo's hand. Margo unwrapped one, but instead of placing it in her own mouth, she offered it to her mother. "The body of Christ," she said solemnly.

Mary Fran recognized Father Bork's deep tone. She sighed, extended her tongue, let Margo place the peppermint on her tongue.

"You have to say *Amen*," Margo said, and Mary Fran said, "Ah, men."

It was good enough for Margo. She settled comfortably against Mary Fran's side. "I'm never going to get married," she said, unwrapping a peppermint for herself.

"Fine by me." Mary Fran stroked her daughter's matted hair.

The doors to the ballroom opened, and Hilda Liesgang strode between them. At sixty-nine, she moved with the easy leggy gait of a much younger woman. Her height gave her movements an authority, a deliberateness, which made Mary Fran—who always felt herself to be shorter and stockier than she actually was—want to stick out a foot and trip her. Hilda's pepper-and-salt hair boasted plenty of natural black, glossy as crow feathers; her eyes were green as tea. She never exercised, never watched what she ate. And yet— as she'd tell anybody—her triglycerides were low, her blood pressure average, her good cholesterol high. She weighed exactly 138 pounds, which was what she'd weighed on her wedding day.

"It's *freezing* in there," she exclaimed, not waiting for the heavy doors to ease shut behind her.

Mary Fran nodded noncommittally, but Hilda settled beside them on the hearth as if this had been an invitation and started picking bobby pins out of Margo's braid. "Well, you're not missing much," she told Mary Fran. "They're wrapping things up with more of that poetry."

"I *like* poetry," Mary Fran said.

Hilda ignored this and removed a large hairbrush from her purse. The truth was that she liked poetry, too, but she'd figured it was the sort of thing that Mary Fran would make fun of. She'd made the complaint as a friendly gesture, forgetting that Mary Fran would contradict, out of habit, anything Hilda said. The fact was that Hilda had come out of the Chapel to offer Mary Fran her assistance, to suggest that Mary Fran go back inside—it was her daughter's wedding after all—while Hilda kept an eye on Margo. But Mary Fran would have refused her help even if Margo was still screaming like a stuck pig, tearing her clothes and kicking the furniture and toppling the plants, which Hilda knew she was perfectly capable of doing. And no wonder—the child had been raised without rules, without firm boundaries or consistent discipline. Elmer was trying to rectify that, taking the girl to Mass, setting a good example; Hilda hoped with all her heart it wasn't too little too late. It had taken this business with April—lost since the day she'd set foot on a college campus—to make him see what was at stake. Her marriage out of the Church was a tragedy, yes, but no one could pretend it was a surprise. There'd been plenty of warning shots fired across the bow. Her paintings, for instance. They'd changed overnight from civilized landscapes to things nobody in their right *mind* would hang up on a wall: nudity and promiscuity and, well, *pornography*—Hilda Liesgang wasn't afraid to call a spade a spade. And then, for a while, there'd been that vulgar nose ring.

"Most girls want a ring on their *finger*," Hilda had said, the first time she'd seen it. She was only trying to make a joke, ease the tension. Nobody had laughed.

How she wished April had married Barney Lohr! It didn't seem to matter where the girl punched a hole, or what new, crazy thing she did to her hair. He had always worshiped the ground she walked on. Had, in fact, barely let her out of his sight.

She finished Margo's hair, tucked the brush back into her handbag, then rummaged around in its depths until she found a dusty compact. "Shake your head," Hilda told her.

Margo did, without enthusiasm. The chignon stayed in place.

"See?" Hilda said, holding up the compact. "Now you look fancy, just like your mother."

Mary Fran pursed her lips, made a rude, wet sound.

"Well, you *do* look fancy," Hilda said. From the looks of things, Mary Fran had actually taken a brush to her short, permed curls. She'd even sprayed them into a semblance of order, rather than leaving them to dry every which way like she usually did. Why couldn't she just say thank you? That was what you did when someone gave you a compliment, even if it was someone you didn't particularly like. That was how you set a good example for little pitchers who had big ears and bigger eyes and who would grow up to follow in your footsteps.

But Hilda had more important things to think about than Mary Fran's bad manners. It was nearing five o'clock, and she still hadn't found her penny. Usually, she found it by early afternoon, three o'clock at the latest. Before the ceremony, she'd walked between the rows of folding chairs, expecting she would see it any minute. Now she began to pace the lobby, making neat, deliberate lines as if she were pushing a vacuum cleaner, or plowing a field. Not that she usually found her penny by looking for it. No, it generally *appeared* to her: in an ashtray, wedged in a sidewalk crack, under a newspaper or napkin or cup. Nobody seemed to notice it until she picked it up. For the past nineteen years Hilda Liesgang had found a penny every single day of her life—with a few rare but notable exceptions. On each of those days, someone had died: a family member or friend, an important political figure, a cherished pet.

She'd found her first penny on the day of her husband's death. It was New Year's Day, 1979, when something went wrong inside Bart Liesgang's heart. As his body stopped its jackrabbit thrashing, a penny—bright as a marigold—rolled out of his pocket. Hilda had saved that penny and all the others she'd found since. She kept them in mason jars in the spare bedroom, lined up on the shelves he'd built to hold his lead-soldier collection. Several times, she'd been written up in the papers, and last year a talk show had flown her to Chicago to be interviewed along with a man who erased surgical scars with his hands and a woman who always knew who was on the phone before she picked up the receiver. Overall, Hilda had had a nice time—the lady talk-show host knew how to put a person at ease—but she'd suffered from nightmares ever since in which she found herself back on the show, wearing nothing except a pair of bedroom slippers.

"What're you looking for?"

Hilda looked up to see she'd caught the desk clerk's attention.

"A penny," she said, wishing the boy would mind his own beeswax. If he truly wanted to be helpful, he could turn up the heat in the ballroom. She could see the thermostat on the wall behind him, secured underneath a Plexiglas box. This made her relent a little. The poor kid probably didn't even have the key.

"I think I got one," the boy said, and he dug around in his pocket, but Hilda shook her head. It didn't count, if somebody just gave you one. She felt Margo's hand slip into her own, warm as a baked potato.

"I'll help," she said.

"Here," the boy said, holding out a handful of coins.

"She's got to *find* it," Margo said, making a scornful face.

The boy looked hurt. He tucked the change back into his pocket. For a moment Hilda thought she saw a flash of copper between the leaves of a plastic potted plant. But it was only the fancy foil from one of the complimentary candies on the counter, nicely displayed in a pewter bowl: mints and chocolates, peppermints, small individually wrapped caramels. Hilda could see why people who didn't know about the Chapel might think it was a nice place, even though one of the men in her bridge club had assured her that nothing had really changed. All you had to do was ask for suite thirty-three; a girl would be knocking at your door within the hour.

No, no, his wife said, I heard it doesn't matter which room.

That's true, another man said. You just leave a note for the manager that reads, *Give this to the President*. And then write down your room number. They send the girl—no questions asked!

Yeah, well, I got a question, his wife said. How come you know so much about this place?

That was the kind of conversation any mention of the Lodge churned up. That, and talk about Gretel Fame's ghost, which was said to appear from time to time, striding through the ballroom in a bright red dress.

Still, Hilda couldn't help thinking that all the Christmas-tree lights were festive and pretty. The neon wedding bells over the ballroom doors were tastefully done in purple and white, clear clean colors that raised a person's spirits just to look at them. And that grand moose was a homey touch.

"Did it hurt, when the hunters shot him?" Margo asked, studying its enormous brown eyes.

"Absolutely not," Hilda assured her. The desk clerk still watched her with his own wounded look. "The hunters shot him right through the heart. He didn't feel a thing."

Mary Fran got up and walked over to the counter. Her dress was dull yellow, the color of blackboard chalk, tight as it could be across the rump. Hilda thanked the Lord that she herself had been born with a good metabolism. "My mother-in-law finds pennies," she heard Mary Fran explain in a voice that was low, confiding, bemused.

The boy said, "Huh?"

"You know," Mary Fran said. "Like some people are always finding four-leaf clovers?"

Hilda felt her face flush; she held dear little Margo's hand more tightly. How like Mary Fran to reduce her to a foolish old woman in search of lucky charms. She couldn't quite hear the boy's reply, but there was no way not to hear Mary Fran's laugh, which was more like a bark, a one-note call. And she recalled the first time she'd heard that laugh, nearly twenty-three years earlier, when she'd risen in the middle of the night for a cold glass of milk. It was late summer, hot and still. Every window in the house stood open, the curtains limp with humidity. In the kitchen, she'd heard whispers, the scuffle of fabric, and then that awful laugh. There they were on the porch, leaning up against a pillar: Elmer, her youngest son, her favorite child, her special soldier, and common-as-nails Mary Fran Schrunk, who would become Mary Fran Liesgang within the year and give birth to a nine-pound baby everybody would pretend was premature. Hilda predicted it all, right then by the glow of that harvest moon. She turned on the porch light, counted to ten, and when she stepped outside, no one was there. But halfway down the steps was a pair of cotton panties. Hilda swept them off the steps and poked them under the house with the handle of the broom.

Now she considered trying to explain to the boy herself about the penny. How it wasn't at all like four-leaf clovers, which was a superstition and, therefore, against the teachings of the Church. How it wasn't something she *chose* to do. How it was, like any talent, a gift from God. But if she opened her mouth, there would be a row. If there was a row, Hilda would come away looking as if she'd started the whole thing, while Mary Fran—innocent Mary Fran!—would simply be the victim of Hilda's oversensitivity. Hilda might be oversensitive, fine, but wasn't that better than being *in*sensitive?

Turn the other cheek, she reminded herself. Jesus was persecuted by those who did not believe. And with that thought, she understood she wasn't going to find her penny, not today. Perhaps, with the strain of the wedding, she'd overlooked it, passed it by. Whatever happened next would be her fault, a result of her distraction. Her inability to see what was right beneath her nose. A wobble in the iron-firm grip of her faith.

"Gram?" Margo said. "Are you *sure* that the moose didn't feel anything?"

Unable to reply, Hilda dropped her granddaughter's hand and pushed open the heavy storm doors leading to the front porch. She stood in the small entryway, arms folded, recovering herself. Even here, it was cold enough so that she could see her breath. Through the glass, she watched the snow drifting over the deck chairs and iron tables. The hanging planters swung back and forth, violently, a line of silent bells. Without hope, she lifted the floor mat with her toe.

No penny.

It was out of her hands now and into the Lord's.

From inside came the faint sound of applause; Hilda guessed that the service was over. And she was right. Caleb and April, arm in arm, were coming back down the nuptial stairs; the photographer knelt on the landing to capture the proper angle of their triumph. The assembly rose to congratulate them, everybody surging forward. In the kitchen, Emily Bamberger was putting the finishing touches on the chicken à la king while two assistants, stout, unhappy women in their forties, clattered white plates into stacks and loaded them onto the serving cart. Two more assistants—younger, lovelier women—had already removed every trace of plastic wrap from numerous platters. One arranged white and pink carnations in a vase; the other released the ice swan into the punch bowl. Both wore crisp white aprons around their narrow waists. They fluffed their bangs, freshened their lipstick, mouthed, *Do I look okay?*

In the dining room, the bartender was throwing ice into glasses.

In the game room, the assistant bartender was setting up a keg for after the sit-down supper. In the back office, Ralph Bamberger was listening to travel advisories on a small radio. Early reports suggested the next few hours would be intense. He glanced out the window in the direction of the Lodge, trying to figure out if there was any way to charge people who decided not to risk the roads and, instead, share rooms with legitimately registered customers. Probably not. Though he'd certainly raise his usual cot fee whenever cots were requested. He reminded himself to send Dimmer down to the game room where there were several additional cots tucked away. Frankly, these weren't quite up to snuff, but who was in a position to quarrel in the middle of a whiteout?

In the ballroom, Dimmer was setting up the long reception tables as Jeffery worked his way down the rows of freshly vacated chairs, folding each one and stacking it onto the large, wooden dolly. The two were brothers, bachelors at the lip of middle age, but they moved like men who were considerably older, mindful of brittle bones. "Some storm out there," Dimmer said, passing by. And Jeffery echoed Dimmer, as he always did, "Some storm." Guests milled about, getting in the way. Gradually, they were figuring out that only pop and nonalcoholic punch would be served at the reception tables in the ballroom. The cash bar was in the dining room, and the only way to *get* to the dining room (aside from vaulting the dolly, which blocked the east archway) was to join the wavering line of people that snaked its way toward the west archway, where the bride and groom still stood at the foot of the balcony stairs. Not until one had shaken hands and murmured all the appropriate things might he or she pass into the promised land. Then there was wine or a sweet drink for the ladies, perhaps a Manhattan, an occasional rum and Coke. Beer and gin and tonics and blended whiskey for the men. Blood sugar was low. Tempers were hot. *What do you mean, a shot*

*of Jack Daniel's costs five bucks? FIVE BUCKS? When I can walk
across to Bittner's Plaza and buy the whole damn bottle for TWENTY?*

*What do you mean, you don't have change for a hundert-dollar bill?
All I got is dis hundert, and my money is green as da next fellah's.*

*Yeah, a Mutant Monkey, that's what I said. No, I don't know what-
all is in it—hey, Marta? What's in those monkey drinks you like,
brandy and something, right?*

OUT in the Hideaway Lodge, the hall lights flickered. The wind
shaved the fat, marbled icicles from the eaves, and the sound was
like so much breaking glass: plates and cups and silver thrown during the most bitter and foolish of arguments. By now, the wedding
guests were all at the Chapel, and most of the suites stood empty:
hot tubs steaming up the windows, ice from the machine in the hall
thundering down into the holding bin. But wait—there was someone in suite eleven. A retired couple traveling from their weekend
cottage back to their home in Oak Park, Illinois. When they'd heard
the travel advisories, they decided to hole up somewhere. What else
did this couple have but time? So they arrived home on Sunday, or
even Monday? The days of morning rush hours and harried weekends catching up with household chores were long gone for them
both. These days, they tooled around on their pontoon boat. They
fished. They watched the birds. And each time they passed the
billboard advertising the Great Lakes Chapel and Hideaway Lodge,
either going to the cottage or heading back home, the man put his
hand teasingly on his wife's firm knee and said, "Maybe we ought
to try out one of those hot tubs sometime."

And she said, "You know what those little places are like. They
probably don't even change the sheets."

But today, with the storm coming on and that coaxing hand, she'd agreed that a dip into a hot tub might be just the thing, and they were settling down to business in the Frank Sinatra Memorial Suite when the wind picked up—surely it was the wind!—sudden as a woman's scream. "Dear Lord, did you hear that?" the woman whispered, groping for her towel, and the man whispered back, "I'm sure it's nothing." They didn't hear anything more. But the suite's cozy feeling had soured, and neither the man nor the woman could relax until after the man had pushed the small breakfast table in front of the door and piled their luggage on top of it.

In connecting suites twenty-six (Deep Space) and twenty-seven (Music of the Spheres), a mother and father and their two teenage children were playing cards. They, too, were waiting out the storm. Yes, they thought they heard a few thumps and crashes in a nearby room, perhaps a man's hoarse shout. But when the father rose to open the door, the mother told him to sit back down, you never knew what went on in a place like this and, besides, it was none of their business. She turned up the television so they wouldn't hear anything more.

In suite thirty-one, the Hunter's Suite, a salesman slept with an open Bible on his chest. His wife would have gladly testified that even a train wreck could not wake him. But the wide-eyed bucks on the wall pricked up their ears with concern. After all they had witnessed over the years, they were not easily deceived. They'd been watching on the night a well-known senator, dressed in a Batman costume, had leapt from the dresser and knocked himself out while attempting to save his sweet young wife, tied prettily to the bed. They'd been present when that boy from Ohio had written letter after letter—to whom? If only they might have craned their necks to see!—then torn them all up, swallowed two bottles of pills, and shot himself in the head. They'd seen great sex and lousy sex and lots of sex that fell into that nameless category in between. They'd heard flamboyant fights and lean conversation, belly laughs and long deliberate nights of weeping. They'd seen hundreds of suitcases unpacked and repacked, their contents—like the contents of the human heart—both identical and unique.

And in suite thirty-three a man and his wife were arguing. At least, they had been arguing. Now the man was talking to himself, for the woman had fallen asleep. Or maybe she was only pretending to be sleep; the man could not be sure. They'd been married three years, and the man's wife often pretended to sleep when she was tired of listening to him. Now she lay on her back in the bed, the pillow covering her face as if she could no longer bear to hear another word. But the man kept talking anyway. He'd made this reservation months earlier, and he'd had such high hopes for this Valentine's Day weekend—for the two of them, together—that he was reluctant to admit that nothing was working out.

Suite thirty-three was the Western Suite. The headboard was shaped like a wagon wheel, and there were oil paintings of cowboys rounding up dusty cattle. The hot tub gurgled like a fat, happy baby, and whenever the timer wound down with a *ding*, the man reset it so that the water would be nice and warm when his wife woke up. He speculated on how much that hot tub had cost, how much energy it took to run it. There was a carved wooden sign on the bathroom door that said POWDER ROOM, and the man wondered how old it was. Another sign hung in the kitchenette, and it read RUSTLERS WILL BE SHOT. The man thought this second sign was particularly funny. He'd made his wife read it several times when they'd first checked into the room. That had been—when? Somewhere around four? He couldn't exactly say. It was already snowing pretty hard by then. Anyway, she hadn't thought the sign was all that amusing. She said she loved him, she truly did, but things really weren't working out between them, and she thought it would be best if they separated for a while.

The man had sighed, and since they were going to get into an argument anyway, he'd opened the bottle of brandy he'd smuggled along—there was a nice box of chocolates, too—concealed in the ski sweater she'd given him last Christmas. He didn't particularly like the sweater, but he'd brought it along to please her. The Lodge brochure had talked about a natural environment and country roads and walks on the beach, and he'd had an image of the two of them, hand in hand on some snowy trail, the dark green pines all around them tall and strong as guardian angels. Her nose would be pink, her dark braid undone; snowflakes would sparkle in her hair. He'd say, "Happy Valentine's Day." He'd bend to kiss her and she'd kiss him back, her hands all over that sweater.

But he guessed none of that was likely to happen now.

"If you're going to spend the weekend drinking," she'd said when she saw the brandy, "I'm going to get my own room."

It was likely that the argument had started then, though the man couldn't exactly remember. It did seem like a long time ago. Ages. Another lifetime. He checked the bedside clock.

Half-past five.

His wife slept on, still in her clothes, her hair a tangled halo over the pillow's blank face.

Why was it, the man wondered, that people just wouldn't listen when you told them something? That was his wife's problem. He'd tried to explain about the natural environment, about the walks on the beach, but she wouldn't listen. She never did listen to anything he said.

He went back to the dresser where he'd left his drink, and he picked it up, but then he put it down again. He didn't know what he wanted, but this certainly wasn't it. He hoped that, once his wife woke up, she'd give him another chance. Maybe they could have a nice dinner at the little strip mall across the intersection. Or, if there wasn't any sit-down place to eat, they could pick up some beer at the package store, some bread and cheese at the minimart. They'd lie in bed and cuddle up together, and if that was all she wanted to do, he wouldn't press. It might even be a turning point in their marriage. Who could say? Maybe they'd come back to this same place, year after year, and stay in this same sweet little room, and talk about how well everything had turned out. By then they might even have a kid to bring with them. That would be just fine. The man thought he'd really like having a kid, a boy or girl he could teach things. He hoped that the kid would like him, and admire him. Maybe even listen to him sometimes.

Something caught his eye: a flash of copper on the bed, half-hidden in the twist and tumble of sheets. The man hesitated before he picked it up. It was a penny. A lucky penny. It shone as if it were made of gold.

RECEPTION

*I*F you turned left out of the Great Lakes Chapel parking lot and followed the road west across the interstate, past the Budgetel, past the Simplicity dealership, past the ostrich farm and its small petting zoo closed for the season, you'd eventually come to a T where there was a defunct gas station, the pockmarked foundation of an old church, and an ancient stone tavern called the Mother of Pearl. Mother's was squat and rectangular, with a steeply pitched roof and a single, crooked pine tree beside it. A Miller Lite sign hung above the chipped cement steps, a pale eye shot through with neon letters like bloodshot veins, and it stared balefully across the flat frozen fields, blinking in time with the wind. Men and women entered with expressions of reverence, glasses fogged, stamping their boots and whistling *whew* beneath their breath. They ordered double pitchers and buffalo wings, turned their chairs toward the new color TV, and watched the Bucks dash up and down the sunny yellow length of court as if there was no such thing as winter, snow, irritable spouses, and restless children, everyone either getting over a cold or catching another.

It was here that Barney Lohr sat now, stuffed into the same tuxedo he'd worn to escort April Liesgang to her prom, boring the living hell out of his best friend, Albert Groscholz.

Albert Groscholz, alias Coot—"as in *drunk as a*," he'd explain if you asked—wistfully eyed Barney's Schlitz even as he downed his third ginger ale. But Coot was driving and besides, he had his baby with him, a one-year-old boy named Albert Jr. whom everyone had already started calling Cootie. Cootie slept in his car seat, sweet as a flower in the center of the table, and he seemed oblivious to the ratcheting sound of the cigarette machine, the squeak of the men's-room door, the flood of commentary that bubbled from Barney's mouth. Coot knew that Barney was still trying to decide whether or not he should go to April's wedding, but you had to know Barney pretty well to figure this out, because he'd said nothing about the wedding, and he hadn't even once mentioned April's name. Instead, he'd been talking home improvement. His parents' place was out-dated, and he'd decided to fix things up. Over the course of the past two hours, he'd discussed removal of asbestos, lectured on the pros and cons of vinyl siding, and instructed Coot on the importance of a quality carpet pad.

Barney Lohr could talk more and say less than anybody Coot had ever known. Now he'd drifted onto the topic of fences. Coot sighed. He stifled a carbonation belch. He studied the droplets of moisture on Barney's Schlitz, sweet as the sweat on a woman's upper lip. He had heard from his wife, Annie, who'd heard from one of her sisters, that Barney had been seeing some kind of shrink. Not that it was any of Coot's business. But if it *were* true, it sure didn't seem to be helping any. Barney carried his torch for April Liesgang just as hard and high as ever.

"Me, I'm partial to a nice grapesteak fence," Barney said, arranging a handful of complimentary popcorn to demonstrate the pattern.

"Prettier than a palisade design. And you don't have to worry about finials, like you do with your post and board."

"Look, Barn-boy," Coot said. Cootie's pacifier kept slipping from his mouth, but at the very last minute, just when Coot was certain it would fall, the kid sucked it back up. "Annie'll scorch me if I don't get the baby home by six."

"Now, *here's* your post and board," Barney continued, shifting the kernels around.

"Six o'clock's his feeding time."

"You see? It's a classic design."

Cootie opened his eyes a little, slurped that pacifier in.

"The ceremony's *over*," Coot said. "She's a married lady now." He stood up, fished his gloves out of his pockets. "You've got three choices here," he said. "One: I drive you home. Two: I drive you over by your folks so you can tell them everything about asbestos and siding and fences that you've been telling me. Three: I take you to the Chapel, and you hope to hell they don't throw you out on your ass."

"I have an invitation," Barney said. He stood up to wrestle it from his tuxedo pocket; he'd discovered it, by chance, in the kitchen trash at his parents'. "Look. *The Lohrs*. She could've just said *Larry and Alma Lohr*. She probably thinks I'm still living at home—"

Coot had seen that invitation before, had heard its convoluted analysis. "Who knows what she meant?" he said. "The question is, why put yourself through this? You think you feel bad now, man, wait till you see her in her wedding dress." He felt for the guy, he really did, though he'd never believed that Barney and April had any long-term chance. Anyone except Barney could have seen the breakup coming a mile away, and it had nothing to do with his and April's last big fight, a real whopper, from what little Barney'd say

about it. Frankly, if he had been Coot, he would have told April
good-bye after her first year of college when she started doing those
modern-style paintings. Naked women and shit. Sometimes naked
men, too. Good-bye, he would have told her, don't let the door bang
your butt on the way out. Sometimes a man and woman simply
weren't compatible, especially if the woman could render other
men's cocks in such accurate perspective.

But the truth was that Barney had always *known* that he and April
were incompatible. And he knew it had nothing to do with anything
that had happened since they'd moved to Madison, where April
became the controversial star of the art department while Barney
remained just another drama major, failing his core courses, calling
home far too often to hear his mom and dad say not to worry about
it, and they missed him so much, and what was the point of college
when there was a perfectly good job waiting for him at home? He'd
seen this breakup coming already back in high school, when she'd
draw something perfectly and then tear it up, insisting it wasn't any
good. He knew when she'd point to paintings in the huge, glossy
books she ordered through the library, talking about composition,
tension, texture when all Barney saw were blobs and streaks that
weren't nearly as nice as, say, the watercolor of Lake Michigan she'd
given him for their six-month anniversary. (It still hung over his bed.)
They'd meet at her house for study dates, and he'd watch her reading
Jane Austen or Virginia Woolf, the book cradled in her hands like
the heavy head of a lover, and know she was already leaving him,
walking a path he could not see toward a place he'd never find. He'd
watch her preparing for calculus, copying each formula in her crisp
businesslike hand, and when she'd solved a particularly tough problem, he recognized that soft, satisfied sigh.

And right there in the kitchen, sitting across from her at the
Formica table, he'd have to fight to win her back to himself, nudging

his sock-footed toe between her thighs, teasing his way up under her skirt. Her little brother and sister racing around the table. Her mother's sharp voice in the other room saying, *Kids, let your sister study.* How his foot ached from holding his big toe erect, careful of the blunt-cut nail, offering only the damp cotton ball of his toe like a generous tongue, rubbing and twisting until she rocked toward him, her shadow falling over the rows of penciled numbers, the book dropping from her hands.

He'd been her first lover, one warm June night after a movie that hadn't been very good. They'd ended up at his house two hours early, his parents still out at a party. How happy he was, now, that he'd never told her that he'd been a virgin, too. Instead, in the spring of their senior year, when it seemed things between them were heading that way, he'd ordered a book from the back of a catalog, studied it the way he'd studied football plays before he'd torn both Achilles during that terrible game junior year. In his mind, he ran through sequences, practiced fakes and passes and runs. At last he'd let himself go all the way. Touchdown! As soon as he'd recovered, he practiced the whole thing again. This was nothing like the self-abuse Father Bork had warned would drain his strength, muddle his thinking, and cause his face to break out. This was hard training, a serious business, and the night he and April were finally together, Barney did every last thing he'd memorized, and in the same sequences the book suggested, no matter how it made him feel, no matter if it even disgusted him a little, and afterward, when she'd held his face in her trembling hands, he felt as if he'd done something meaningful and lasting, something that, no matter what else happened, could never be taken away.

Barney knew he should feel bad about making Coot drive out of his way to the Lodge. Snow spilled over the snow fences and drifted across the highway; Coot's Rodeo slipped and slid, despite the four-wheel drive. But Barney wasn't nervous about the weather anymore. He knew everything would be okay. Because when Coot had presented him with his choices, he'd suddenly understood that he had never really had a choice at all. Of course he would go to April's wedding. Of course he would congratulate her, wish her well. His parents might be angry with her, outraged on his behalf, but for God's sake, this was *April,* his dearest and oldest friend, his first and only love. Over time the bad stuff that had happened between them would fade away and they'd remember good things, good times. Eventually, he'd get married, too. They'd still see each other at sports events, at festivals and picnics. They'd have a chaste drink and talk about their families, catch each other up on local gossip. The doctor he'd been seeing didn't think this was likely, but how could he understand? The doctor had never met April. And he'd only known Barney since December, since a few days after Barney had walked into the woods behind his parents' house and taken off his clothes—except for his underwear—and lain down in the snow. He'd heard somewhere that this was the least painful means of suicide. But his mother had seen him walk into the woods. She'd had a bad feeling. She'd followed him. Now he had to drive to Cedarton once a week, where there was this doctor, this head doctor, who came all the way from Milwaukee.

"I'm going to have to let you off here," Coot said, stopping in the mouth of the Chapel parking lot. "I can't risk getting stuck."

Cootie fussed behind them in his car seat. It was almost six o'clock.

"Thanks, man," Barney said. He cracked his door; the resulting blast of cold brought tears to his eyes. "Say hey to Annie for me."

"Annie won't want to hear it," Coot said glumly. "Annie's gonna frost my ass worse than any storm ever could."

"Sorry," Barney said. He'd known Annie nearly as long as he'd known April—all of them had been Class of '92. He'd even dated Annie himself a couple of times.

"Just behave yourself," Coot said. "I ain't coming back out in this weather to post your bail."

THE ceremony was indeed over. Now the reception had arrived as proof. Who hasn't endured those blocks of white and yellow cheese, the dull knives poised between them? The crackers lined up like schoolchildren in neat, precarious rows? The single perfect strawberry no one dares to touch standing guard over acres of pale melon cubes, corralled by scant bunches of sour green grapes? Too many vegetables, especially radishes. Not enough chive-and-onion dip. The olive tray already empty. And, at the center of it all, a small crumb-speckled plate, rumored to have held toast points spread with smoked trout pâté.

The photographer was hard at work on the balcony stairs, maneuvering April and Caleb into position one step below Elmer and Mary Fran, with Hilda Liesgang and Corrine Shannon arranged like bookends, holding them in on either side. How the photographer wished the bride's dress was a little more flattering, something with ruffles to enhance the bust, perhaps a more tightly fitted waist. At least her train was pretty and full, and he'd managed to twist it to conceal the smudges where she'd stepped on it. "Hold your bouquet a little higher," he said. "Look a little more to the left. *There* you go, sweetheart, *there* you go!" At least the camera would like the older women. *Corrine, Hilda*—even their names suggested good taste and breeding. The photographer had been married to such a lady once, and though the marriage had ended twenty years earlier, he still kept their wedding picture next to his bed. The couple in that picture was in love, and would always be in love. You couldn't put a price on a picture like that. Such pleasure it gave him, even now, to look at it.

Children raced across the ballroom floor, slipping and sliding in their smooth dress shoes. A few people sipped glasses of nonalcoholic fruit punch beside the reception table; others headed for the lobby to use the rest rooms, or else chat beside the crackling fire. But the majority of the guests had elected to remain on the other side of the twin archways, where the cash bar was suffering heavy losses. Outside, the wind churned the snow into peaks; with each gust, the lacy curtains shivered wantonly, deliciously. Everyone seemed to realize they wouldn't be going anywhere for a while. What could a person do about it? Nothing, that's what. Easier to reason with God Himself than argue with the weather.

Might as well have another drink.

Bamberger had been in the business for fifteen years, and he still found it difficult to predict how much liquor each wedding would require. The most innocent-looking family of minister fathers and church-lady mothers, volunteer sisters and born-again brothers, would drink until they wept and fought and eventually dropped to the floor while, at the biker wedding the following night, brutally tattooed guests would peacefully sip club sodas, swapping wistful stories of life before AA.

Easy does it, man, they told Bamberger. Let go and let God.

It was good advice to live by, especially on a night like this one when bad weather was inflating the conservative numbers Bamberger had been given by the groom. Hard liquor seemed to be everybody's preference. The bride's father in particular had four thirsty brothers, all of whom had married thirsty wives. On top of that, the bride herself had a number of youthful friends who hadn't lost their college-level tolerances. There were also artists present, and no one drank more than artists—except maybe lawyers, and Bamberger was beginning to suspect the crowd harbored several of them as well. Already, they were running dangerously low on blended whiskey. And forget about the complimentary Goldfish crackers.

Bamberger sent Dimmer and Jeffery across the intersection to the liquor store at Bittner's Plaza. Then he stood on a chair and tried to get everyone's attention. He encouraged the guests to circle past the bar and back into the ballroom, where there was plenty of room, now that the chairs had been folded away. He spoke seductively of the vegetable platter. He gave the cheeses enticing names: Wisconsin Dells Cheddar, Midwestern Farm Colby. He even referred to the toast points, knowing full well they were gone, eaten by two adolescent boys in one swift inhalation. Ladies and gentlemen, if I could please ask—

If you would simply—

If you might—

But no one seemed eager to forfeit his or her place near the bar, and when the brothers returned, snow caked around the cuffs of their trousers, bent beneath jugs of Bacardi and Old Grandad, a cheer went up. It wasn't a happy cheer, either. It was more like the sound hockey fans make at the first sight of blood on the ice. People surged forward, brandishing wallets and purses like pistols. Libby Merideth—legally, she was still Libby Schrunk, though now that Aaron had remarried she was finally taking steps to remedy that—rode the crest of the wave, arrived in a splash with a twenty already in her fist.

"Scotch," she said, sliding the bill across the fine marble top.

"Five dollars." The bartender was already making the change.

"Put fifteen bucks' worth in a cup and keep the rest."

He looked up wearily, looked again. Somehow, during the course of the past difficult year, she'd become the sort of woman men looked at twice. She'd begun dressing elegantly, simply, in the bright colors Aaron always hated. Sorrow had melted twenty pounds from her stomach and hips. Her recent promotion to events coordinator at the Milwaukee Holidome had given her the air of a woman used to accommodation.

"Lady," the bartender pleaded. "The most I can give you is a double."

"This is the last you'll see of me, I swear."

The bartender sighed. "One sec," he said, turning away, and when he returned he was holding a tall glass with Coca-Cola written in cursive down the side. "The last I'll see of you," he repeated.

"Scout's honor," Libby said, skimming a little off the top. As she turned away, she caught a glimpse of her oldest child, Mickey. He and Stanley Liesgang were skulking along the wall by the NO SMOK-ING sign, where three of April's gallery friends were defiantly lighting up. Libby sincerely hoped that the boys would spend the evening raising Cain. A small fire, such as the one they'd set at the Liesgangs' house last summer, would do nicely. And if Mary Fran got her pant-ies in a twist because Mickey had led dear, innocent Stanley into trouble again, Libby would tell her, Boo-hoo. Stanley was, after all, thirteen years old, two years older than Mickey. Stanley should be the one with enough maturity and common sense to say *no way, José* when Mickey suggested doing things like seeing if an inflam-mable mattress really *was* inflammable.

She worked her way toward the EXIT sign above the archway, passing through clots of Elmer's brothers and their wives, Mary Fran and Elmer's neighbors, April's friends from the gallery—each wear-ing nearly identical black dresses. (Carefully mussed hair and ma-roon nail polish seemed popular as well.) She wriggled around the epicenter of a political argument, holding her drink high and out of harm's way, and when her breasts brushed the forearm of a handsome, bearded man with pepper-and-salt hair, he smiled and said, "Why, thank you," but she let it go, spun forward into a group of Elmer's coworkers from the city, who'd been called in for a long night behind their plows, due to emergency road conditions. All were jolly at the prospect of the overtime, buying quick drinks for a flock of Mary Fran's flirtatious cousins before heading out. Some of these cousins Libby had met. All of them knew—she could see it in their faces—the saga of Aaron and Sara. Hurrying past, she tripped over the high, polished toe of a man's cowboy boot. Had its owner not caught her, she'd have hit the floor spectacularly, still clutching her drink like a bad promise.

"I'm sorry," she said as he released her.

"No harm done," the man said, though he lifted his foot to inspect it, as if hoping for damage. Everything about him looked gloomy: his thin chapped lips, his watery eyes, his suit with its fussy double-breasted cut. His head was like the dome of a peeled boiled egg, peppered with moles, salted with tiny albino freckles. A single, vigorous tuft of hair remained above his forehead, but he'd cropped it close, as if to quell its enthusiasm.

"You remember me, of course," he said.

"Of course." He was one of the cousin's husbands, but which?

"Well, I remember you, *too*, my dear, but I'm afraid I've forgotten your name."

The bastard. "Oh, I'm Libby—" she began, but then she faltered. Any last name she offered would involve a complicated explanation. The single name hung between them, like the name of a supermodel, or a rock star.

"All of this seems rather sudden, Libby," the man said.

She realized he was referring to the wedding, and not their introduction.

"Love at first sight, I suppose," she said, taking a polite step back.

The ice in her drink was making wet, tempting sounds. "I hear they're honeymooning in Mexico."

"I never did see the point of a honeymoon," the man said, "for couples who have already engaged in cohabitation."

Libby said she thought that couples who were already engaged in cohabitation were the ones who *most* needed a honeymoon. Then she laughed, a high little cheery nervous laugh, which eventually died of loneliness, for the man did not join in. He didn't even smile. He said that was certainly an interesting way of looking at things, but he wasn't sure her ideas could be supported by the teachings of our Lord Jesus Christ. Mumbling something about the ladies' room, Libby fled through the archway, into the spacious quiet of the ballroom.

Bliss. She took a victory slug from her cup, let that good, golden heat soften what had lately become a constant lump in her throat. Folding chairs had been arranged in a row along the wall; she chose one, sank into it gratefully. At the Holidome, she was the one who made certain receptions like these ran smoothly, and what a pleasure it was to sit back, relax, let somebody else head off the snafus.

A pack of children tore through the ballroom, Libby's own Sam among them; she noted, absently, that he wasn't wearing shoes. Jenny, she assumed, was still with Aaron and Sara—she'd seen the three of them heading toward the lobby. Mickey and Stanley were nowhere to be seen, and neither was Margo Liesgang, thank goodness. Libby felt for the little bottle of hydrogen peroxide she'd tucked into her purse—it was better to be prepared than deal with a staph infection later. But if Jaws bit one of her kids *this* time, Libby wouldn't let it pass with a splash of antiseptic. *This* time, Mary Fran and Elmer would have a lawsuit on their hands. It would serve those Liesgangs right if Libby sued their asses—and with that thought, her mood toppled into despair. How *could* they have invited Sara to the wedding? How *could* they have betrayed Libby that way? All through the divorce, Mary Fran had promised that things would stay the same between them. Their kids would grow up together. When it came to family gatherings, Libby would always be invited and Sara—well, wouldn't you think that Sara would just *want* to stay home?

Blinking back tears, Libby slurped off a little more whiskey. Until the incident before the reception, she'd been absolutely fine, telling herself again and again that, considering her sixteen years of marriage to Aaron, it was *Sara* who should feel out of place, and it was *Aaron* who should feel embarrassed. But in the confusion following the ceremony, Libby and the kids had ended up behind Aaron and Sara in the receiving line. At first, Libby hadn't even noticed. She was preparing herself to avoid Mary Fran's eye, to congratulate April and Caleb in a voice that betrayed nothing. Gradually, she realized that the man in front of them looked familiar. Something about the back of his head, the shape of his ears—

"Mom," Mickey whispered, "are we supposed to talk to him or what?"

And with that, Aaron turned around. "Kids?" he said. "Well, hello there!" Jenny and Sam launched themselves into his arms; Sara bent to kiss them, too. Jenny, who was eight—too old for such shenanigans—put a hand on Sara's stomach and announced, in her best made-for-TV voice, "That's a ba-by in her tummy."

All around them, people smiled indulgently.

"That's right, sweetie," Aaron said, hamming it up, too. "Your stepbrother. Just two more months till he's done and then the doctor can take him out of the oven."

"The *oven*?" Libby said. She hadn't planned to raise her voice. "The word, Aaron, is *uterus*."

They had reached the front of the line. The wedding party stood in a row like beads on a chain: Mary Fran and Elmer and Hilda; April and Caleb; Corrine Shannon and her grandchildren, Anderson and Lacey. Legally, they were all family now. And yet, at this moment, they might have been any random group of people waiting in line to see a movie. Someone had just popped a stick of gum. Juicyfruit. The sweet smell enveloped them all.

"Well," April finally said. "Thank you for coming, everybody." She stuck out a polite hand to Aaron, but he swept it aside.

"Is this how you treat your favorite uncle?" he said, crunching her in a big bear hug. A few pearly beads sprang from her dress, but Aaron didn't seem to notice. He congratulated Caleb. He complimented Elmer on the service, Mary Fran on her dress, Hilda on her glorious corsage. Next, he turned to Corrine, telling her how much he and Sara had just *loved* Nashville! Why, they'd spent a whole weekend at the Opryland Hotel. They'd taken a shuttle down to Second Avenue and gone line dancing at the Wild Horse Saloon. Sara was a big fan of country music, wasn't she, honey?

Sara nodded at the prompt.

Corrine Shannon was a heavyset, handsome woman, the sort of person who took her time before she spoke. She studied first Sara, and then Aaron, as if she were piecing together a story she did not particularly care for. Then she said, rather stiffly, "I *do* hope y'all realize there's a little more to Nashville than the *Wild Horse Saloon*."

Libby looked up. Could it be that there was *someone* in the world who saw Aaron for the unctuous phony he really was? Libby wanted to seize Corrine's hands and confide that Aaron had still been a married man when he'd sneaked off to Opryland. She wanted to tell her the joke he'd told Libby whenever he'd catch her listening to *Country Countdown*:

What happens when you play a country music record backward? The men sober up and they get their women back.

Aaron and Sara moved on, Sara holding Jenny's hand, Aaron with his arm slung around Sam's shoulder. Libby stood before the wedding party, eyes downcast, as if before a court of law. Aaron had already said anything she might think of to say.

"Oh, Aunt Libby," April said miserably, and Mary Fran started forward, but Libby felt Mickey's arm on her sleeve—dear, loyal Mickey—and she let him guide her away.

Now the group on the balcony stairs was breaking up. Mary Fran took April's bouquet; they exchanged a few words, then looked directly at Libby, mouths pinched with concern. Libby got busy examining her cuticles, but moments later, when she heard, "Aunt Libby?" what could she do but look up into the face of her favorite niece, her godchild? The billowing dress made April look like a swan. The bodice, which was bald in patches, made her look as if she was molting.

"I know, I look dreadful," April said. "But it meant a lot to Mom that I wore her dress."

"It's very pretty," Libby said, looking away.

"Yeah, right," April said. "Now let me talk, okay? I want to apologize for what happened in the receiving line. Mom's sorry, too. Sara—well, she just decided to come."

Libby shrugged, but she could feel herself wavering. Mary Fran was watching them from across the ballroom. Another bead popped off April's dress; this one landed with a *plop* in Libby's Coke glass.

"Shit," April said. "Please don't hate us. It's just really stressful, all this wedding stuff."

"You should have eloped."

"No kidding we should have eloped, don't tell me we should have eloped, that's what we wanted to do in the first place until my dad—" April pulled up a folding chair, yanked the train around, and tried to beat down the skirt of her dress so she could sit. But the chair shot backward with a screech when she attempted to lower herself onto it. "Fuck it," she said. "I'll stand. Look, can I get you another Coke?"

"You won't find another like this one," Libby said, relenting. She offered April the glass.

April sniffed, then took a long swallow. "I needed that," she said, and hit it again before handing it back. "God, this dress *itches*," she said, reaching deep into the bodice of her gown to scratch.

"What made you get married in a place like this?" Libby said. "I would have gotten you a summer deal at the Holidome. Indoor pool, shuffleboard—"

"We didn't want to wait that long."

"You're not pregnant, are you?"

"Is that what people are saying?" She was still scratching. "Christ, this thing is worse than a hairshirt."

"I just wondered," Libby said.

"I'm not pregnant," April said. "I'm in love. I'm happy."

Suddenly Libby felt ashamed. "Can I see your ring?"

April held out her hand; Libby touched the simple gold band, its diamond chip. Her own wedding ring was in her top bureau drawer. She couldn't figure out what to do with it. "So what's Caleb like?"

It was clear that April had been asked this question more than once since the reception began. "He grew up in Nashville. His dad's a minister, and it's kind of a sore point that Caleb didn't want to follow in his footsteps. He got a scholarship to this college, you probably haven't heard of it, but it's called Barton? Nobody has majors there, except for liberal arts, and they do all these apprenticeships in Minneapolis. That's how he got the job he has now with this law firm—"

"I didn't mean his résumé. I mean, what's he *like*."

"Oh." April smiled then, thinking. Across the ballroom, Caleb and his mother were looking out one of the tall windows, watching the falling snow. He was listening to something she was saying, his head bent toward her, earnest, attentive. "He's considerate," April said. "And honest. And relaxed about things. We don't have to be together all the time. And if something's wrong, he just tells me what it is, you know?"

Libby couldn't help laughing. "That sounds like any normal relationship."

"You would think," April said, glancing at her. "But it's all new to me. I mean, I knew things were never right between Barney and me—"

Libby was amazed. "But everybody thought you two were perfect together."

"Everybody thought you and Uncle Aaron were perfect, too."

Libby blinked. "Touché."

"I don't mean it that way," April said quickly. "It's just that nothing is ever the way it seems. From the outside anyway. Mom was always saying, look at how he talks to you, look at how he wants to spend time with you, you're so lucky. And I thought maybe I was lucky, only I didn't know it. Everybody liked him so much. Everybody had us married already when we were still in high school."

"So you outgrew each other, then? Is that what happened?"

"Something like that," April said, and then she said, "Crap." The photographer was waving her over. Mary Fran and Elmer were back on the stairs, this time flanked by Stanley and Margo. All of their mouths were set in the sort of flat lines which, on a heart monitor, would indicate the patient has died.

"Mom wants a family shot," April said. "Look—we'll talk more later, all right? I just didn't want you to think we planned on Sara's being here."

"Don't worry," she said. "I'm fine about it now." It was almost true. The whiskey was finally working. The thumbnail of pain that had lodged itself deep in her skull had given way. Sara's face drifted into her mind, but the image was no more significant than a single fluffy cloud on a beautiful day. At last she understood that everything was just a matter of perspective. Take that whole receiving-line fiasco. You just had to see it in the right light. Aaron and his ovens! As April headed for the balcony stairs, leaning slightly forward to offset the weight of her train, Libby imagined a little gold timer going off deep inside Sara's belly. The doctor putting on a pair of oven mitts. The baby, curled in its roasting pan, steaming and pink.

Libby smiled. Anybody for a drumstick?

From all the way across the room, posed with one arm around his wife and the other around his mother, feeling like the conduit between two highly charged batteries, Elmer Liesgang studied Libby's smile. Admired it. Strove to emulate it as the photographer tweaked April's bouquet, then fluffed her train into a glossy wave around everyone's feet. This, Elmer understood, was the sort of smile the photographer was trying to coax from them all: pleased and spontaneous. Delicious. The sort of smile memories are not so much made of as repaired by. The sort of smile that, pressed securely into an album, inspires silky waves of nostalgia. Nobody would remember Stanley's sullenness, Margo's glassy-eyed silence. Nobody would remember that Elmer and April hadn't exchanged a single word since he'd walked her down the aisle.

"Papa?" the photographer said, lowering his camera. "How about a little smile?"

Elmer recovered himself, bared his teeth all the way back to his first row of molars. Two were cracked; they hurt when he drank his morning coffee. *Stress,* the dentist had said. *Have you been clenching your teeth?* He stared at the top of April's head, the whorl of cowlicks at the crown that had been there since her infancy. He remembered how it had felt to stroke her baby-fine hair, how Mary Fran had scolded him: *Don't you know you never touch a baby's head?* No, he hadn't known anything—about babies, about children, their bodies so frail and needing. He hadn't known anything about adolescents, their attitudes and angers, their stunning flashes of sweetness. He was doing better with Margo, he could already see that, but April was lost to him forever. That moment in the lobby before the ceremony tortured him. *I don't expect your blessing, Dad . . .* Helplessly, he watched the future unfold: the infrequent holiday visits, the stilted phone calls on Father's Day, the photographs of grandchildren he'd never really know.

"Papa?" the photographer said pleadingly, and Stanley said, "Can I *please* go now, *please*?"

The photographer sighed. Then he said, "Okay. Why don't we try a couple shots with just Papa and Mama together?"

"Great idea," April said. "I'm gonna get rid of this train."

She hurried up the stairs toward the dressing room; Stanley wriggled through the banister supports and hit the ballroom floor at a run. Margo would have jumped, too, following his example, but Hilda took her arm and forced her to walk down the stairs in a ladylike way. This left Elmer alone with Mary Fran, who said, "Like rats from a sinking ship." He stared at her, appalled. How could she joke at a time like this?

Fortunately, as the photographer's camera chattered and popped, he remembered to take a deep, cleansing breath. After the Church had given April the big thumbs-down, he'd approached Father Corcoran, the assistant pastor at Saint Michael's, and begged him to ask Father Bork to reconsider that decision. He told Father Corcoran about April's youth and promise, about the double bed and Caleb's unremarkable livelihood, Mary Fran's indifference to the

Church, her refusal to attend Mass with him, his fear that there was something, you know, *hormonally* wrong with his son, who would be a freshman in high school next year and could still wear the same clothes he'd worn in fifth grade and whose voice sounded no different than his eight-year-old sister's—

Father Corcoran had listened for a long time before interrupting him to point out that Elmer's breathing patterns were shallow and irregular. "Peace of mind begins with the breath," he explained. Father Corcoran was a young man, fresh from seminary, known for his radical ideas. He fixed Elmer a cup of catnip tea, something Elmer found remarkably soothing. Then he and Elmer had breathed together, deep shuddering cleansing breaths, until Elmer started to weep. "Good, that's very good," Father Corcoran said, and Elmer, whose sobs had turned to childish hiccups, said the real trouble was he hadn't made love to his wife in almost two years and Mary Fran was mad at him and everything was pointless. "Everything is pointless," Father Corcoran said, "but it isn't *hopeless*." Then he suggested Elmer might want to come for regular visits, just for a while.

Deep cleansing breaths, one after the next. The camera chattered, the flash popped; still, Elmer felt his mind begin to clear. Once, Mary Fran's elbow stuck him in the ribs ("Are you catching a cold or something?" she said. "You sound congested."), but he let it go, returned to the breath, which was the beginning, and the ending, and all that was between. He began to see a radiant circle of light between his eyes, a light which, according to Father Corcoran, some cultures considered the soul. Is that what it is? Elmer had said, and Father Corcoran had said, What do *you* think it is? Elmer pondered this question now, his mind bathed in the exquisite shadows cast by the light, until he noticed one shadow that seemed different from the others. It lumbered along the light's perimeter, bumping against the smooth surface, a persistent sperm circling a placid egg. Something about it seemed familiar, and before Elmer realized what he had done, he had followed it back through time and space and into the confines of the ballroom, where, at the other end of the dance floor, the figure made its way around and around the reception tables, scavenging for whatever was left.

Good God. It was Barney Lohr.

Mary Fran must have seen him, too, because her elbow left another indentation in his ribs. Like sleepers caught in the same bad dream, they watched Barney feed the last snippets of cheese from the platter directly into his mouth. They watched him pick over the broken ends of the crackers. They watched him pluck the big decorative strawberry, suck it from its hull. How long had he been in the ballroom? Had he watched as the earlier pictures were taken? Had he stared at them all, at the living portrait of Liesgangs, at the family to which he'd never belong?

Mary Fran's sister, Melissa, had noticed Barney, too. She'd just finished her martini—Brian had gone off to get them two more—when she'd noticed him foraging for scraps among the decimated reception platters. Looking at his forlorn tuxedo, she could practically smell the mothballs. Poor bastard, she thought, surprising herself. It was, perhaps, the first sympathetic thought she'd ever had for Barney Lohr, whom she'd always considered the human equivalent of a floor rug hooked from a kit. For five long years she and Brian had tried—not always subtly—to drive a few well-placed wedges between Barney and April. In fact, during April's junior year at Madison, they'd even offered to sponsor a year abroad. But April said she wouldn't go unless Barney could go with her, and Barney's parents said Madison was far enough from Holly's Field. That had been the end of it.

Mary Fran, of course, had been no help whatsoever. "It's her life," was all she'd say.

No, Melissa had thought. It's yours and Elmer's all over again. Two incompatible people clinging to each other out of habit.

Caleb Shannon, on the other hand, seemed a step up the evolutionary scale. Capable of silence when silence was appropriate. Capable of a conversation which didn't center around carpet fibers, or whatever tired musical the community theater was planning next. Melissa hadn't met Caleb before today, but she'd spoken to him on the phone. He'd called to ask if she might be willing to lead the midnight toast. "Maybe you'd have some advice for us," he said. "Something that comes out of your own experience. April says you and Brian have been married—how long? Twenty years?"

"Twenty-two," Melissa said, pleased. Honored, in fact. That had been two weeks earlier. The problem was, she still hadn't been able to think of anything to say.

At forty-six, Melissa was the CIO of a Chicago-based software company; she dictated, on average, three dozen letters each day, not to mention countless e-mails, memos, and progress updates. Why, then, was she suddenly at a loss to find the words for what she wanted to say? Something about love being more about curiosity than passion—but no, that wasn't it, not exactly. Something about seeking out stormy seas and riding the waves instead of cowering in the shallows . . . gag. Something about the difference between forgiving and accepting—merciful Christ, now she sounded like a priest. It was nearly seven o'clock and, still, she had nothing more to go on than the few key words she'd jotted on the palm of her hand: *expectation, honesty, fulfillment.* So she was awfully happy to see Brian reappearing with those drinks—until she glanced over at Barney again. She sighed. She knew she ought to do the right thing and take him her drink. After all, if she'd seen a wounded creature on the highway, she'd have made the effort, backed up, aimed the wheel at its head. But, mercifully, one of Elmer's brothers intervened before she had time to do anything.

"Barn-boy!" he yelped, pumping Barney's hand. "Glad you're not a stranger! So how's your mom and dad?"

The older Liesgang brothers looked so much alike that few people could tell them apart. Barney, not having seen them together in a while, was no exception. Still, he gratefully shook the hand that was offered, said his mom and dad were doing fine, and before this particular Mr. Liesgang could reply, another had clapped him on the shoulder. They were thick-wristed men with the hunched, industrious look of beavers; they favored plaid sports coats, wide ties, pants in the highwater style. Only Frank had distinguished himself on this particular evening. A member of the Holly's Field Police Force, he'd worn his sharply creased dress blues.

"How about lettin' Frank there buy you a drink?" the second Mr. Liesgang suggested. "Seeing he's too good to touch the stuff himself."

"Sure, I'll buy him a drink," Frank said mildly. He'd been sober for almost a year, and not one of his brothers had forgiven him for it. "Why the hell not?"

Poor bastard, Frank thought, throwing an arm around Barney and guiding him—over his feeble protests—toward the cash bar. There, the crowd had thinned considerably, but April's college girlfriends were still perched on their stools, drinking martinis and chatting with the fourth Mr. Liesgang and several of the Mrs. Liesgangs. The younger women flirted with Barney sweetly, demanding that he taste their martinis, while the older women patted his arms and asked, So how's the carpet business these days?

Poor bastard, thought the bartender, who'd picked up the story in bits and pieces. Poor young fellah. But wasn't that just the way it always went? Young girl goes off to school and gets ideas and flies away. He filled a foamy cup, passed it over to the wretched kid. "On the house," he said.

"Here, here!" people said, and everybody raised their glasses in a toast.

"We're still friends, you know. Me and April," Barney said, as if it wasn't clear who he was referring to. The beer was like WD-40 on his tongue, loosening the limber muscle beneath it, greasing his soft palate, the hard uncompromising acorns of his vocal cords.

"That's the way to handle it," somebody said.

"She invited me herself," Barney said, nearly ripping the frayed invitation in two as he pulled it from his pocket, but everybody told him to put that away, of course he was invited, of course he was welcome, they sure were glad to see him, you betcha, and one of the Mrs. Liesgangs patted Barney's arm again and murmured about plans for new carpeting in the rec room, possibly the upstairs guest room, too, she would give him a call, and soon.

"No sense in having hard feelings," Barney said, and everyone agreed there was no sense in that at all. "I mean," he said, "we've got all this history between us, and that doesn't change, you know?" And everybody, even the seasoned bartender, leaned forward, nodding, hoping to hear what some of that recent history might be. There were, of course, speculations about the breakup: April had gotten fed up because Barney hadn't finished his degree. April had fallen in love with Caleb much earlier than anybody realized. April just got too big for her britches, left the poor bastard behind.

"To history," one of April's friends toasted, when it was clear that Barney wouldn't or couldn't elaborate further.

Everybody echoed, "To history!"

"To the future," said a handsome, bearded man with pepper-and-salt hair. His name was Darien Cole, and he was Elmer's second cousin from Indianapolis. Years had passed since anyone had seen him last; now he was a lawyer, some kind of big shot. "Spilled milk can only sour, you remember that."

"Listen to the man," Frank Liesgang said. "That's why they pay him the big money."

"Well, it's free advice, so take it as such," Darien Cole said, and everybody laughed and agreed and accepted another round of drinks, which Darien generously paid for. More toasts were made. More rounds were bought. People raised their voices to be heard over the sound of tables being set behind them, coffee cups clattered onto saucers, the musical argument of knives and forks and spoons. Soon the warm, salty smell of chicken à la king thickened the air like fog. It was ten minutes till dinner. Last call. Anybody still thirsty? Anybody willing to risk conversation with a table full of strangers over tepid Asti Spumante alone?

Barney tried to buy the final round, but no one would even hear of it. He wrapped his fingers happily around his fragile cup. He'd made the right decision, coming to the wedding. There was no doubt about that now. Sure, it had been painful when he'd first arrived and seen April on the balcony stairs. She looked older, more professional. She'd cut off her pretty long hair. And when she'd linked her arm casually through her new husband's—stop it, he told himself firmly. She was married now. That was that. The next time he saw her, he'd simply walk over and congratulate her. Maybe he'd give her a brotherly peck on the cheek. If that seemed to go over all right, he might even take the liberty of a hug, closing his eyes to better smell the sweetness of her neck.

But he hadn't seen her anywhere since the photographs had been taken. In fact, no one else had, either. April was still upstairs. Stalling. She had left the heavy train in the dressing room, draped across the daybed like a dry, yellowing skin. She'd killed some time in the bathroom, running a brush through her short hair—*snap, snap, snap*. Now she sat down on the closed toilet seat, pawed at the toilet paper, and blew her nose, hard. One wedding down, one to go. Tomorrow, instead of flying straight to Mexico for their honeymoon—they had reservations at a little town in the Bajas, well off the beaten track—she and Caleb were stopping over in Nashville, where Caleb's father would perform a second ceremony at the New Life Christian Joy Fellowship. They'd been unable to get out of it. Corrine had tried to intervene, but the Reverend Arthur Shannon had insisted, and the congregation had gone ahead and arranged everything. And when Caleb had phoned his father to object, the Reverend—instead of arguing back—had broken down and wept. Caleb, helpless before his father's tears, had promised they would be there. How could April explain to Elmer that she was being married in a fundamentalist church after refusing to consider a Catholic service? She could not. And so the second wedding was a secret. This nondenominational service—which she'd hoped would satisfy both families—had satisfied no one at all.

She got up and went back into the dressing room, stared at her reflection in the mirror over the daybed. It was as if she'd stepped into a painting, something not terribly original, yet poignant for all its diligent detail. The bulbs in the lamps were tinted pink, and this made her skin look unnaturally rosy, tubercular against the stark whiteness of the dress. There were dark circles under her eyes, a glint of steel reflected in each pupil. She knew that it was time to head back to the ballroom. She needed to make sure her mother didn't want any more pictures. She needed to try, yet again, to patch things up with her father. She needed to circulate among the guests, some of whom she was having trouble recognizing: friends of her parents, distant cousins, people she hadn't seen in years. She needed to rescue Caleb from her relatives' painfully earnest questions about Dollywood and Graceland.

Instead, she compulsively checked their plane tickets, their passports and traveler's checks. She went through their carry-on luggage, making sure that nothing had been forgotten: their books, her sketchpad and pencils, candy bars. Pepto-Bismol and prescription medication for the diarrhea everybody promised they would get. Birth-control pills. Condoms in case she missed a pill, which she always seemed to do whenever it was crucial that she didn't. Then she took the service elevator down to the game room, the way she'd done just before the ceremony. Before she was married. She realized that she'd expected to feel different now. The elevator warbled and groaned, descending so slowly that it didn't even feel like it was moving, and she remembered a vacation she had taken with her parents, long before Stanley was born, when they'd crossed the Wisconsin line and entered the state of Minnesota. She'd been four or five, and how she'd waited for that moment, expecting—what? Even now, she couldn't say. She knew only that she'd been disappointed when the road continued uninterrupted, and the landscape stayed the same. If somebody hadn't put up a sign, there'd have been no way to know that anything had changed.

The elevator landed; the inner door gave way. April opened the metal, outer cage and stepped into the game room, twisting to tug her skirt through the narrow door. When she turned around, she jumped and said, "Jesus!" Caleb was sitting on the edge of the air-hockey table.

He grinned at her. "Busted."

"I was going to come right back."

"You were going to hide down here till suppertime."

It was the truth, and they both knew it. She said, "Maybe not quite till suppertime."

The game room looked and smelled like the cellar that it was. The ceilings were low, the beams exposed. The cement floor was partially covered by large rubber mats. Here and there, lightbulbs swung from cords, the glare softened somewhat by dented green shades. There was a warped, plywood bar with a half-dozen bar stools, a mirrored wall that reflected a waiting keg, cocktail napkins, stacks of plastic cups. A pool table set too close to the air-hockey table. Ping-Pong. Pinball machines. A battered dartboard.

"Come over here," Caleb said.

She went to him gratefully, leaning into him, the skirt of her dress spilling over his knees. "Can we go home now?" she asked, and he kissed her, the answer she had wanted. Reflectively, he licked her lower lip. Touched it with his finger. "Where'd you get the whiskey?"

"Libby."

"Did I meet her?"

"In the receiving line."

"The one who's mad at your mom because the new wife showed up."

"Very good."

They kissed again, her arms about his neck, his fingers snagging in the ruffles around her hips.

She said, "I can't believe we're married."

"Why not?" He'd slid off the table to hold her against him; now he turned them both around so she could hop up.

"It's just weird," she said.

He rubbed her thighs with the flat palms of his hands. "I think it's nice." They could hear the wooden footsteps of the guests overhead, the rasp of a chair pushing back, a high, strange wail of laughter. He was trying to lift her skirt, clumsily searching through the thick folds of material.

"Are you crazy?" she said.

"Look at me," he said, but she was looking at the stairs leading up to the lobby.

"Nobody's coming down here," he said. "It's closed until the dance."

"People will be looking for us."

"So let them find us. We're legal now, remember?"

She laughed, tried to wriggle off the table, but he linked his hands behind the small of her back. "Would you please just look at me?"

Up close, his green eyes always seemed golden. He was breathing through his mouth, like an eager child. He said, "Don't you know we're going to be great together?"

And with that, the strange feeling she'd carried since the ceremony left her. "I know it," she said.

He was fingering the folds of her skirt again; she clawed the whole mess into her lap and let him ease her back onto the table, one hand cupped to pillow her head. Pinprick airholes scraped the skin between her shoulder blades, bare beneath the scooped back of the bodice.

"Nothing fancy," she said. She'd already kicked off her shoes, and now she struggled out of her panty hose, fighting the cloudy haze of dress.

"We have time."

"We don't. Come here."

"This won't exactly be ladies' night."

"I don't care," she said, pulling him up by the boxy shoulders of his tuxedo. And this was the thing that amazed her again and again: how effortless it was, this physical affection, as if sex were just another kind of conversation, another way of saying something that needed to be said, the continuation a story that had begun on the day they'd met and was still unfolding, even now, as they cleaned the apartment or went to work or shopped for the groceries. A story that returned to its source now and then, the way all good stories do. Repeating favorite punch lines. Going over and over the best moments.

He was fumbling in his trouser pockets.

"What?" she said.

"Hang on." He reached somewhere just beneath her. There was a clank, and then the table started to hum. Cold air rushed up through the hundreds of pinprick holes, and they shook against each other, laughing, as the skirt of the wedding dress billowed around them.

THE man in suite thirty-three was restless. He paced the length of the room. A couple of times he parted the curtains to peer out into the storm. Something was bugging him, he couldn't say what. Maybe a nice supper would put everything right. Order was the best remedy for disorder; experience had taught him that. No matter what fell from the sky all around you, you just went on going to work and coming home and eating and sleeping, and before you knew it, the storm had passed and the sun came out again. The trick was making certain you never looked back, like Lot's wife—what was her name? Did it even matter? Forgive and forget, that's what mattered. Let bygones be bygones. Turn the other cheek, that's why God gave you two. This was the secret to a happy marriage, maybe even a whole happy life.

The woman, his wife, was still sleeping. The man couldn't wake her up.

The thing was, he'd already forgiven her for everything that had happened during the long afternoon. In fact, it all seemed like something he'd dreamed or made up, a story in the newspapers, or on

TV. It was only when he decided to get himself cleaned up to go out that he noticed their suitcase wasn't on the luggage rack anymore. He found it in the kitchenette, cracked open like an egg, clothes and toiletries scattered everywhere. Another funny thing: there was a good-sized gouge in the wall where the RUSTLERS WILL BE SHOT sign had been hanging. Now the sign was on the floor, the glass cracked into daggers. One of the chairs lay on its back, legs thrust into the air, and it looked like an animal, a turtle or a beetle, foolishly struggling to right itself.

The man was truly surprised by what he saw, even though he'd been the one to hurl the suitcase at the RUSTLERS sign and kick over the chair and generally tear the place apart. When his wife had made a run for the door, he'd beaten her to it and yanked it open, ripping the chain clean out of the wall. "C'mon," he'd said, daring her to get past. "What's the matter? Not so brave all of a sudden, huh?" She'd surprised him, though, by starting to yell, something she rarely bothered with anymore, and what she yelled was *Fire! There's a fire! Call 911!* at the top of her lungs, which was something she'd read in one of her women's magazines. She liked to read them at night, after work, and sometimes she'd read aloud to him—mostly just the questionnaires, but every now and then she'd say, "Hey, listen to this," and he knew he'd have to sit through an entire article, which really bugged him, the way it bugged him when she'd read aloud from the morning paper. This time, though, he'd made a point of looking at her, because he was so relieved she was speaking to him again. Things had gotten a little out of hand the previous evening, but everything was pretty much blowing over, as these things usually did, and the memory seemed, well, kind of embarrassing really, silly even, to look back on now that they were fine again, better than fine, a nice couple sitting in their living room discussing something one of them had read.

The article said that if a woman was being attacked, she should yell *Fire!* instead *Help!* or *Rape!* or whatever you'd think she would yell.

That's crazy, he'd said.

It's based on statistics, she said. They say that if you yell *Rape!* or *Murder!* it scares people off. Nobody wants to get involved.

If you were being murdered, how could you yell "murder"? the man said, to change the subject. But his wife wasn't listening.

I suppose these days nobody would help you, no matter what you yelled, she said. And then she went back to her reading, just like that, as if they'd never even spoken.

But the man couldn't stop thinking about their conversation. What was wrong with people? What was happening to the world? If *he* ever heard a woman yell *anything,* he'd be there in a flash. Sometimes, he even imagined encountering a situation where a young woman was being forced into a car. How he'd wrestle her attacker to the ground, take command of the gun or the knife. How he'd hog-tie the scumbag with his own belt. The would-be victim's gratitude. The admiration of the police, just arriving on the scene. The write-up in the paper, in which he'd state emphatically that he was not a hero, that he'd simply done what any decent citizen would do.

Recently, he'd been driving home from a friend's place—it was somewhere close to midnight—when he'd seen a girl walking by the side of the interstate, all alone. When he pulled up beside her, he could tell she couldn't decide if she was more afraid of riding with him or staying where she was. C'mon, he told her, I'm not going to hurt you, and he flashed his wedding ring like a badge. It turned out that her car had broken down. She was just sixteen, had been walking for over an hour. He drove her all the way to her mother's house, and later his wife had said who knew what might have happened if he hadn't stopped and been the Good Samaritan. It was nothing, he told her, proud and pleased, and she said, I'll tell you what, sometimes I think there aren't any Good Samaritans left in the world.

But she must have still hoped there might be a few, yelling *Fire!* with her head tipped back and her mouth opened wide as it could go right there in the middle of the goddamn Western Suite. It was the damnedest, funniest thing, and he'd laughed—he couldn't help himself—and she started laughing, too, and the two of them just stood there laughing like best friends, like old drinking buddies, like they'd just heard the best joke in the world. When he grabbed for her, though, she twisted away and chunked a lamp at him, a good-sized fucker, too, probably would have brained him if it hadn't missed him altogether and then he had her pinned down on the bed. She bit him pretty good when he got his hand over her mouth, so he let her yell into the pillow for a while. He kept expecting a knock at the door, a stern voice asking what the hell the problem was, but nobody came, and after a while, he couldn't say how long, he began to calm down a little and he thought what in hell was wrong with the world that someone could scream *Fire!* or *Help!* or *Dear God, please!* and neither God nor man would lift a finger to see what the trouble was. His wife was right. There were no Good Samaritans. There was nobody to stop him from kicking the living shit out of her, again and again, no matter how much he wanted to be stopped, no matter that afterward he'd want only to die and the one way to keep from blowing his brains out, from slitting his wrists, from stripping away the veins with his own bared teeth was to hop back on the horse, old sport, get back on the track. Go to work and come on home, go out for a nice supper somewhere and wait for the whole goddamn thing to blow over and then don't look back, forgive and forget, let bygones be bygones, isn't that what Jesus said?

All he had wanted was a happy Valentine's Day, some quality time, just the two of them together. All he'd wanted was to talk and make love and go for long walks on the snowy trails. Even as everything came back to him, he was mystified by the evidence he saw. He began to bargain, make promises. When his wife woke up, he'd do whatever she wanted. He'd take her home, no problem. He'd agree to a separation. He'd clean the whole house, top to bottom, and finally get the snow tires put on her car, and cook for her and wash her hair and rub her feet so tenderly if only she'd turn the other cheek, just this one last time. If only she'd forgive him. If only she'd just wake up.

But she wouldn't wake up, so he got himself dressed in the sweater that she'd bought for him, a nice pair of pants to match. He had a few more gulps of that brandy straight from the bottle, then walked down the hall and let himself out through the heavy storm door. The storm hit him in a blast of stinging cold and white; he staggered back before catching his balance. A nice supper, he told himself, slogging along what he hoped was the trail, trying to keep the wavery light above the Chapel's front porch in view. He'd planned to get something from the pizza joint across the intersection, but by now the snow was falling so hard he couldn't see even that far. Darkness had fallen, a terrible ignorant country darkness, the sky like the endless roiling belly of a whale. The man took deep burning gulps of cold air—he was crying, why was he crying?

The porch light shivered and burned.

When he walked into the lobby, the warmth of the fire made leftover tears leak from his eyes. He stood by the door, slapping snow off his pants legs.

"Are you here for the wedding?" the desk clerk asked.

"Yeah," the man said, wiping his eyes, and then, "Yes," more firmly. Why not? He might end up with a free meal. The boy was looking doubtfully at his casual pants, his down-filled parka, but all he said was, "May I check your coat?"

"I'm fine," the man said.

"Well, okay," the boy said. "But supper's already started, and it's no fun eating with your coat on."

The man hesitated. Then he shrugged, unzipped his parka. "Thanks," he said, handing it over. He smoothed out the sweater; it was a nice sweater, at least. Surely, with the weather like it was, a few other people would be underdressed. The boy indicated a set of heavy doors.

"Walk all the way through the ballroom," he said. "The dining room's on the other side."

The man did as he was told, scuffing his wet work boots against the smooth pickled floors. Christmas-tree lights filled the room with quiet starlight. He could smell the yeasty dinner rolls, the salty meat. Already, he was feeling better. Maybe all he needed was some food in his stomach. Some wine, some good conversation. Back on the hobbyhorse, back on the track. The nuptial canopy shone violently white as he walked on toward the dining room and the dark, musical murmur of people settling down to a meal. The tables were arranged in long, parallel rows; he stood back, watching, until he noticed an open place setting. Then he headed for it and, without hesitating, pulled back the chair.

"This seat free?" he asked.

"Help yourself," said the young guy across from it. "You with the bride's side or the groom's?"

Too late, the man realized the young guy was a talker. "Which are you?" he asked.

"Bride's," the young guy said. He seemed surprised that the man would ask.

"Groom's," the man said, playing it safe.

The young guy's eyes narrowed with something like curiosity. "I'm Barney Lohr," he said, extending his hand, but the man pretended not to see it. He reached for the breadbasket. He broke open a dinner roll. He kept his gaze fixed on his shining plate. A face stared back up at him, the features blurred, indistinct. Both familiar and unfamiliar. It might have belonged to anyone in that room.

SUPPER

y seven o'clock, the storm was setting records. Power outages trailed behind it like a broad, black wake. There were reports of high winds, drifting snow; a forty-mile stretch of the interstate had been closed. But none of this deterred the house band as they flew through the fields on their snowmobiles. The Chapel shone on the horizon like a strange and wonderful planet, appearing briefly—an impossible mirage—before vanishing altogether into the next whiteout. Praise the Lord for Bittner's Plaza! Had they not glimpsed the bloody pulse of its sign, they might have charged straight on past the Lodge and into Lake Michigan. Instead, they circled back, weaved their way through the Chapel parking lot, and plowed into the tall drift running the length of the porch.

Laughter. The death rattle of the last choked engine. A few good-natured curses, one following the next, like a child's merry round. The band was red-faced beneath goggles and ski masks, not so much from the cold as from a two-hour stopover at the Mother of Pearl. The In-Laws, they were called. Their wives, who were sisters, had named them. Ten years earlier, there had been five In-Laws, but clogged arteries and hypertension had trimmed their membership to three: Jackie Vogel, the handsome lead singer, who also played backup accordion; John-John Waranka, the backup singer—not so handsome—who played accordion and squeeze box and, during certain numbers, his armpit and bare belly; and Lou Fojut, the tuba player, who was shaped like his instrument, and wore the high-shouldered, pleading look of a child who longs to be invisible. Of course, he suffered from paralyzing stage fright, and thus it was moral duty—this alone!—which had forced Jackie and John-John to lubricate him thoroughly at the Mother of Pearl. After all, as they loved to tell their wives, you can't endure surgery without a *little* anesthesia! You wouldn't want the poor man to suffer, now, would you?

No one appeared to be suffering now.

In the lobby, they stomped the snow from their boots and blew their noses lustily. "She's a honey out there," Jackie told the desk clerk as they trooped into the back office. "You ain't getting home tonight."

"You see him worrying?" John-John said. "He's already countin' his overtime."

The lights flickered and the desk clerk said *Fudge!* for he'd been entering data into the computer. "What overtime?" he called after them. "I'm lucky if Bamberger doesn't bill me for a night's stay."

Everybody had a good laugh at that one. They all knew Ralph Bamberger: tighter than bark on a tree.

These days, the In-Laws kept their instruments and gear in a closet off the planning parlor. As young men, they'd rehearsed in each other's homes, but the truth was that they hadn't learned a new number in years. Why shake folks up? Audiences knew what they wanted to hear: the "Beer Barrel Polka," the "Too Fat Polka," "Who Stole the Kishka?" with a few contemporary numbers thrown in. "Rhinestone Cowboy." "Rawhide." The inevitable medley from

Fiddler on the Roof. Sometimes, Jackie stepped off the stage, chose a pretty gal, and spun her around the dance floor. The audience, led by John-John, egged him on. "A telephone book apart!" John-John would yell, and Jackie would holler back, "Telephone *book*? I thought it was a telephone *number*!" Bad jokes like these were part of their repertoire, the kind of thing Bamberger paid them for. (How can you tell if a train's passed through? By its tracks!) The older couples loved it. The younger brides and grooms were, well, less than charmed. But avuncular antics and a rollicking repertoire tugged at the tender heartstrings of their parents, and tender heartstrings—like the kneebone to the shinbone—were connected to stubborn purse strings. A breathless bunny hop or a tipsy hokey-pokey greased the hinges of the tightest purse clasp, smoothed the folds of the stiffest wallet. You get a crowd shouting *E-I-E-I-E-I-OH* and they weren't about to quibble over dollars and cents.

Bamberger was waiting in the ballroom, looking up at the flock of plaster cherubs as if he were hoping one of them might descend, should the band not show, and sing a joyful song. When he saw Jackie, he bellowed, "You fellahs know what time it is?"

"There's a little bit of snow on the road," Jackie told him. "Thought I'd point that out to you, in case you didn't notice."

Bamberger ignored this. "They're already into the main course," he said, waving his hand at the dining-room archway. "They're drinking like soldiers."

"My kind of crowd," John-John said, shrugging his shoulders through the straps of his accordion. Lou embraced his tuba, tongued the mouthpiece, let loose with a nervous *blat.*

"Speaking of soldiers," Jackie said, nodding at Lou, "this particular regiment's parched."

"Not likely," Bamberger said, but he whistled to Dimmer and Jeffery, who were trotting carts piled with dirty salad plates toward the kitchen. The lights flickered; Bamberger heard the nervous gasp of the crowd. There wasn't much left on those plates, and he knew this was not a good sign. Usually half the salads came back mostly untouched, though politely rearranged. This, after all, was a canned-vegetable crowd. Fresh vegetables were acceptable only if cooked beyond recognition or, better still, served creamed. The salad was something to be endured, like endless previews before a long-awaited movie, or perfunctory flirtations before the satisfying rigors of sex. Perhaps someone might spear a few limp pieces of iceberg lettuce while waiting for the breadbasket to pass. Most guests, however, licked the dressing off their forks, ate the single cherry tomato, and held out for the meat.

Real food for real people. This country wasn't won on lettuce.

But the storm was making them uneasy. They weren't nibbling, they weren't eating; they were indiscriminately gorging. An age-old animal part of their brains was telling their bodies to bulk up. Bamberger stood in the archway, watching quarter sticks of butter disappear into the hot, open mouths of fresh-sliced dinner rolls. Grease glistened on lips and chins. When the lights flickered again, a woman fished the lemon slice from her water glass, bared her teeth, and stripped it clean.

Bamberger shivered. He thought of Donner's Pass, pushed the gruesome image away. If the power went out, which it frequently did, there was always the emergency generator, which towered between the road and the edge of the parking lot like a piece of modern art. It spit enough juice so the pipes wouldn't freeze. In the meantime, guests would be able to see by the light of the candles on each table, and Emily had set out a dozen fresh boxes of Fancy White Tapers just in case. If the highway was still closed in the morning, there was meat in the freezer, powdered eggs, and milk. No, it was not the prospect of cannibalism that troubled Bamberger.

The true source of his anxiety was potential loss of revenue. If the power stayed out for any length of time, Lodge guests would demand full refunds, insisting there was no way in Hoover they'd pay for partial services. No matter that they'd already messed up their rooms, showered and changed, enjoyed the TV. No matter that, if they didn't like the weather, they should take up the issue with God Almighty instead of an innocent businessman. The savvier ones wouldn't argue; they'd simply stop payment on their Visas. And forget about cot fees! Forget, too, about charging for whatever Emily might scrape together in the kitchen during the course of their entrapment.

Bamberger scanned the rows of boisterous middle-aged uncles, the parallel universe of boisterous middle-aged aunts; the artsy crowd arguing heatedly at the single, round table by the window; the miscellaneous tables holding school friends, family friends, coworkers, and neighbors. Usually, he could spot the malcontents, potential ringleaders and troublemakers; he'd target them for special attentions, a cordial hand on the shoulder, maybe even a free drink or two. His gaze skipped neatly over the children's table—nothing to worry about there—and landed at the head table, its finery and flowers, the towering cake photogenically stationed on a sideboard just behind the bride and groom. The photographer shuffled between the tables, shooting sweet old couples and attractive young women and, here, a group of middle-aged men who were emptying the contents of their pockets onto the table, shouting, "Yeah, but look at this, see this?" And here was the main course, right on time, servers gliding up and down the rows as gracefully as dancers, each bearing steaming plates of chicken à la king.

The guests tucked in. Let the lights flicker. This was Grade-A comfort food. Nothing too spicy, nothing unfamiliar. Nothing too colorful, crunchy, textured. Plenty of white sauce to smother it all.

How lovely it was to have a nice hot meal. How lovely to enjoy it without a tower of pots and pans in the kitchen casting their long shadows over the moment at hand. And how particularly lovely not to have to eat with the children for a change. To erect the complex scaffolding of adult conversation without risking injury to little pitchers' ears. Complete sentences bridging metaphors. Curses punctuating complaints. And the children just as happy at their own special table, making new and wonderful friends.

STANLEY Liesgang thought that the chicken à la king looked exactly like barf. Mickey Schrunk, taking another hearty bite, disagreed. "Barf wouldn't have so many chunks in it," he said, with his mouth full.

"Yes, it would," Stanley said irritably. Why did Mickey always have to contradict him? Stanley was, after all, thirteen years old—two years older than his cousin. "If it was freshly eaten. It takes a while for stuff to digest."

"I'm warning y'all," said Lacey. She reached for the salt, her bracelet brushing Stanley's hand. Lacey's breasts were almost like real ones, not the painful-looking bumps most junior-high girls had. Her bangs were teased into a short, stiff shelf which shaded her face like an awning. Her lip gloss left faint, bloody kisses on her napkin, cruel tattoos on the paper's pale flesh, and Stanley found himself wondering how he might get hold of that napkin as a keepsake. He imagined the smell of it, something feminine and fruity. He imagined the pressure of it tucked inside his trouser pocket.

Lacey was the single redeeming feature of the children's table, where Stanley had been confined along with the Tennessee kids, plus Mickey and Mickey's kid brother and sister, a handful of Liesgang cousins, and a couple more kids nobody knew. Everyone was pretending it wasn't thoroughly humiliating to be drinking 7UP out of Disney cups and eating off Disney plates at a table spread with a Mickey Mouse oilcloth. The first time the server had come around in her crisp, white apron—a stout woman with a thick square belly like a vault—they'd all sat in mutual, miserable silence as she told them how, should they need something, they were expected to raise their hands, any questions?

Anderson, without raising his hand, had asked for coffee and was refused.

Now Anderson said, "*I* threw up a whole hot dog once." He had wide shoulders, narrow hips. Razor stubble separated his nose from his upper lip like a thriving hedge. Like Stanley, he was an eighth-grader, but he was already fourteen and he looked like a sophomore in high school. You could just tell he was the sort of kid who was popular at school. The sort of kid who was good at sports. The sort of kid who made passing through the halls akin to running the gauntlet if you happened to look like, say, Stanley Liesgang. The sort of kid it seemed more and more likely that Mickey Schrunk would become. But the wedding had shaken everyone free of his or her perch on the social food chain. Like shipwreck survivors, they'd landed on an island where regular rules did not apply. The fight for the giant conch was on. Anything might happen.

"It was in three pieces," he said. "You could still see the tooth marks."

Lacey said, "Grow *up,* y'all, I mean it."

Normally, Margo would have been in the thick of a conversation like this one, offering anecdotes drawn from her own wide range of experiences. But today she'd given Stanley a murderous look and carried her plate to the head table. It was the first time she'd even acknowledged him since he'd said that thing to her during the ceremony. It was something he'd heard at school. A boy had said it to a girl nobody liked, and Stanley had laughed at the time. But the more he thought about it, the more it seemed like a terrible thing to say, especially to your little sister. Earlier, when they'd had their pictures taken, he'd tried speaking to her, but she'd pretended not to hear.

Now he still felt guilty, yes, but he also felt a little relieved. Without Margo hanging on him all the time, clamoring for his attention, he was free to talk to whomever he pleased. Lacey, for instance. The thing was, he didn't quite know how to begin. He remembered Mary Fran telling him that, if you wanted to make a friend, you should ask a question. It was the sort of *Sesame Street* advice that usually made him want to punch someone, but his mother was a girl, and Lacey was a girl, so maybe, in this particular situation, Mary Fran did know what she was talking about. He thought about a question he might ask. Something about the wedding. Something about the Chapel. He thought about a story kids told about a high-school boy who'd broken into the ballroom on a dare. He'd fallen asleep and dreamed of a beautiful woman in a cherry-red dress. Do you want to kiss me? she'd asked. It's all right, go ahead. But each time he kissed her, he got a mouthful of rice. Finally, he said, You're really beautiful and all, but how come each time I kiss you I get a mouthful of rice? And she said, Oh, that's not rice. It's worms. I've been dead for fifty years.

He wasn't sure that this was what Mary Fran had had in mind. Besides, it wasn't a question. "What suite are you guys staying in?" was what he finally came up with.

"Suite thirty-five," Lacey said, and she made a face. "It's full of unicorns. There's a rainbow painted over the beds."

"Thirty-five?" Mickey said, with his mouth full. He swallowed, and Stanley could see cold envy in his eyes. "You mean you're, like, right next to suite thirty-three?"

"So?" Anderson said.

Could it be that he and Lacey didn't know? Stanley and Mickey exchanged disbelieving glances. Mickey started to speak, but Stanley interrupted him, eager to be the one to explain.

"There's prostitutes in suite thirty-three," he said. "That's how this place makes its money. The wedding stuff is, like, a front."

"Yeah, right," Anderson said.

"It's true," Mickey said proudly. "All you have to do is tell the front desk you're looking for a friend in suite thirty-three, and they'll know exactly what you mean."

"Nuh-uh," Stanley said. "What you have to say is, 'Has the President checked in?' And when they say, 'What room?' you tell them, 'Suite thirty-three.' And then they send somebody to your room."

"How would you know?" Mickey said.

"They'll send any kind of girl you want." He was improvising now, but it was working; Lacey had put down her fork. "You can even go visit them, pick one out."

"The only thing *you'd* know how to pick is your nose," Mickey said scornfully.

"Bite me."

"Y'all are making this up, right?" Lacey said.

Somebody started tapping a knife against a wineglass. Within seconds the sound spread, swelling until the whole room sparkled with it. Now everybody was tapping their glasses—everybody, that is, except those seated at the children's table. Plastic cups just didn't have the same ring. There was nothing for Stanley and the others to do but watch as Caleb and April rose and kissed each other. It was a long kiss, too, even though they'd had to do it just a few minutes earlier. Stanley wondered if they were using their tongues. He wondered if Caleb had a boner. Shame lapped over shame. The sad fact was that he could barely even glance at his sister in her wedding dress without succumbing to thoughts of the wedding night. Such thoughts were gross and exciting and exquisitely painful all rolled up into one weird feeling. Perhaps the adults felt the same way, for they hooted and clapped even after the tinkling of silver died away.

The lights flickered, popped off. Popped on. For a moment nobody spoke. Gradually, the murmur of conversation resumed.

"If one of us *did* throw up," Mickey said, reclaiming the conversation, "and the power goes out? I bet we could, like, serve it to somebody? And they'd *eat* it."

"Whenever our dog throws up, he eats it," Anderson said.

"*That's* it." Lacey stood up, glared at each of them in turn—it seemed to Stanley that she looked at him a bit longer than the others—and then stalked away. Anderson was laughing, a deliberate I-want-you-to-hear-me kind of laugh, and when Mickey accidentally-on-purpose made the milk he'd been drinking spurt out of his nose, the entire table erupted into squeals and shrieks. Stanley said, "*Grooooss*," but the truth was that he was, well, bored. How many times, over the years, had he seen his cousin do the same thing? And not just with milk: lemonade and Hawaiian Punch and even cherry pop, though Mickey had done that only one time because the bubbles had given him a headache. Suddenly Stanley was tired of Mickey, tired of his leaky nose and potty mouth and inevitably sticky fingers, tired of setting things on fire, tired of the familiar, homey talk of barfing and farting and belching, tired of making the same old crank phone calls and playing the same old practical jokes. He was ready, he felt, for something more left-brained. Boundaries, guidelines. Focus. He believed that a time of great change was upon him, the way his latest horoscope had said. These days, he had to read the weekly horoscope in secret because Elmer disapproved. Elmer said that if Stanley wanted to know the direction of his future, he should pray for God's guidance. The trouble was that Stanley usually didn't remember to pray until it was time to get ready for bed. And getting ready for bed meant taking off his clothes. And taking off his clothes meant being naked. And being naked meant that certain thoughts swarmed into his mind like flies, settled upon the dung heap of his soul, and feasted upon the rich variety of pornographic carnage that festered there.

Ruefully, Stanley watched Lacey set a steady course toward the nearest ballroom archway. He knew she didn't look much like girls who were supposed to be pretty, the girls on the pom-pom squad at school with their skinny legs and snub noses, or the grown-up ladies in the copy of *Ouch!* he'd swiped from an older kid's gym bag. Lacey was what Mary Fran called *big-boned*. She'd bitten both thumbnails down to the quick. She had acne along her jawbone, the beginnings of a double chin. Somehow, none of that mattered. Or made things better. He couldn't say which.

Lacey. The long, velvet curtains in Stanley's living room were trimmed with lace. He and Margo were forbidden to touch them, but sometimes Stanley did anyway, sneaking into the room to crush the exquisite fabric between his thumb and forefinger.

He could hear the polka band warming up, the slur and slide of accordion scales, the hollow grunt of the tuba. What would it be like to dance with Lacey? Stanley was a good dancer—though he'd never tried dancing with a real girl. Just April. Back when he was still in grade school, she'd come home from college in one of her rare, exuberant moods, wearing old-fashioned clothes ("Vintage," she called them), globs of paint stiff in her hair. "C'mon, sweet feet," she'd say, and instead of going over to Barney's right away, she'd put on one of Mary Fran's old LPs and swing him around the house. Her hands would be rough from building frames and stretching canvases, the edges of her nails discolored from paint thinner, her breath sweet from the clove cigarettes she sneaked in the upstairs bathroom.

By the time he was ten, Stanley could polka. He could fox-trot. He could do the Robot, the Swim, and the Dirty Dog. But after he started junior high, Elmer took him aside and told him he was a little too old to be dancing with his sister. She seemed to come home less and less anyway. Even after Barney dropped out of school, he usually went to visit her in Madison, rather than the other way around. Besides, Margo was getting old enough to want to dance, too, which was fine, except that she wanted Stanley to dance with her, to play with her, to *be* with her *all the time*. If she sensed his attention wandering, she'd pinch herself on the arm, twisting the skin, goose-style. Then she'd run to show Mary Fran the bruise, claiming that he had done it.

The last time Margo blackmailed him into dancing, Stanley had swung her into a doorjamb, which he'd meant to do and not meant to do in exactly equal proportions. Regardless, her lip required three stitches, and no dancing had been permitted in the Liesgang household since. But as Stanley watched Lacey's receding back, his feet remembered every joyful step, every skip, every *slide cha-cha-cha* he'd ever known, and he did not even realize he'd risen to his feet until he was stumbling after her, trousers slipping low on his hips, his father's gargantuan tie flapping between his legs. What if somebody noticed him? What would he say if someone asked where he was going?

He risked a glance at the head table, saw with relief that his parents were too busy picking at each other to notice anything or anybody but themselves. Elmer and Mary Fran's fights, if you could call them that, reminded Stanley of the plots of the old-timey books April liked to read. Nothing seemed to actually happen in those books. You could flip through them and glance at, say, every tenth page, and it would seem like all the same people were still in all the same rooms, talking about all the same things. But, at the end of the book, you'd discover that, just like the landscape before a glacier, things had gradually changed after all. People had fallen in love and men had gone to war. Hunters had returned from safari. Downtrodden families had avenged their good names.

Stanley much preferred the way that he and Margo fought. Their fights were like an action movie, complete with explosions and chemical warfare. Often, they both were left horribly wounded, clutching cracked ribs, groping for missing limbs. Then it would be over. Like cartoon characters, they'd jump to their feet, dust themselves off, and forget the whole business. Or, at least, that's how things usually went.

Stanley wondered what would happen if Margo never forgave him for what he'd said. He wondered what would happen if his parents split up. He wondered which one would remarry first. He wondered who he'd live with if that happened. He wondered if he would pass his driver's test when he finally turned sixteen. If it was true that high school would be worse than junior high. If April was really going to hell for getting married out of the Church, the way his grandmother said. If the stories about suite thirty-three were true. Why he wasn't growing, the way people thought he should be growing. Why his voice hadn't changed. Why he'd catch his father studying him the way he might study a malfunctioning bicycle.

These were the thoughts running laps in Stanley's mind as he slipped through the archway to freedom.

It was cool in the ballroom. The plaster cherubs swayed very slightly around the chandelier. On the small stage, the band had stopped their warm-up to rehash the Bucks game, gesturing at each other with their plastic cups of beer. Stanley had had a beer last fall, or part of a beer. Elmer had given it to him. "Try it," he'd told

Stanley. "It'll put hair on your chest." As soon as Stanley smelled it, yeasty and sour, he knew he did not want to drink it. But what could he do? He sat down on the couch beside Elmer. He took little teensy sips the way he did when his grandmother made him drink buttermilk, which she promised would "put some meat on those bones."

Meat on his bones. Hair on his chest. Sometimes, he'd sneak into his parents' bedroom and stand naked in front of his mother's full-length mirror, twisting this way and that to see if he had any flattering angles. He did not. The sad fact was that he looked like a hobbyhorse: tall thin pole of a body, yarnlike tuft of hair on top, enormous, painted eyes. He was crazy to think that Lacey would want anything to do with him. Not that he wanted to *do* anything— not like that. Well, maybe he did. But what he really wanted was to memorize the dip of her shoulders. To run his finger along the bumps of her spine. Later, after she'd gone back to Nashville, he could reassemble these delicacies like a complicated layer cake, devour the sweet thing whole.

"She went that way, boy," said one of the accordion players.

"Huh?" Stanley said.

The accordion player jerked his thumb at the lobby. Grinned. There was plenty of hair on *this* man's chest. It rose from beneath his open collar like the thick smoke from a scrub fire. Stanley tried not to stare at the man's belly, a slice of which hung down below the waistband of his embroidered vest. All the men wore identical vests, and lederhosen, and funny hats. Embarrassed for them, Stanley hurried on into the lobby.

But Lacey wasn't there, either. The fire in the fireplace had burned down to a single charred log. The phone booths were unoccupied. Stanley checked the coin returns; the last held a quarter, which he slipped into his pocket. Then he turned, studied the registration desk. No one was behind it, though he could hear somebody moving around in the back office. His attention was caught by a wall of keys, each hanging from its numbered hook as neatly as an earring from a woman's ear. Sometimes, a peculiar sensation came over Stanley, the feeling that he was not himself so much as somebody *watching* himself, and whenever he got this feeling, he did things he ordinarily would not do. As if he'd been planning this all along, he ducked around the counter and, in one fluid motion, selected the key labeled "33." By the time the desk clerk appeared, Stanley was himself again, back on the lobby side of the counter, studying the bowl of complimentary candies.

"These free?" he asked.

When the desk clerk looked at Stanley, he didn't see a hobbyhorse mounted on a pole. He saw the sort of sullen kid who might slip outside and key his car. Reluctantly, he nodded. Stanley picked out all the Hershey's kisses, pushed them into his pocket where the stolen key and the quarter he'd found *click-clicked* together, a soft secret sound.

"Thanks," he said.

The desk clerk forced a smile, reminding himself that this boy was one of God's children, too.

Stanley pretended he was heading back into the ballroom, but at the last minute, when he saw the desk clerk return to the back office, he veered toward the door marked GAME ROOM. The doorknob turned easily as sin beneath his hand.

Downstairs, Lacey stood behind the bar. It was as if she'd been expecting him. She didn't even bother to say hello. "What a dump," she said instead, turning toward the mirrored wall, and Stanley watched her hands alight seductively upon a keg, a stack of plastic cups, a small metal box marked CASH. She picked up the box, shook it. "We might-could pick it, if you have a knife."

Ruefully, Stanley shook his head. In fact, he owned a pocketknife, but Mary Fran wouldn't let him carry it.

"It doesn't matter. You want something to drink?" Without waiting for an answer, she selected a cup and expertly tapped the keg. For the first time Stanley noticed a second cup, half-full, sweating on the bar. He felt a flicker of kindness toward his father—it had been uncharacteristically thoughtful of Elmer to anticipate a situation just like this one, to make sure Stanley knew what beer tasted like in advance, so he wouldn't be surprised or embarrassed. "Cheers," Lacey said, and they clicked their cups together. A tingling wave from Stanley's crashed over their knuckles.

"Sorry," he said.

Lacey sucked at her glistening rings, lapped the back of her hand. Then she leaned toward him, elbows on the bar's rough, plywood top. "You need to relax," she said.

"I know."

"Are you always this way?"

"Pretty much," Stanley said miserably. He took a sour sip of beer, then swallowed the rest like a life sentence. Lacey downed hers as well.

"This tastes like piss," she said. "You want some more?"

"Not really," Stanley said. There was a funny noise in his head. Suddenly his brain teemed with polliwogs, a quivering mass of heads and tails and useless feet, a feeling he remembered from the beer Elmer had given him—only then he'd assumed it was only nerves, a result of his father's hopeful scrutiny, which was making him feel this way.

"Maybe we better wait." She took his cup, inspected the foam at the bottom, compared it with her own. "Cheap beer," she said, and then she stacked both cups at the bottom of the clean ones and came around the bar to join him. "Let's play something. Air hockey. Got fifty cents?"

Stanley had only his quarter.

"Ping-Pong, then. It's free."

The polliwogs made it impossible for Stanley to assemble a convincing excuse. "I suck at Ping-Pong," he admitted.

"What *are* you good at?"

He could feel the tight muscles in his arms and chest loosening. It seemed as if his heart and lungs and a few less recognizable organs might, at any moment, spill in a slithering mass on the floor. *Spleen,* he heard his biology teacher whisper in his mind's inner ear. *Duodenum. Vas deferens.* "I can dance," he finally said.

"Ping-Pong's easier than dancing," Lacey assured him. Without warning, she tossed him a paddle; angels intervened and he actually managed to catch it. "I mean, all you have to do is hit the ball."

For some reason, this observation made Stanley laugh so hard he had to sit down on a bar stool for a minute. But Lacey pulled him up by the hand—triggering another helpless fit of giggling—and they managed to bat the ball back and forth. And after a while, Stanley realized he didn't suck as badly as he'd thought. The trick was not to get excited. To keep breathing, steadily, in and out. Not to think about the ball so much as its motion between them.

Ka-tick, ka-tock.

Inside Stanley's pocket, the key and the quarter clicked, clicked again. Deeper still, the Hershey's kisses melted, one by one.

"Where did you learn to play Ping-Pong?" he asked.

"Youth group," Lacey said. "At our church."

"Your church has Ping-Pong?" Stanley said.

"And tennis courts. And a big-screen TV and an Olympic-sized swimming pool in the community hall. There's a restaurant, too. You could practically live there."

Stanley thought about Saint Michael's, the hard pews, the beady eyes of the saints. "We have an organ," he said.

"We don't," Lacey said. "That's against church law."

Stanley didn't know what to say. *Ask a question,* he heard Mary Fran prompting. "What church do you go to?"

"The New Life Christian Joy Fellowship," Lacey said. She sounded surprised that he would ask. "My grandfather started it. We call him the Reverend behind his back—even my grandmother does. He's, like, totally strict. No booze, no cards, no dancing."

"No dancing?" Stanley said. He could understand banning organs, he didn't much care for them himself. But *dancing*?

"My grandmother's more relaxed about things. That's why she likes to go on trips without him. Like this. She calls them her sanity excursions. Last year, she went to Las Vegas."

Stanley tried to imagine his own grandmother in a place like Las Vegas. The effort caused him to miss the ball. He chased it down, set it back in motion.

Ask another question.

"How come your mom and dad aren't here, too?" Stanley said.

"Oh, they're with the rest of the family. They're going to the other wedding at the Fellowship."

"What other wedding?" Stanley said, and Lacey caught the ball and said, "Shit! I wasn't supposed to tell anybody that."

Whenever Stanley swore, his mouth felt thick, the way it did on recitation days in his German class: *Guten Tag. Wie geht's?* But *shit* rolled off Lacey's tongue as easily, as elegantly, as the name of a fashionable wine.

"It's okay," Stanley said. "I won't tell."

"You promise?"

"Cross my heart." Stanley traced an invisible X across his suitcoat pocket.

"Well, okay," Lacey said. "Uncle Caleb didn't want a Fellowship wedding, but The Reverend went ahead and set one up, anyway. So Uncle Caleb and your sister have to stop in Nashville on their way to Mexico." She lowered her voice. "They don't know this, but The Reverend? He said God told him to swallow fifty aspirins if they refused a sanctified union."

"Why?" Stanley said.

"To bear witness to his faith," Lacey said. "My grandmother said that, if he'd done it, God could have taken him to the hospital, too."

"Would fifty aspirin kill you?" This question stuff was getting easier and easier.

She thought about it. "I think it would just make you sick."

"God helps my grandmother find a penny every day," Stanley said. "On days she doesn't find one, somebody dies."

"Somebody dies every day," Lacey said skeptically.

"I mean, somebody we know. Or else somebody famous. And she didn't find her penny today."

"Somebody might have froze to death," Lacey said. She didn't seem particularly bothered by the thought. "Hey, thanks for not telling," she said.

"No problem," Stanley said.

They began again.

Ka-tick, ka-tock.

She said, "There's a lady at our church who reads people's futures in their dryer lint. She doesn't charge you for it either."

Someone was coming down the stairs. They dropped their paddles, sprinted around the bar, but before they could duck, they saw it was only Anderson, smirking on the landing.

"Hope I'm not *interrupting* anything," he said.

"Shut up," Lacey said.

More footsteps on the stairs, light and quick. Mickey.

"Did you get it?" Anderson said, and Mickey unbuttoned his sports coat, pulled up his shirt to reveal the bowl of complimentary candies tucked against his stomach. It wasn't a little boy's stomach, either. It was hard and flat. With a little tuft of hair at the navel. Stanley laid a protective hand across his own soft puppy belly. There must be something wrong with me, he thought. There just must.

Mickey emptied the bowl onto the bar, the candies skittering and scattering like roaches. When he saw the keg, he dropped the bowl, clicked his heels, and saluted. "A kegger!" he cried. "Is it armed?"

Anderson shouldered past him, spewed a foamy jet onto the floor. "Looks like Spacey left us a little."

"Fuck you, Android," Lacey said, unperturbed. She massaged a caramel from its wrapper, looking squarely at Mickey. "I can't believe you swiped all these," she said. "I can't believe you didn't get caught."

Mickey grinned, and if Stanley could have locked him outside in the snowstorm to freeze, he would have done so. Everything was spoiled—the Ping-Pong game, the polliwogs. "I already swiped the best ones," he said, knowing his offering would be too little too late, but as his fingers groped for the softened Hershey's kisses, they snagged the key to suite thirty-three which the *other* Stanley had stolen.

The key! The real Stanley had nearly forgotten.

"And I swiped something else while I was at it," he said, his voice lower now, almost drawling with anticipation. When he tossed the key onto the bar, it landed with its plastic tag face-up.

For a moment no one said anything.

"Holy shit," Mickey finally said, and Stanley knew that this moment alone would be worth any future consequences: punishment, imprisonment, torture, even his own electrifying fear of unlocking whatever lay behind that door.

Anderson said, "That's the room y'all were talking about?"

Stanley said, "Yeah. I thought maybe we could check it out."

Lacey said, "You mean, like, just walk over there?"

"Sure," Stanley said. "Why not?"

THEY were finishing their main courses, tipsy with what they'd done in the game room as much as from champagne, when April fell suddenly silent. Caleb heard her breath catch hard—"What's wrong?" he said, thinking she might be choking—and she said, in a strange, small voice, "Oh my God, he's here."

"Who's here?"

But she'd already turned away from him, leaning past her father to say to her mother, "Mom, he's here. *Barney's* here."

"So you've seen him," was all Mary Fran said.

"Why didn't you tell me?"

"We couldn't find you," Elmer said, significantly. "*Either* of you."

April blushed, retreated.

"Which one is he?" Caleb asked, but he recognized him even before she pointed him out. He'd studied the photos in April's high-school yearbook, her college scrapbook, the dusty frames lying face-down, forgotten, on the closet shelf in her parents' guest room, the way he might have studied fragments of a larger map to some old, lost treasure: April at her prom, April building sets for the Holly's Field Playhouse, April in her Madison apartment, April at her first group exhibition. Always, Barney Lohr beside her. He looked heavier in person. His blond hair had darkened. He was eating like an obedient child, steadily cleaning his plate.

"What I can't figure out is why he'd *want* to be here," April said, tossing off the rest of her champagne.

"Maybe it's a closure thing," he said. "Maybe he needs to see you married, the way some people need to see"—he realized it wasn't the best analogy, but he'd already launched himself into it—"the body of a loved one."

"That's harsh," April said.

"You know what I mean." He touched her arm, was surprised to feel her flinch.

"I'm sorry," she said. "I just wasn't expecting to see him, that's all."

She'd told him a few things about Barney, not much. She said that they'd gotten engaged in high school, and that her parents had loved him, and his parents had loved her, and that this had made it especially hard to break things off when they got to college. She said he'd been possessive. Jealous. That they'd fought about her paintings, which he'd called obscene, and her use of live models— mostly other artists for whom she modeled in return. He'd had a quick temper, though he was always sorry, afterward. And, yes, he'd slapped her once, nothing serious, just before they'd broken up.

"First time you're a victim, second you're a fool," she'd said, and then she'd dropped the subject forever, for which Caleb was grateful. He'd never loved a woman who hadn't, at some point, told a story like that—maybe not *exactly* like that, but similar. Sometimes worse. And then she'd look at him, expecting something from him that was nameless and impossible. Something that had to do with an apology, or maybe forgiveness, he couldn't say. All he knew was that he'd felt hopeless in the face of it. But April had never looked at him that way. For the first time he wondered if maybe she wasn't fully over this guy. Why else would she be this upset?

As if she'd read his mind, she kissed him then, a sweet, unexpected kiss. "It doesn't matter," she said. "I shouldn't let it bother me. I mean, I still think it's weird, but it's a free country, right?"

He said, "We could have somebody ask him to leave. Maybe your uncle would do it. The cop."

"Uncle Frank?" April said. "Uncle Frank loves Barney. Everybody loves Barney."

"I don't love Barney. I'll ask him to leave."

But she shook her head. "Maybe that's what he wants. Some kind of scene. So that whenever I remember our wedding, I'll have to remember him, too."

And before he could say anything more, Hilda Liesgang chose that moment to interrupt. "What are you lovebirds whispering about?"

"Nothing," April said quickly, and Caleb said, "Would you like more champagne, Mrs. Liesgang? Mama?"

"Just a splash," Corrine said. "Now come on and be sociable. You two have got the rest of your lives to be alone."

"The Lord's truth," Hilda said, holding out her glass.

Originally, Hilda was to have had the place on the other side of the table, beside Mary Fran, but Mary Fran had let Margo take that seat—Margo, who was not even supposed to be at the head table to begin with! That left Hilda with nowhere to go. "I suppose *I* could eat at the children's table," she said, raising her voice so that Elmer would hear. If it had been up to him, Hilda was certain, he would not have indulged Margo's temper. But Mary Fran wore the pants in Elmer's family. She said, "Sit wherever you're comfortable, Hilda."

Beside her, Elmer studied his plate.

"For heaven's sake, we'll just ask for another place setting," April began, but then Corrine kindly intervened. "I believe there's one beside me," she said, and before Hilda could protest, Caleb rose to pull out the chair. My goodness—a real Southern gentleman! Hilda accepted the seat. She hadn't known such a thing as a gentleman existed anymore, in the South or anywhere else. And now she found she was enjoying herself, despite Mary Fran's intractable rudeness, the flickering lights, the penny which still weighed on her mind. Corrine Shannon was a charming woman, a lady of impeccable taste. Such a shame she hadn't managed to keep her figure, the poor dear. And those deep crow's-feet around her eyes! No doubt it was due to a lifetime spent as a minister's wife: all those ladies' teas and weekend potlucks, the enormous smiles that went with them. A difficult life, Hilda imagined, and when she broached the subject, Corrine agreed.

"Never a moment of privacy!" she exclaimed. "Always seeing to the needs of the flock. Always setting a good example." She shook her head, sipped her freshened champagne. How wonderful it was to have a little drink, out of sight and out of mind of the Fellowship. It was not that she condoned *heavy* drinking, but a little glass of bubbly now and then—well, shoot. Even her husband, back in his day, had bent his elbow a time or two. And she couldn't believe the good Lord would begrudge a mother a drink on her only son's wedding day.

Caleb laughed, draped an easy arm around her shoulder. "Go on and live a little, Mama," he said. "No one's telling the Reverend." When Corrine swatted at him, he grinned, kissed her cheek. Hilda smiled, too, but a lump had risen in her throat at the sight of a grown man touching his mother that way: affectionately, unself-consciously, almost like a daughter. She tried to recall the last time any of her sons had touched her, aside from the perfunctory back-slapping hugs she received on holidays. Of course, there were always flowers on Mother's Day. Rose-scented soaps at Christmastime. Each year on her birthday, all five pooled their money to buy a single, expensive gift: last year, for example, it had been a trash compactor. They were good boys, she reminded herself, looking around the dining hall until she'd located the oldest four. They were sitting in a boisterous row, identical as apples. Each wore his belt too low and the hem of his trousers too high—even Frank in his officer's dress blues. Each had the same easy temper, the same bad habits (though Frank had quietly climbed up on the wagon), and the joke people told was that Bart Liesgang had discovered cloning way ahead of the scientists.

And then there was Elmer, so different from the others: fine-boned, almost delicate, in spite of his generous height. Hilda knew there were whispers about a mongrel in the kennel. She also knew that, in their hearts, these same gossips believed it had been her lifelong yearning for a daughter which had altered the physical characteristics of her youngest son.

Now she prayed that the penny she'd failed to find wasn't in the pocket of one of her sons, jangling against the other, innocent coins like a small alarm. Death would be sudden: a heart attack, a clot in the brain. Or perhaps the penny had been spotted by one of her daughters-in-law? She glanced hopefully at Mary Fran. But Mary Fran, of course, was the picture of health, certain to outlive all the others. The penny, the penny—no matter how she might attempt to distract herself, there it was, shining in its absence like a full moon behind an unexpected curtain of clouds. Who else could possibly have it? Good heavens, not a grandchild! And with that terrifying thought, she noticed the empty seats at the children's table.

MARY Fran had been helping Margo pick the peas out of her chicken à la king when she heard Hilda call her name in the sort of theatrical whisper that was meant to grab everyone's attention.

"I don't suppose you know where Stanley is?"

And before Mary Fran could reply, Hilda was accusing her of spoiling her youngest while leaving her middle child to run wild. It didn't matter that Anderson and Lacey had wandered off, too. It didn't matter that there was no sign of Mickey, who inevitably initiated these things. To Hilda, this was just another example of Mary Fran's irresponsibility. For Pete's sake, Hilda cried, what if they'd left the Chapel? What if they were out in the storm?

At this, Corrine stood up, wide-eyed.

"I'm sure they're in the lobby," Mary Fran assured everybody. "I'll go check. They're probably calling strangers to ask if their refrigerators are running."

Frankly, she would have been grateful for *any* excuse to get away from her mother-in-law for a minute. When she found the children, she would thank them. But, to her surprise, the lobby was empty. Even the desk clerk had abandoned his post; Mary Fran could hear him shuffling papers in the back office. There were no giggles from behind the fireplace, no whispers from along the wall of phones. She checked the front porch, the ladies' room, the mens'. Supposedly, the game room didn't open until the dance began, but when she tried the door, she found it was unlocked. *Gotcha,* she thought, clumping down the stairs. Overhead, the light fixture swung very slightly, as if had been tugged by a sudden breeze. Candy and wrappers were scattered everywhere. Had Mary Fran looked behind the bar, she might have seen four half-drunk cups of beer, one overturned, dull yellow liquid pooling on the floor. But she didn't. She was distracted. She had started to cry.

Well, this is dumb, she told herself, scrubbing at the tears with a cocktail napkin. Back when she and Elmer first were married, she'd believed that Hilda would warm up after the baby had been born. And then, when April's birth made no difference, Mary Fran

hoped that Stanley—conceived in legitimate wedlock—would become the bridge between them. By the time Margo arrived, she
understood that grandchildren would never change her status, but
she'd felt certain that the accumulating years would count for something. Now she understood this wasn't so. Hilda would never forgive
her for that first, unplanned pregnancy. It wouldn't matter how long
she and Elmer stuck it out, through thick times and thin—and for
the past few years it had certainly been the latter. He was with-
drawn, irritable, unaffectionate. What remained of his sexual interest in her had evaporated altogether.

"Nothing's wrong," he insisted, when she tried to talk about it.
"Nothing's wrong."

Over the summer, Mary Fran had finally said, "I may have to have
an affair." She'd been trying to joke away her own embarrassment—
he'd just refused her again—but he'd put one cool hand on her arm
and said, without emotion, "If you want to, I understand." And she'd
thought of Libby the night she'd phoned to say that Aaron had left
her. *He was crying,* Libby said, in her new, strange voice. *He said
that he was sorry, he was just so goddamn lonely all the time.* For the
first and only time in her life Mary Fran felt close to her brother.

Over the summer, Mary Fran had considered leaving Elmer.
She'd scanned the rental notices in nearby Cedarton. She'd made a
few calls to find out the cost of going back to school, completing
her degree. She'd called on a few help-wanted ads and accidentally
left the red-circled paper on the table. Elmer brought it to her,
placed it on her knee. They stared at it together. Through the open
windows, they could hear the happy sounds of children playing kickball in the street. "Don't leave till Margo's in high school," he'd said
sadly, as if this was something they'd been discussing all along. By
now, they'd lived together twenty-three years. He knew her heart,
and she knew his. "I'm not going to leave you," she said.

Enough. She blew her nose, picked a peppermint up off the floor. Studied it. Unwrapped it. Popped it into her mouth. Hadn't the desk clerk promised it would take the taste of crying from her mouth? She sucked it furiously. It was time to return to the dining room. With any luck, the children would already back in their places by the time she arrived.

But the children were not in the dining room. When they'd heard the sound of footsteps on the stairs—too heavy, too foreboding to belong to anyone other than a parent—they'd swigged a few last hasty gulps of beer, scrambled around the bar and over the pool table, and then flat out ran toward the back of the cellar, tripping over crates, toppling boxes. Stanley discovered some kind of door, oddly heavy, no time to consider where it went. Next came total darkness, some kind of closet, or cage—was it a trap? Flailing wildly about, he encountered a small raised button. On popped a dim, jaundiced light; a metal door unfolded, closing with a clang. There was a hard jolt, and the cage began to rise.

They were in the service elevator.

"Going up," Mickey said.

When it lurched to a stop, Anderson pulled back the door, and they stepped into a small, plushly carpeted room. Only then did they understand that they were up in the balcony. So this was the bride's dressing room! They stopped short at the sight of themselves in the large, decorative mirror: giddy with beer, rumple-headed and red-faced, the boys' shirts buckling out of their trousers. Stanley sank onto the daybed, crushing the bridal bouquet, half-concealed beneath the massive detachable train. Mickey investigated the wardrobe where a dress hung sweetly, expectantly, while Anderson poked at the garment bag waiting on the luggage rack, stretched open like a bear trap. Lacey seated herself at the dressing table. She selected a bottle of hair spray, shook it, sprayed and scrunched her hair. She dusted powder over her nose and forehead, freshened the blush on her cheeks. Then she sniffed at a tiny bottle, held it out to Stanley.

"What do you think?" she asked, and when he innocently bent toward the bottle, she misted him with what he instantly recognized as April's perfume. Mickey shrieked, "Ooh, Stan-ley, you smell so purty!" and he laughed until he toppled backward into the wardrobe. Stanley had to do something, so he twisted the bottle out of Lacey's hands ("Ow, my rings!") and doused Anderson, who kept saying, "You wouldn't dare, you wouldn't dare."

The fight was on. Shoes, hairbrushes, and decorative pillows rocketed through the air. The garment bag toppled off its rack; the bridal bouquet bounced across the floor, scattering petals like tears. Mickey vaulted it, landed on the bed, the dress from the wardrobe still hugging his shoulders. Anderson grabbed a small duffel bag, chucked it at Stanley like a football. Its strap swept everything off the top of the dressing table while the bag itself, dragged off course, missed Stanley altogether and crashed, hard bright buckle first, against the mirror. The mirror divided, divided again, more and more rapidly, like cells under a microscope at school. The bag released its contents in a colorful splash of cosmetics and combs, keys and pens, books and airline tickets and candy bars and—what was this? Condoms and a tube of spermicidal jelly.

Everyone sobered up. The spinning world halted, slipped off its axis. The shattered mirror reflected back a skewed, unsympathetic tableau: fractured arms and distorted faces, chaos, entropy, the Big Bang.

Gingerly, Mickey picked up the condom package.

"Ribbed," he read solemnly, "for her pleasure."

With that, the power went out.

*   *   *

A howl of pleasure rose from the guests downstairs. Wasn't this naughty? Wasn't this fun? The food on their plates gave them a jaunty confidence they hadn't had before. What, after all, could possibly go wrong in the middle of this lovely hot meal? There were mock screams, lewd accusations, the delicate chime of dropped flatware. It was suggested that the men better watch out or the ghost of Gretel Fame would make off with them, one by one. From the ballroom came an accordion's rendition of a horror-flick chord. Then everybody quieted down, the way people do when they tire of a joke. Enough is enough, they were thinking. Okay. Very funny. Now let's get things back to normal.

So they waited, table after table of jovial guests, wax dribbling like tears down the sides of the Fancy White Tapers. Ladies tugged their panty hose into place and gentlemen adjusted their trousers. The darkness gave permission to such things, and others. A man scrubbed his front teeth with his napkin, dislodging a tormenting shred of chicken. A woman patted her hair with anxious fingers; another pulled up her bra straps. There was a rash of vigorous nose blowing, and everyone who had an itch, scratched. Staring, rude only moments earlier, was now perfectly acceptable, for it was hard for people to see each other's faces without leaning forward and squinting. Touching, too forward under normal circumstances, was now necessary, reassuring. Shoulders bumped, knuckles clicked. Hands overlapped when the breadbasket passed. Feet ventured forward, nuzzled other feet like the long, shy noses of dogs. Those closest to the Asti Spumante gave in to longing and captured the last lonely inches for themselves. And Libby Schrunk, soon to be Libby Merideth, leaned over and kissed the open, waiting mouth of Elmer's second cousin from Indianapolis. Darien Cole's pepper-and-salt hair was softer than she'd expected; his tongue tasted whiskey-sweet. Vaguely, she sensed the dismayed buzzings of Mary Fran's cousins, who'd cleverly ditched their husbands in order to seat themselves across from her, faces bright with sympathy and something sharper, shinier, knifelike. Clearly, they'd expected to extract the messiest details of Aaron's affair. Oh, how they'd wanted it all: the betrayal, the shock, the devastation. Get an eyeful, girls, Libby thought, coming up for air.

"Why, thank you," Darien said.

Already this was a joke between them—the first words he'd ever spoken to her, back at the reception. He'd since apologized for that. Even before they'd finished their salads, he'd explained that he was an attorney, specializing in some obscure ("and very dull," he'd added) form of tax law; generally, he found it tough to get away. But the invitation to April's wedding had arrived on the same day his divorce was finalized, and he'd decided this trip might be just the thing he needed to counteract any last, sentimental regrets.

Doubtfully, Libby had looked at her own ringless hand. "You're *happy* to be divorced?" she said. "You must have been the one to file first."

"Guilty," he'd said, and though his tone had been light, there was something more complicated in his face. "You see, she'd fallen in love with a wonderful man, and I just couldn't stand in their way."

Now, as he slid his hand along her thigh, Libby couldn't decide what was more pleasurable—the fish-eyed expressions on the faces of Mary Fran's cousins, or the snatches of conversation drifting, like perfume, like an exquisite tropical breeze, from the table behind them.

"A glass of wine, Aaron, it's not like I'm asking to snort cocaine."

"It's my goddamn body and I'll have wine if I want it."

Once again, Libby and Sara had been thrown together. In their rush to avoid each other, they'd inadvertently seated themselves back-to-back.

"My mother drank wine every night when she was pregnant. My grandmother drank gin, for Chrissake."

Though Libby couldn't make out Aaron's responses, she recognized the wheedling tone in his murmur: he was telling Sara to be reasonable, that he had her best interests at heart, that she was always overreacting to things; *why* did she always overreact?

"*You* calm down! *You're* the one who's being ridiculous!"

"So where are you spending the night?" Darien asked.

"Here," Libby said. "We have the Gardener's Suite."

"*We?*" Darien said. "Who's *we?*"

And, as if cued by the hand of a merciless god, Mickey materialized to drape himself over the back of Libby's chair. "*Mo*-om," he said, singsong.

"*Mick*-ey." How odd. The child reeked of perfume.

Darien's wandering hand withdrew.

"When are they going to turn the lights on?"

By now Mickey had her in a full nelson, the weight of his head against the back of her neck nearly pinning her chin to her chest. Mickey was a slumper, a leaner, an affectionate sloucher—provided none of his peers were watching.

"Never," Libby said. "We shall live in darkness for the rest of our lives. How are Sam and Jenny holding up?" She tickled his ribs to free herself, half rose in her seat. By candlelight, at least, everything at the children's table looked fine, although a dark shape she recognized as Mary Fran's was leaning over the scrawny shadow that was Stanley. The dark shape waved its arms. The shadow bowed its head.

"Sam's cool," Mickey droned, settling back against her. The sharp point of his chin dug against the crown of her skull. "Jenny's cool. Ev-erybody's cool."

"So how come you smell like a lilac?"

"I dunno."

"What's Mary Fran going on about?"

"Nothing."

"Nothing?" Libby sniffed the air, caught a whiff of something stronger beneath the floral scent. "Come let Mama smell your breath."

But Mickey reassembled his limbs in one fluid motion, gave the back of Sara's chair a vicious bump (Sara gasped; Aaron said, *Careful, son!*), and then returned to the children's table, where Mary Fran turned to include him in her lecture. Well, Mary Fran could handle it, whatever *it* was. Probably the kids had swiped somebody's beer, tried to conceal the smell. It happened. Punishment was part of the pleasure.

She glanced at Darien, who was busily buttering a roll. "That's one *we*," she said.

"There are others? A wee *we*, perhaps?"

"Jenny's eight and Sam is nine. That was my big boy, Mickey. He's eleven."

"He looks fourteen."

"And acts it. Girls already phoning him and everything."

Darien nodded, but his hand had not returned to her thigh. Instead, it was operating his fork, shoveling chicken into his mouth with all the matter-of-factness of a man at a business lunch. No romantic overtones in the regular *chomp-chomp-chomp* of his jaw. Well, it was inevitable. And, to tell the truth, Libby was relieved. What on earth was she thinking, going on like that with a complete stranger? And someone so much older. Experienced, no doubt. He looked to be in his late forties, though who could say what that beard concealed? Libby was thirty-six. She hadn't dated since the divorce, had no idea where to start. Aaron had been her high-school sweetheart, the third person she'd ever dated, the only person she'd slept with. Ever. She couldn't imagine making love to another man's body. Sex was a language she'd been forced to abandon, the lost mother tongue, a casualty of war. Whenever she tried to think about it, the only image that came to mind was Mr. Myers, the widower down the block. Mr. Myers collected beer cans. He made his own lawn ornaments from scraps of plywood he stole off construction sites. If he saw Libby at the mailbox, he'd trot down the sidewalk and yelp, "When ya gonna join me for a beer?" Libby knew just what he was thinking, for his was the smile of a man who knows he has all the time in the world. Eventually, he was quite certain, loneliness would bathe his bulk in a kinder, more flattering light. That gal would be over for a beer, you betcha. With three kids—well, the bucks wouldn't be lining up at *her* front door any time soon. And Libby, commuting home from the Holidome night after night— barely enough energy left to make a decent supper and tuck the kids in, much less go out and try to meet somebody—had started to fear he was right.

"You have kids?" Libby asked, not knowing what else to say.

"A daughter," Darien said.

"Is she—living with you?"

Darien seemed surprised. "Well, no," he said, and then—what was this?—he touched her hand. Smiled. Moved his chair a little closer. "I have three grandchildren," he said.

Libby tried to do the math without looking too conspicuous, but Darien seemed to be doing some figuring of his own. "Tell me something," he said. "How does someone with three young children find time for her own private life?"

She laughed. "*What* private life? I go to work, I come home, I take care of the kids."

"You're not seeing anybody?"

She shook her head, stared into his unlined face. How old *was* this man?

"Me, neither," he said. "I suppose I could make time. But my— ex-wife and I were together almost thirty years. It's hard to think about starting over."

They were silent for a moment, and then Libby said, "Did she tell you about him—I mean, the other man. Or did you just find out?"

"She claims she told me in a hundred ways," he said, and then he shrugged. Grinned. Put his mouth to Libby's ear. "I wish we could be together tonight."

Libby stifled a laugh. "On what planet?" she said. "I think the kids would notice if I brought you back to our room."

"Wishing doesn't cost anything," he said. "Wishing is the one thing in life that's always free."

"One goddamn glass of wine," Sara was saying. "You can't imagine how my back is killing me."

"So what about you?" Darien said. "Where is the father of your *we's* these days?"

"Turn around."

He didn't seem surprised. "Which one?"

"Power tie, low criminal forehead—"

"I can't take much more of this, Aaron, I swear I can't."

"—young, pregnant wife."

"Ah, yes," Darien said. "And they're getting on so nicely."

"He says that he told me in a hundred ways, too."

"You didn't know, either?"

Libby shook her head. Even now, thinking of it brought something unyielding into her throat. "Not a clue."

A beam of light crisscrossed the room as Ralph Bamberger,

clutching an industrial-strength flashlight, approached the head table to make an announcement. In the hearty voice of a game-show host, he assured everyone that there was no need for concern. He'd already sent two of his assistants out to get the generator running. In the meantime, people would have to make do with candlelight, but what could be more romantic? The cake would be cut in another ten minutes. The band would still play as scheduled. Bamberger heartily suggested that everyone plan to dance. It would get the blood moving, keep the fingers and toes toasty warm!

"While I'm up here, let me propose a toast," he cried, hoping to jump-start the guests' plummeting mood. "To Caleb and—" What was the bride's name? Some month of the year—May? June? Best to play it safe.

"To the new Mr. and Mrs. Shannon!"

A few glasses were raised but, for the most part, the toast fizzled. Nobody was listening. Those with reservations at the Budgetel were speculating on whether or not the power outage extended as far as the interstate. Those without reservations anywhere were discussing the pros and cons of the lobby floor. Some were in favor of leaving immediately, taking their chances on the roads, while others felt that waiting was a better option—give the plows time, let 'em get things opened up. The servers were trying their best to clear away the dirty dishes, rolling carts along the edges of each table, but everyone politely ignored their requests to hang on to forks, pass plates. People recalled the storm of '88, when power had been out for over a week. Surely this wouldn't be as bad—but, still. Did anyone remember that widow who'd survived by sleeping in the barn with her sheep? Did anyone remember the Hammerschmitts coming home from vacation and finding all the pipes had burst? "We live up the street," a man said proudly, "and it was true—you could've gone skating on the kitchen floor."

Gradually, the noise began to fade as people realized that the bride and groom had risen. A few members of the head table clinked their silverware. The bride's dress, illuminated by candlelight, made her look as if she was floating in the dark, cooling air.

"Thank you for the toast," Caleb Shannon said, "but we thought you should know April's keeping her name. I guess that makes us the new Mr. Shannon and Ms. Liesgang."

There was a murmur of opinions, a dry-leaf scattering of applause. Barney Lohr did not applaud, although he wanted to. In fact, he wanted to leap from his chair and do cartwheels and handsprings. So she hadn't taken the bastard's name. Certainly, she'd have taken *Barney's* name. They'd even talked about it once, after a certain conversation with April's Aunt Melissa, who didn't like them to call her "aunt." She and her husband, who didn't like to be called "uncle," had invited them both to Chicago for a weekend, and on the way home, April said she hoped that when she and Barney got married (back in those days, they'd both said *when,* never *if*) they would have the kind of relationship that Melissa and Brian had: everything equal, both people working, the housework divided, that kind of thing.

"But what if you had a baby?" Barney said. "Somebody would have to take care of it."

April said she'd been thinking about that. She said maybe she'd stay home with it for the first few years, and then they'd switch and he could stay home, and what did he think about that?

"That's ridiculous," Barney said. "I couldn't just stop working and then go back."

"Sure you could," April said. "Your parents would give you time off, if you asked. Or they'd let you work flexible hours."

"Well, I wouldn't ask," Barney said. "I mean, I'm supposed to run the business someday, right? It wouldn't make me look real, you know, responsible."

They'd driven on in silence, and he knew he'd done it again. He'd made her mad. He was always making her mad. You would have thought he lay awake at night, thinking of ways to do it. And that was the farthest thing from the truth. The truth was that he worried like crazy that they didn't get along the way they used to. After a while, to apologize, he'd said, "It's different for Melissa and Brian because they *don't* have children. They don't even have the same last name. It's like they're just living together or something."

But that pissed her off all over again. "Lots of married women don't change their names."

"Like who?" Barney said, and now he was pissed off, too. "I don't mean some movie star. Somebody we know besides Melissa. Somebody from Holly's Field."

She was silent, and Barney said, "Besides, how would people know we were married if we had different names?"

"Why would it matter whether people knew or not? What difference would it make?"

"What *difference* would it make?" He was trying not to yell.

"I just mean," April said, "it's nobody's business but our own."

"When we get married," Barney said. He swallowed hard, started again. "When we get married, I'll want everybody to know. I'll be proud, I mean, won't you be proud? Unless you're ashamed of me or something." He'd only said that because they were fighting, but as soon as it was out, he thought it might be true. She was going to finish college and he wasn't. She was much smarter than he was, and more talented. She had made dozens of friends in Madison, while he still spent half his weekends in Holly's Field, driving around with Coot.

"I *won't* be ashamed," April said. "Look, this is stupid. I'll change my name, okay? It doesn't really matter to me, and it matters to you, so it's fine."

The stranger seated across from Barney hadn't spoken much—to Barney or to anyone else. He said he'd arrived late because of the weather, hadn't had time to change clothes. His wife was worn-out from the trip, so he'd left her sleeping in the room. Barney complimented the stranger's sweater; it made him think of cross-country skiing trips he'd taken with his parents long ago. But when he'd asked if the stranger liked to ski, the stranger merely shrugged and said, "It's okay once in a while."

It was clear that he didn't want to talk.

Now, however, the stranger surprised Barney by leaning forward into the candlelight. "Me?" he said. "I wouldn't marry a girl who didn't want my name."

"Me neither," Barney said eagerly, gratefully. "No way."

The stranger mopped his plate with the last of the bread, held the dripping piece aloft to inspect it before popping it into his mouth. "You want more?" he said. "I want more." He signaled one of the kitchen staff by lifting the empty breadbasket high in the air.

"Just a sec," she said, treating them both to a smile. Her hair was very straight and fine, held back from her face with two heart-shaped barrettes. Her sleeves were rolled to her elbows, revealing sweet, freckled forearms.

"No rush, sweetheart," the stranger said.

Together, he and Barney watched her walk away.

"Cute," Barney said.

"Cute enough," the stranger agreed, but then he sighed. "I wouldn't know about it," he said. "I'm a married man."

"Yeah?"

He nodded, looked at Barney, as if to size him up. "How about you?"

Barney narrowed his eyes. Everybody knew about him and April. Then he remembered that the stranger was a guest of the groom.

Maybe he hadn't heard. "Engaged once," he said cautiously. "It didn't work out."

"That's too bad," the stranger said, and his voice was sincere. "What happened?"

Barney licked his lips. Nobody had ever asked him that so directly, not even his mom and dad. "I screwed up," he said, and it was such a relief, releasing those words, like being a little kid again and walking out of the confessional, late on a Saturday afternoon, enough daylight left to play ball before supper, his heart feeling clean and light and sweet as a piece of angel food cake.

"Screwed up," the stranger repeated. "Well, God knows we all do that."

Barney thought it was a kind thing for the stranger to say. "You said your wife is here with you?" he asked.

The stranger nodded. "Back at the room. The Western Suite. You should see it. There's this sign over the kitchen sink: RUSTLERS WILL BE SHOT."

Barney laughed.

"My wife didn't think it was all that funny," the stranger said regretfully. Suddenly he looked concerned. "You think she'll get cold out there?" he asked. "With the power out and all?"

"Not for a while," Barney assured him. "It takes time for things to cool down."

"I'm saving this for her," the stranger said, and he patted something small and round and white beside him. Leaning closer, Barney could make out a dinner roll wrapped in a napkin. "Made her a little bread-and-butter sandwich," he said. He seemed pleased to have thought of it.

"She'll like that," Barney said.

The stranger nodded. "It's the little things in a marriage."

"I wouldn't know," Barney said. "I screwed up."

"I screw up all the time," the stranger said. "What can you do?"

"Not much," Barney said.

The stranger patted the sandwich. "The little things," he said, and then he drained the last of his Asti Spumante. "Lousy champagne," he said. "Always gives you a killer headache."

The girl had returned with the breadbasket. "Thanks," the stranger told her, and she gave him another one of those smiles. Barney wished he knew how to flirt like that. He wondered if flirting was something the stranger had learned. He wondered how old the stranger was—maybe thirty, thirty-two? He wished, as he so often did, that he had an older brother, somebody to look up to. Somebody he could ask the sort of questions you really couldn't ask regular, normal people, and at the same time you needed to ask normal people, because they were the ones who knew. Sometimes, Barney thought that normal people had a single, perfect microchip implanted inside their brains. God had put it there before they were born so they'd always know what to do, what to say, the proper way to behave. How had Barney missed getting his own microchip? Well, probably he hadn't been listening when God said, *Line up over here.* Or else he'd flown off on his tiny baby angel wings to use the angel can. By the time he returned, all the microchips were gone. His mother was already going into labor. It was time for him to assume the fetal position and be born. Of course, Barney didn't truly believe this, but it seemed as likely an explanation as any for why he understood so little, why everybody else seemed to know so much. That was what he loved about acting: the lines were put down for you, and all you had to do was memorize them. Selling carpeting was pretty much the same. You always knew the right things to say and do.

April had never seemed to care about saying or doing the right things. If she wanted to dye her hair pink, she did it. If she painted something their high-school teachers didn't like, or understand, she never changed it just to please them. He admired her for this. Envied her, too. It was the thing which had attracted him to her in the first place. It was also the thing which, as soon as they'd started college, pulled her away from him forever. And yet, he hadn't been able to let go of her, even though he'd known—at least, sometimes he'd known—that he should. He'd been so happy to be engaged. To believe that his life was neatly settled. The future clear. Safe.

From outside came a sound like a buzz saw as the generator growled, caught, sputtered out. People murmured hopefully, twisted in their seats. "I wish I'd gotten married in a place like this," the stranger said.

"Like *this*?" Barney said.

"What's wrong with this?" the stranger said.

"It used to be a brothel," Barney said.

"Naw."

"The woman who ran it got murdered by one of her lovers. The place has been haunted ever since."

"Are you serious?"

"When my dad was in high school?" Barney said. "And this place was still boarded up? Him and some friends broke in one night and they're sitting around drinking, you know, and they start hearing music. Real faint and all, but still. And then the woman who was murdered? They saw her. Gretel Fame. She came walking down the stairs in a bright red dress."

The generator started up again; the sound was louder, throatier. Faint yellow light poured from the ceiling fixtures, and then the PA system in the ballroom squealed horribly. Guests cried out, stuck their fingers in their ears; the light bled back into darkness.

"Sorry!" somebody hollered from the ballroom.

The stranger said, "What were they drinking, turpentine?"

"It's a true story," Barney said. "People see her ghost even today. They never caught the guy who killed her. Stuff like that doesn't just go away."

The generator released another tortured roar, and this time, the dim light held. People applauded, whistled, cheered, the same way they'd done when the power first went out. But the dining hall wasn't nearly as bright as it had been, even after Bamberger and his staff turned off whatever lights and appliances weren't absolutely necessary. And the floodlights that the photographer had erected so painstakingly emitted a faint humming sound and nothing more. Regardless, he was determined to get a good a shot of the bride and groom cutting the cake. Already, he'd set up a tripod; now he was changing lenses and film, ordering all nearby candles snuffed. The resulting photograph would be theatrical, of course, the tension of deep shadow offset by the whiteness of the dress, the cake. And the cake was a beauty, three tiers in all, sweet smelling as a beehive. Someday, the bride and groom would appreciate all he had done for them. Someday, they'd thank their lucky stars that there'd been an innovative photographer on the premises. Someday, too, they'd both look back and wish that the bride had taken the time to find her bouquet—glaringly absent from all recent shots—which she'd somehow managed to misplace.

"It doesn't matter," she told him impatiently. "It was bothering my allergies anyway."

The photographer sighed. "Everybody ready?" he said. He explained that the shutter speed was at its lowest setting. Nothing and nobody could move, understood? He positioned April and Caleb to the right of the cake, with April holding the knife. He directed Caleb to cover her hand with his own, as if he were assisting with the first, difficult cut. Then he scuttled back to his tripod to make a few last adjustments.

Hilda watched uneasily. She was breathing too fast; her heart bucked against her ribs. Since the children's safe return, a new thought had crossed her mind. Perhaps today's penny had been meant for her. Perhaps her own time had arrived. Sixty-nine wasn't that old, but it wasn't any spring lamb, either. She imagined Bart waiting for her on the other side, reaching out as if to assist her across a small, bubbling stream. She could see the hand he offered her, the palm yellowed with calluses that cracked and bled in the wintertime. The stern frown of dirt beneath his thumbnails. The naked fourth finger where his wedding band was not. He'd taken it off early in their marriage; nothing personal, he'd told her, he just didn't like to wear rings. By the time he'd died, it no longer fit his finger anyway. She'd given it to her oldest son, Frank, who now wore it on the fourth finger of his right hand. How strange she felt, whenever she noticed it—as if Bart had been resurrected. But she herself had seen him buried, and in his oldest suit, despite the boys' protests.

Why waste a good suit? she'd told them.

Good girl, she'd heard him say. *If I'd lived another couple-three years, you'd have turned into a practical woman.*

For as long as she could remember, he'd accused her of being wasteful. *Prone to excess,* was how he put it. *Slave to happy impulse.* In bed, he was businesslike, his hands predictable as the hands of a clock, sweeping left breast to right breast, then down to her buttocks before he opened her legs with his knee. If she went to bed early, he'd wake her; if she went to bed late, he waited. Once, she ordered a book, a sex book, from the back of a magazine. That had been the only time, to her best recollection, that he'd ever meant to be cruel. "Maybe," he'd said, "if you looked like these here women, I'd want to mess around with stuff like that."

Then came those years after the oldest boys were born when he'd simply not touched her, for two years, for three. When her belly began to swell with Elmer, he said nothing; at the hospital, he'd brought her a dozen roses, just as he'd done when the others were born. But after that, the sex began again, mornings now, Wednesdays and Sundays. Left breast to right. That monstrous wedge of knee. Never a word spoken between them, not then, not ever, about the child he'd raised as his own.

And then he was gone. Just like that. He'd left a fat life insurance policy in addition to his generous pension. Father Bork, attempting to comfort her, assured her that Bart was preparing a place for her in heaven, taking the same care he had taken in life to make certain she'd be comfortable. And as Hilda watched April wield the cake knife, long and blunt as a dagger, she realized that it wasn't death itself that frightened her. Who wouldn't be willing to die right now if death meant only sleep? It was the thought of Bart, waiting for her; the way he would grasp her hand. The way he'd lead her to the heavenly home he'd prepared, where everything that had occurred on earth would continue through all eternity. The smell of his clothes when he came home from work. The stain on his pillow where he rested his head. The monotony of meals. His arguments with the boys. Those mornings, rolling her over. Those clockwork hands. Row after row of lead soldiers on the shelves above their bed, and the hours he'd spend arranging and rearranging them, inflicting wounds with the tip of a paintbrush, repairing them with thin strips of muslin torn from his great-grandmother's dress. Always preparing for the next battle. Always repairing the damage from the last.

"Hold very still," the photographer said.

Hilda Liesgang obeyed. She kept as still, as silent as gold. Her gaze was frozen upon the blade, where it rested upon the sweet, white cake.

DANCE

HE woman in suite thirty-three awoke when the polka band started to play. The last time she'd been to a real polka dance she'd been a little girl, dancing on her father's feet at the summer festival, saddle shoes slipping and sliding off his wing tips. She remembered the hot, sweaty crush of the beer tent. The odor of sawdust and bratwurst. The whoops and catcalls of the band. Her father's hands beneath her arms, half hurting, half tickling. At the end of each number, he'd toss her into the air, let go for a split second before guiding her safely to the ground. This was what made it all worthwhile—that moment in which anything might happen. That glimpse of weightless freedom that was neither up nor down.

The music seemed to be getting louder. More distinct. The woman switched on the bedside lamp, but it gave off only a dull, resentful light. Brownout. It happened a lot in winter. She got up and walked past the cooling hot tub and into the bathroom, where she combed the tangles out of her hair with her fingers. The body on the bed did not concern her. She was wondering where the man had gone, how soon he would be back. She was thinking about the two of them running around and around the room. Like children.

Like lunatics. Fighting the way her own parents used to fight. The thought made her want to laugh and cry at the same time, and she was glad she'd finally found the courage to tell him she planned to leave.

Though now she was starting to worry a little. She wondered how difficult it would be to get a divorce. How expensive. She wondered how quickly the news would get back to people they knew. She wondered if she'd have to stand up in a courtroom and listen to words like *abuse,* like *battery,* like *domestic violence.* Those words seemed to be everywhere these days: on TV, in the papers, on the radio. She was sick to death of them, who wasn't? And she just didn't think she could use them. That wasn't what any of this felt like, not to her, not really. It was more like a private thing between them. A pet name. A bad joke. Something you couldn't explain.

She'd made a mistake, that was all, and now she wanted to get out of it.

She splashed water on her swollen face and dried it tenderly. Smoothed her wool skirt over her hips. Straightened her panty hose. She unbuttoned her cardigan sweater, buttoned it back halfway. Leaned in close to the mirror to examine the dry skin at the corners of her nose. A wrinkle ran parallel to her eyebrows, which were darkening as she grew older. She was soon to be twenty-nine. She gave her reflection a crab-apple leer, and then she went into the little kitchenette to look for her lipstick, which had spilled out of her makeup bag when the suitcase hit the wall. The lipstick was one of those things she had noticed when everything seemed to be happening in slow motion. It had rolled to a stop halfway under the miniature stove. When she picked it up, she felt a small flush of triumph. Tea rose. She never quite felt right unless she was wearing her lipstick. She liked the small kiss of color it left, claiming cups and glasses, pencils and pens, the man's freshly shaven cheek.

Ordinarily, she would have straightened up the room so that, when he returned, it would be as if nothing whatsoever had happened. This would make him feel even more ridiculous and sorry and ashamed. There she'd be, sitting quietly with an ice pack, her hair neatly combed, their clothes hanging cheek to cheek in the closet, the bed like a smooth, blank sheet of paper, toiletries lined up by the sink. She'd give him one cold look, nothing more, for she'd have earned the right not to speak. She'd have earned the right to purchase expensive things, to make long-distance phone calls, to buy foods she particularly liked and eat them, relish them, alone. But tonight something was different. She didn't feel quite herself. She found herself unable to remember, exactly, what all these things—the shirts and socks and deodorant sticks, their textures and colors and smells—were meant for, much less where they were supposed to go. It was the storm, she supposed, which was distracting her. And the polka music, so loud that it was as if she, too, were at the dance.

She opened the heavy drapes, cupped her hands to the glass. The snow was falling diligently now, without drama or gusting remorse. It had a task to complete. It had started this thing, and it would finish it. There was no moon; the stars had been snuffed, one by one. Yet, the woman could see all the way down the path to the Chapel, where a light flickered weakly above the porch steps. She could see inside to the darkened lobby where the desk clerk stoked the fire. How did she know he was madly in love with a girl who thought of him as her dearest friend, who liked to talk to him about the boy she loved, a boy who refused to love her back? How did the woman know that the music was a jolly jackhammer on the desk clerk's heart, that he prayed to Jesus to scour the lustful thoughts from its throbbing chambers? She smelled the piney scent of the logs. She saw the flames reflected in the wide, glassy eyes of the mounted moose. She studied its expression but could not decide if it looked peaceful, or astonished, or terrified, or indifferent. Peaceful, she decided, since there was really no way to tell. Might as well imagine something happy. Might as well make yourself feel good.

And then she was in the ballroom, moving among the guests as easily as a shadow. Briefly, she wondered how this had occurred. If she'd made her way here along the snowy path, she could not remember doing so. Perhaps she'd been transported by the force of her desire, for there was nothing she loved more than a dance. She watched the couples rock and skip across the pale floors, which had been scattered with sawdust: women in their stocking feet, hair falling into their eyes; men with loosened ties, trousers barely clinging to the swing of their hips. She knew their most ridiculous failures, their private loves and polished hates. She could hear the conversations of those who stood in small groups around the edges of the ballroom. She could smell perspiration, the medley of scented hair sprays and cosmetics, foot powders and copycat perfumes. She could hear the *flush-hush, flush-hush* of their hearts, the wheeze of their lungs, the gurgle of their intestines.

Christmas-tree lights hung overhead in bursts—some electrified, some not—like handfuls of glitter tossed into the air. The chandelier was dark. There was no other light save a group of floor lamps, glaring as candlesticks, which had been carried in from the lobby and arranged in a half-moon behind the band. But the low light flattered the In-Laws, cleaned their stained vests, concealed their scarred lederhosen. They hadn't looked this good in years, and the woman from suite thirty-three could tell that each man knew it, even shy Lou Fojut, who risked glancing up from his tuba as Jackie Vogel approached the mike—which, of course, wasn't working—to heckle the aloof, twenty-something bachelors who were holding up the far wall.

"C'mon, fellahs, don't be shy! Look at all those gals lined up by themselves."

"You, there, with the carrot top. Stop makin' cow eyes and ask her to dance!"

"It's a cold night out there, so ya better find a little somethin' ta keep ya warm!"

It *was* a cold night, and there was sense in what the man said. If you had to wait out a storm, wasn't dancing and drinking at a wedding celebration one of the better ways to pass the time? A person could be stranded in a car, for Chrissakes. A person could be at home with the kids, listening to their cries bounce off the linoleum like hard, red rubber balls. There were rumors that a state of emergency had been declared, that the interstate had been closed from Green Bay to Milwaukee, that the power outage extended across the better part of the state. Another run had been made to the package store, and this time, the assistant bartender had been accompanied by three volunteers. No sacrifice was too great where the needs of others were concerned. No risks were too large if circumstance demanded they be taken. The men had bundled up and set out for Bittner's Plaza, guided by identical shining images of themselves. Now they burst back into the ballroom with the look of warriors who have conquered a nation. The woman from suite thirty-three applauded and cheered with the rest of the crowd; the heroes bowed deeply, ice cracking from their coats. "This next number's dedicated to these brave young soldiers," Jackie said, and he signaled John-John, who stepped up to the dead microphone and began an old favorite: "In Heaven There Is No Beer."

"That's why we drink it here!" the crowd sang back.

The woman from suite thirty-three sang along. She was feeling more like herself again. She was happy to be here, at this wedding, at this dance, among people who were enjoying themselves.

It was then that she saw the bride—a young girl, bright as a coin in her full wedding dress. She was dancing with the groom, his broad hand splayed across the small of her back, and she was laughing at something he had said. The woman from suite thirty-three approached her, closer, closer still, passing through the other dancers as if they were not even there. She was overwhelmed with a tenderness so great that it bordered upon longing. It was all she could do not to reach out and touch the bride's shoulder, stroke that sweet, cropped head. They were almost exactly the same height. They probably wore the same size shoe. She believed that if they pressed their hands together, palm to palm, their fingers would match exactly, and how it pleased her, thinking of this!

At the end of the song, the bride and groom left the floor, and the woman fell into step behind them as they walked the perimeter of the ballroom. Here and there, the bride paused to introduce the groom. The bride's mother came forward, leading the bride's little sister, who hung back, suddenly shy. And when the bride turned to speak to the girl, asking, Was she having a good time? a flashy young woman in a white, sequined dress pounced on the groom and dragged him back to the dance floor.

You don't mind if I borrow him? she called to the bride.

Would it make any difference if you did? the mother muttered. Who the hell is she?

Five dollars, the sister said.

Lanna Yoderman, the bride said. From the gallery. I couldn't invite the others without inviting her, too.

The woman from suite thirty-three watched Lanna Yoderman lasso the groom with both arms. The groom made a private face for the bride, who made a private face back. The mother was still staring at that shimmery, white dress.

Does she think *she's* the bride?

The bride laughed, and her sister laughed, too, although it was clear she didn't know why. But then the mother said, Have you talked to Barney yet? and all of them stopped laughing.

I haven't seen him since supper.

As long as he's here, you could at least talk to him.

If he wants to talk to me, I'm easy to find. I'm the other woman wearing a white dress.

Maybe he's afraid to approach you, the mother said. She shifted foot to foot, and the woman from suite thirty-three knew how much her shoes were hurting her.

Maybe he should be.

Why?

When the bride didn't answer, her mother said, Are you ever going to tell me why the two of you broke up?

The woman from suite thirty-three saw the bride's body tilt away from the mother's; she saw the bride's sister look up, startled, her plain face creased with worry. She hoped that, in the morning, the mother would have blisters on her heels. And sore ankles. A hangover, too. It was all so very obvious. Why couldn't the mother see?

Irreconcilable differences, the bride finally said.

The mother sighed. I don't mean to pry. I was fond of the guy, that's all.

So marry him, then. I hear he's free.

Are we having a fight? the mother said, and the bride said, Not really, and the mother said, I'm relieved to hear it. For a moment neither of the spoke. Then the mother linked her arm through the bride's and said, Maybe we can fix him up with Lanna Yoderman. The bride laughed then, and the little sister laughed, and everything was okay.

But the woman thought of her own mother, who was always going on about *girls today*, how *girls today* were spoiled, how *girls today* were always running off to court over every little bump and bruise. No different than two-year-olds, she liked to say. They get a little scratch, they scream bloody murder. An image came into the woman's mind, floated there like a dust mote: her mother on the couch, holding one arm, her mouth swollen and red. Her father kneeling before her, as if in prayer. And her mother's face shining like Jesus. At least Daddy would never know that her own marriage hadn't worked out. Her mother liked to believe he was an angel now, looking down upon them all, seeing everything his daughter did and registering his disapproval—but the woman herself did not think so. She had seen her father's body. She'd watched them put it in the ground. It had never made sense to her the way some people went on and on about heaven and what a wonderful a place it was. If that were the case, then why didn't everybody just go ahead and kill themselves right now?

"Why do you suppose they don't?"

The bride and her mother and sister were gone. A woman was standing beside her, instead—had she been there all along? She wore a cherry-red dress with a low-cut neck, and there was a peculiar smell about her, like onions and spoiled grain. Like the bitter-tapioca smell of unwashed sheets. But she was the first person who'd spoken to the woman from suite thirty-three all evening long, and the woman from suite thirty-three was grateful, even though she didn't know how to answer the question.

"I guess the people we love keep us here," she finally said, but this just made the other woman laugh.

"What does that word mean? *Love*." She said it the way someone else might have said *sin*. "I'll tell you what—anything sticks to you long enough, you'll wind up calling it love. A child, a sickness, a particular chair. A mean idea. You lean on it or hide from it or walk around it long enough—" The woman in the red dress stopped, fingered the locket she wore around her neck. It was large, cumbersome, the sort of thing you might inherit from a grandmother and cherish, but never wear. The woman from suite thirty-three tried to glimpse the picture inside it, but the woman in the red dress hid it away before she could get a good look at the man's face.

"Oh, yes," said the woman in the red dress. "I was once in love myself."

"That's nice," said the woman from suite thirty-three. Silverbellied images flashed through her mind: roses, diamonds, chocolates in a heart-shaped box. An infant in a cradle, the passing years. Holiday dinners with wine and candles and deep, woven baskets of bread. Grandchildren flowering on a green summer lawn. The woman in the red dress stared at the woman from suite thirty-three in a way that wasn't unkind.

"I know about all those things," she said, "but I'll tell you what. If he were on fire before me now, I wouldn't spit to put out the flames."

The woman from suite thirty-three didn't know what to say to such a thing. She turned back toward the dance floor and saw that it was empty. "What's happening?" she said, and the woman in the red dress said, "They just announced the father-daughter dance."

Now the bride stepped forward into the middle of the room. She was blushing deeply, uncomfortably. Men whistled. She kept her head down. Her father approached her slowly, as if she were a task, a complicated tool, as if he were sizing up an unbearably heavy object he must carry for an impossible distance. His shoulder blades beneath the thin fabric of his suit coat were as sharp and poignant as a child's. When the band began "Is This the Little Girl I Carried?" he didn't move, didn't even lift his head. The guests murmured to each other. Somebody called, "Hey, Elmo, want me to show you how it's done?" but only a few people laughed. And then no one was laughing.

Please, thought the woman from suite thirty-three. She could feel the same plea unspoken in the throats of the guests who were watching, waiting, not knowing what to do. The bride turned to look at her mother, who made the slightest pleading motion with her hands.

"Anything familiar," the woman in the red dress said. "Good or bad, right or wrong. One day you wake up and you can't imagine how it was to be without it." She fingered that locket again. "So you give it a name. You call it love. You pretend it's the thing that you wanted in the first place."

The woman from suite thirty-three remembered her own wedding dance with her father. His hands, even in later years, were big as tortoiseshells, each one grappling to keep its perch upon the small, rounded stones of her shoulders. He'd talked softly about love, how it was a grave responsibility, nothing like she was imagining and full of every kind of hardship. He said she should listen to her husband, and put him first, and not let friends or future children come between them. He said over time she would learn to think of her husband as part of her own self, and her husband would come to think of her the same way. He told her how, when she was being born, he'd doubled up with cramps so bad the doctors had to give him a shot, too. "Sympathy pains," he said. "I never told anybody that. We've had our tough times, your mother and me, I won't try and fool you, sweetheart. But whatever happens to one of us, it happens to us both. We're lonely sometimes, that's the honest truth. But it's better than *being* alone."

If only this father would speak his heart! The woman from suite thirty-three understood there were so many things that he wanted to say: *All I've ever wanted is your happiness,* and *I wish I could give you the formula for joy,* and *I cannot believe how the years do pass,* and *I'm terrified by the force of my love.*

But he said nothing. At last, it was the bride who stepped forward. With great, deliberate tenderness, she placed her hands on his shoulders. Slowly, automatically, his hands rose to settle on her waist. They circled the dance floor once, twice, like sad performing bears.

"Anything familiar," the woman in the red dress said. "It don't matter, good or bad."

The bride was speaking now, rapidly, earnestly. Slowly, the father lifted his head.

"CALL your pocket," said the man. "I got to go check on my wife." He'd honestly planned to return to suite thirty-three immediately after the meal. So how had he wound up in the game room, playing pool? He'd enjoyed his food well enough—he couldn't complain about the price, at any rate. Still, he was feeling a little bit restless, and he'd hoped that knocking some balls around might settle him down, take the edge off. But it was so damn dark you could barely tell the solids from the stripes. The only source of light was a jaundiced bulb that hung from the ceiling, its shade removed. A few men were drinking at the makeshift bar; in the corner, kids were clustered around a single pinball machine which, ludicrously, was chirping and chiming at full power while the rest in the row stood silent, dead. The assistant bartender told them it had been prioritized along with the water pump, the kitchen freezers. "That's the best one—a real moneymaker," he said. "Kids play all night, like they're hypnotized."

"Call," the man said again, although by now it was clear that Barney Lohr hadn't really wanted to play. What he wanted to do was fish for information about the groom. The man had tried his best to offer vague, noncommittal answers, but these only seemed to stir up a new hornet's nests of questions, especially after he said that Caleb and April (he'd managed to deduce their names) had met in college. At that, Barney Lohr became so agitated he put down his cue stick. "They were seeing each other even *then*?"

"Well, yeah," the man said. He was getting in over his head, he could tell. Best to go on the offensive. "For someone who's a friend of the bride, you don't seem to know her very well."

"It's just—she was supposed to be seeing some other guy, when she was in college," Barney said. And then he said, "I mean, she was supposed to be seeing me. She was the girl I was engaged to. You know. The one things didn't work out with."

Oh, Christ. The man considered admitting that he didn't know the groom from Adam, but then he decided against it. He was already in too deep.

"Your shot," was all he said.

Barney shot and scratched. "I can't believe she'd do that to me," he said. Then he laughed bitterly. "But what the hell. I can't believe it's over between us even though she's just gone and married the guy."

For some reason, this made the man think of his wife, the look on her face when she'd insisted they were through, but then he dismissed the thought. She'd been tired, upset, that was all. She hadn't known what she'd been saying. He'd go back to their suite with the dinner roll, and they'd snuggle up and laugh about that stupid business earlier, and then he'd tell her all about Barney Lohr because there was nothing she loved better than a story, especially one that involved relationships. At the retail distribution center where he worked, he'd fallen into the habit of eavesdropping as people chatted about who was dating whom, and what they'd done over the weekend, and how so-and-so's kid was in trouble again.

Then he carried these stories home, the way another man might have brought a bouquet.

But the story Barney Lohr was trying to tell was hard to follow. For one thing, his voice was barely loud enough to hear, and he kept glancing anxiously around the game room, as if he was worried that one of the kids, or the men at the bar, might listen in. He was talking about some fight he'd had with the bride, back when she was still his fiancée, their last fight, in his bedroom at his parents' house. She'd come home for a weekend visit, only it turned out she planned to drive back early. Barney had tried to convince her to stay. She said she couldn't, she had too much work to do. Barney had asked her, right up front, Is there somebody else? and she'd said, No, no, there isn't anybody, for Pete's sake!

The man sank another ball, a clever bank shot, but Barney acted like he hadn't even noticed.

Barney said, "Then my mom came in and saw her on the floor."

The man gave him a peculiar look. "What, did she fall?"

Barney nodded uncertainly, miserably.

"You shove her or something?" Why was the kid telling him this? The man certainly wasn't going to sit around and listen to this bullshit all night long. It was only making him nervous. It was making him think about—well, he wasn't sure what. He was spooked, that was all, what with the storm, the power outage, the fight he'd had with his wife. But Barney wasn't about to let the stranger slip away. He felt as if, at last, there was someone in whom he might confide. A *real* person, not like that doctor, who had to listen whether he wanted to or not. Someone who was older, who had lived in the world and had seen a few things. Someone who could help him make sense of what had happened that night beside his childhood bed, where, once, he'd mapped so tenderly the pleasures of the same body he'd someday rack with such terrible pain. And what he felt for the stranger at this moment was almost like love, like being *in* love, but stronger, and more true. Barney wondered if perhaps, in a former life, he and the stranger might have been brothers, or—weird as this sounded—even sweethearts. He felt as if he had known the stranger since the moment of his own birth, that the stranger had been the one to wipe his body clean, to diaper him and swaddle him in soft flannel blankets. He wanted, at that moment, only one thing, wanted it with the same blind urgency of sex: to offer to this stranger the defining moment of his life, the lens through which he'd come to see everything he was, everything he might become.

"I didn't shove her," Barney said.

His mom had looked between Barney and April, who was lying on the floor beside the bed. Her mouth was open, opening wider, opening like she was screaming, and he knew that feeling, remembered it from that time during football practice—it had only happened once, but it was a thing you remembered—when he'd landed on his back and Chad Eckerd's knee had come down on his chest, and there was nothing he could do but lie there, his lungs flat as leeches, and the pressure was like he'd been flung somewhere beyond the moon and was hanging in that vast, airless vacuum. Only when his vision blurred did he find a way to breathe, and now he could hear Coach saying, "Relax, relax," the way Barney was telling April to do now, rubbing her shoulder, down on his knees on one side of her while Mom knelt on the other, the air tearing into him, jagged sheets like ruptured steel, and he was coming back into himself again. He breathed a little more deeply. Knew that it had passed, that he'd be okay. His teammates helped him off the field. He sat, for the rest of that practice, on the bench.

When April sat up, she kept her arms crossed over her stomach, and her nose and cheek were already swelling on the side where she'd hit the nightstand. Mom said, "Kids, what happened? What happened here? Were you two fighting over something?" And Barney didn't know what to say. I mean, what do you say when your mom says something as stupid as that? He wanted to say, "No, Mom, you know, she just fell down for the hell of it." He wanted to say, "Why don't you mind your own goddamn business?" He wanted to lift April into his arms and take her to the hospital. But April stood up, still doubled over. When she finally straightened, it wasn't all the way.

"What's happened?" Mom kept saying the whole time, and April finally said, "He shoved me. I'm all right."

"He shoved you," Mom repeated, and then she turned to Barney and said, "What on earth? Are you twelve years old and I'm going to have to call April's mother? Do you want me to ground you, or maybe cancel your allowance?"

"Mom," Barney said hoarsely, and if there was ever a time he should have spoken, maybe cried or fallen to his knees, or something—he didn't know what—it was then. And then the moment passed.

"It's okay," April said. Those dead, dark eyes. "I'm not mad. I think I just want to go home."

"Well, sit down for a minute, at least," Mrs. Lohr said. "My heavens, you're white as a ghost."

"I'm fine," April said, but Mrs. Lohr insisted. She led them to the parlor, a room which was only used on holidays, and made them sit side by side on the couch—the plastic seat cover crackled whenever Barney shifted his weight—while she poured them each a cup of coffee, served them on a silver tray. She opened a package of cookies, too. Barney took one. His high-school graduation picture beamed at him from the mantel. April did not reach for her cup.

She did not care for a cookie. Mrs. Lohr talked about appropriate behavior and adult attitudes and how if there was a problem in their relationship, the thing to do was to sit down and talk about it. She said she was always there if they needed an opinion, and so was Mr. Lohr, and she hoped they would feel free to come to either of them. Was there anything in particular they'd been fighting over? Was there something they'd like to talk about now?

Barney didn't say anything.

April said, No, thank you. She really had to go.

"I didn't shove her," he told the stranger now. He could not remember the last time he'd had his face this close to another man's. "What I did was, I head-butted her. In the stomach." He was sweating. He could smell his stink wafting out from under his ruffled dress shirt. "She never told anybody."

The expression on the stranger's face didn't change, and Barney realized he was waiting for him to take his shot.

"She never told anybody," he repeated.

The pinball machine chimed and sang.

"I never told anybody, either." It was true. He hadn't even told that doctor, though he was supposed to tell him everything.

"Uh-huh," the stranger said. He looked uncomfortable.

Barney gripped the edge of the pool table. His knuckles were bone white, rimmed with crimson.

"Look," the stranger finally said. "Don't take it too hard. People fight all the time."

"I heard something break," Barney whispered. "Inside her." But the man made a swift, dismissive gesture, as if he hadn't heard.

"Listen," he said. "My wife and I had a whopper this afternoon. She starts in on how I do this wrong, I do that wrong, she's bored, she's unhappy, she's going to leave and, I mean, when we get into it—" He hung his cue stick on the wall. No use pretending there was going to be a game when there wasn't. "What can you do? Forgive and forget, that's what. Get back on the horse. You can't think too much about it. Drive yourself crazy if you do."

He was soothed by the reasonable sound of his own words. The truth was he'd been a little bit afraid to go back out to the Lodge. He'd had this feeling, as if something terrible had happened, but what could have happened? He and his wife had fought—so what? People fought. Now it was over. It was time for them to make up.

"You ever hurt her?" Barney said. "You two ever hurt each other?"

The man stared at him as if he didn't understand the question. "I've got to go," he said, and then he added, "Sorry things didn't work out with you and that bride."

He took the stairs two at a time. He felt a little sorry, ditching the kid, but clearly he was a person with problems, and people with problems—well, you just never knew. In the dark lobby, he claimed his coat from the desk clerk, complimenting the food, the facilities, the Western Suite. The polka dance was in full swing, and he couldn't resist walking over to the ballroom and standing in the doorway for a minute. There, the light was better, thanks to the strings of Christmas-tree lights. He figured there were probably thirty couples on the floor. The band wasn't miked, but it was plenty loud, the sound bouncing off the hardwood floors. He thought he saw his wife, but that was just a trick of the eye. Suddenly he wished she'd been with him in the game room. She'd have known exactly what to say. It was one of the things he admired about her. She always knew how to make a person feel better.

Somebody tapped his arm. A woman in a red dress was looking at him as if she knew him, as if she were going to accuse him of something. Perhaps she'd mistaken him for someone else. "Dance?" she said, and though her smile was wide, there was something angry about it, too. The light made her face appear gaunt as a skull's; the locket on her chest rose and fell with the labored force of her breathing. "No, no thanks," he said. "I'm leaving."

"Dance?"

He took a step back, unnerved. "I'm on my way out right now."

"Dance?" she said, still smiling that angry smile.

He spun away, crossed the lobby, and pushed through the storm doors onto the porch. There, he stopped to put on his coat. He had the irrational feeling that if he looked back, the woman would be standing right behind him, so he stared straight ahead into the darkness. The bad feeling had returned, stronger now. He thought that he might be sick. What the hell was wrong with him? He still didn't want to return to his room and yet, where else could he go? His wife was in that room. His whole entire goddamn life was in that room.

He felt his way down the steps, which were merely impressions, covered with snow. Still, he sensed that the storm was passing. There was a different feeling in the air. He decided it was a good omen—the second of the evening, in fact. If you believed in omens. If you counted the new penny he'd found in his wife's bed.

BACK in the ballroom, Jackie Vogel shouted, "You've been a great crowd! Who the heck needs Wisconsin Electric anyway?" He waited until the cheers died down. "Gettin' a wee bit chilly, though, ain't it? Guess we better try and get everyone on their feet. This next little tune's dedicated to all you Playboy bunnies out there."

A woman lugging a shrieking toddler was crossing the ballroom floor.

"Why, here's a bunny now!" Jackie cried. "Hey, sweetheart, you wanna come up and show us how it's done?"

The woman, red-faced, didn't smile.

"Aw, a *shy* bunny," Jackie said. "Guess John-John here will have to demonstrate."

John-John raised his shirt, grabbed his big belly, and began to jump up and down in the lamplight, his fat rippling like a living creature. "This how it goes?" he hollered.

"Now, wait just a minute," Jackie said. "I meant the bunny hop, not the hippo hop."

The audience groaned. "We *know* how it goes!" somebody shouted, and someone else hollered, "Get on with it." Already, a line was forming on the dance floor.

"Okey-doke, then," Jackie said. "Those of you unsure of the steps, just get behind the line and—whaddya do?"

He leaned toward the crowd expectantly, put a hand to his ear. The reply came in a ragged approximation of unison. "Kick left, kick right, then hop hop hop."

"Can't hee-ar you!"

"Kick left, then right, then hop hop hop!"

"What was that last part?"

"HOP HOP HOP!"

Jackie cued the band. By the time they'd reached the refrain, the line had swelled from a dozen to more than sixty dancers, hands upon each other's hips, kicking left and kicking right and hop-hop-hopping in a long, snaky line across the ballroom floor: the Minneapolis crowd in their elegant dresses and Italian-cut suits, their manicured nails and thick mascara; the Liesgang women in their floral-print dresses, bulky as ships, short gray hair permed so tightly that the texture, from a distance, resembled the naked human brain; the Liesgang men with their bouncing bellies, their black trousers, white socks, scuffed brown shoes. The cousins and friends and neighbors, some in pale, summer suit coats, some in dark wools, some in striped ties as startling as cattle guards. And, at the end of the line, Elmer Liesgang, hugging the hips of one of April's gallery friends and grinning like a kid on a toboggan ride.

Mary Fran, near the front of the line, twisted to look. She couldn't believe it. Earlier, she'd asked him to dance—begged him, in fact— but he'd refused. "You'll feel better," she'd told him, and he'd said, "Our daughter has married a stranger. The roads are closed. The power is out. I don't see anything to dance about."

That was before the father-daughter dance.

"What on earth did you say to your father?" she shouted to April, who was hopping just behind her.

"Huh?" April stepped on her heels. "Sorry!"

"During your dance together. What happened?"

"Oh," April said. She was out of breath. "I thanked him for talking me into having this wedding. I told him I was having a wonderful time."

"You did?" Mary Fran couldn't believe it.

"Told him"—they hopped three times—"he'd saved me from making a mistake I'd regret my whole life. And I said we'd talk to that new priest he likes the next time we come home to visit."

"You can't mean that!"

April laughed. "Well, no," she said. "But it's true about having a wonderful time. And it made him so happy when I said it. That's all he needs, you know?" she said. "Someone to tell him he's a hero once in a while."

"He's not a hero." Mary Fran was astonished at her own bitterness.

Once again, they hopped three times, then April put her cheek against her mother's.

"Nobody's a hero, Ma," she said.

It felt like an accusation. Mary Fran dropped out of the line. Her ankles were throbbing to a lively little polka beat all their own, so she found a folding chair and sat down. She realized she was scanning the line for Libby; all evening long, she'd been hoping they might talk. But Libby's attentions had been occupied with Elmer's second cousin. Dance after dance, she and Darien Cole had been the most visible couple on the floor. Now both seemed to have vanished. Had they slipped away to the Lodge? Mary Fran supposed it was none of her business. Perhaps it had been unrealistic to imagine things would stay the same between them. Like it or not, Aaron had a new wife—though it appeared that the honeymoon stage was over. Sara had spent the dance sitting on the sidelines, her feet propped up on a second folding chair. Now and then, Aaron left the dance floor to check on her, and whatever passed between them didn't make either of them look any happier. Frankly, Mary Fran felt sorry for her. She wasn't a bad person, really. Just naive. And gut-wrenchingly young. Clearly, she'd had no idea what she was in for when she told Aaron *I do*. Then again, did anybody? Mary Fran sure as hell had been completely unprepared.

She heard the screech of a folding chair being dragged into place beside her, but she continued to watch the dancers, buying time, trying to prepare herself for yet another light, bright conversation about April and Caleb. Yes, indeed, what a surprise this all was, but weren't they just lovely together? And Caleb was such a nice guy!

Somebody nudged a glass into her hand.

"Hi," Libby said. Her cheeks were red from dancing, perspiration forming attractive little spit curls around the nape of her neck. "You look like you could use this."

Gingerly, Mary Fran took a sip. The amber liquid smoldered pleasantly in her throat. "What is it?"

"Single-malt Scotch."

"Wow," Mary Fran said. "You sure you want to give this up?"

"Darien's getting me another," Libby said. "I just saw you sitting here, you know, and I thought—"

"I miss you so goddamn much," Mary Fran said.

"I miss you, too."

"I'm sorry about Sara."

"It's okay," Libby said, and then she added—had Mary Fran heard correctly?—"Poor kid."

The bunny hoppers had formed a great, revolving wheel, and now, as Melissa and Brian hopped past, they tried to pull Mary Fran and Libby into the line. "In a minute, I promise," Mary Fran said, batting their hands away, and Libby said, "I can't, it hurts my knees."

"Sissies," Brian called over his shoulder.

"Now *there* goes a happy couple," Mary Fran said. "You know, I've never heard them exchange a cross word."

"That's ridiculous," Libby said. "Nobody gets along that well."

"They do," Mary Fran said glumly, and then she turned to Libby. "So we're speaking again?" she asked. "This isn't just a momentary lapse?"

Libby shrugged. "Let's just say that certain recent developments have put me in a better mood."

"A good-looking recent development, I might add."

Now she grinned, raised an eyebrow. "He's not too shabby."

"Good dancer, too," Mary Fran said. "I bet he's great in bed."

"Listen to yourself!" Libby said, but she was laughing, and Mary Fran leaned over and whispered, "Imagine those long legs wrapped around your body," and they giggled until Mary Fran slobbered Scotch across their laps.

"Careful!" Libby said. "That stuff's expensive."

"How expensive?"

"Seven bucks for that little glass."

"Jeez." Mary Fran took another, more respectful swallow. "And he's buying you another?"

"He is."

"Sounds like the man is investing money."

"He won't get much interest on his principal."

"Why not?"

Abruptly, Libby's mood headed south. "Why do you think? I have three kids, that's why. And Aaron won't take them for the night, I already asked. Too bad, he says, it's not my weekend. And any minute now, they'll run in here screaming about who did what to whom, and then Jenny will get clingy and Sam will get pissy and Mickey— God, Mickey will have a cow if he suspects some *man* is interested in his mommy."

"Well, I can take them," Mary Fran said. "That's no problem."

"Where will you put them, on the floor?"

"We have a double suite," Mary Fran said. "They can sleep in the kids' room. There are two queen-sized beds."

Libby blinked. "You'd do this for me?"

"God, *yes*," Mary Fran said. "Anything. Anything I can do. It's just that there are some things I *can't* do, and barring Sara from the planet is one of them."

"I owe you," Libby said. "I mean that."

"Pay me back with the details." She leaned over, rested her head on Libby's shoulder. April hopped past again, her cheeks flushed from laughing, the bodice of her gown tugged askew. Behind her, Caleb was laughing, too. He *was* a nice guy. He was open and friendly and warm. He was gainfully employed. He loved April, and she loved him. But hadn't Barney been all of those things? And why not wait another three months, a year?

"Why was she in such a rush?" Mary Fran said.

"Why were we?" Libby said.

Neither of them said anything for moment. Then Mary Fran said, deadpan, "Well, I was knocked up, remember?"

They were laughing as the rest of the line swung past, and when Brian called, "You promised!" Mary Fran got up, kissed Libby on the forehead, and hop-hop-hopped away. Darien was just returning with another single malt; he shook his head politely as people tried to wave him into the line. "The bunny hop," he mused. "Catchier than the macarena, wouldn't you say?"

Libby sipped her drink. "You're sweet to get me another."

"How's Mary Fran?"

"She's fine."

"Elmer seems to be loosening up a little."

"It's something like a miracle, isn't it?" Libby said. She paused, considering her next words. Somewhere inside her, an immense scale teetered between speech and silence. If she told Darien she'd made arrangements for the children, she was committing herself, here and now, to a reckless night. How could she go through it? She glanced at him through lowered eyelids. Mother of God, how could she *not* go through with it? If only he came with operating instructions, maybe a how-to manual . . . but that was silly. It couldn't be all that difficult, making love to another man. Besides, she'd always thought she was all right in bed—though looking back, it was difficult to say. If she'd moved, Aaron came; if she didn't, Aaron came. If she dressed up, dressed down, didn't bother dressing, showered, didn't shower—nothing had seemed to deter him. He chugged away like the little engine that could. "What should I do?" she'd asked again and again, and he'd always said the same thing: "You don't have to do anything."

Maybe Darien would *want* her to do things. Now, wouldn't that be a nice change? Libby had always prided herself on being mechanically inclined. She could drive any kind of car, no problem:

stick shift, automatic, front-wheel drive. But when you drove the same car every day, there was always a certain amount of fumbling around when you first got into another. And if you hadn't had access to a car recently—well, it just wasn't true what people said about riding a bicycle. Last summer, when Mickey had coaxed her onto his mountain bike, she'd crash-landed in the junipers at the end of the driveway.

"People are talking about us," Libby said.

"As well they should." That grin.

"Mary Fran thinks you're cute."

"I *am* cute."

What was she going to do? What the hell did she want? Spine-popping, bone-crushing sex, that's what. No snakes, no snails, no puppy-dog tails, and no strings attached to it, either. And a little bit of genuine affection, after—she wanted some of that, too. A few dreary amoeba shapes drifted into her thoughts: HIV, hepatitis C, herpes, chlamydia. But wasn't that why God made latex? Abruptly, Libby's faith in a Higher Power rekindled, a low pleasant glow in her belly. *Somebody* must have a condom in her purse.

"She's offered to take the kids for the night," Libby said.

THE lobby might have been dim, but it certainly wasn't dark. The fireplace cast more than enough light for the desk clerk to see the boy and girl sitting on the hearth, pale hands and faces savaged by restless shadows. The girl did not particularly concern him. Girls, as everybody knew, were kinder, gentler creatures. But he didn't like the way the boy was staring into the fire in the timeless posture of a hunter plotting a kill. Earlier, this boy had picked all the Hershey's chocolates from the candy bowl; now the desk clerk was certain he'd been the one who'd swiped the whole thing. While the desk clerk didn't care about the candies themselves (okay, well, maybe he did care a little bit about the candies) the pewter bowl was another matter. In Bible study, it had been suggested that each person do one small thing to improve the atmosphere in which they worked, and the desk clerk was pleased at how quickly, how easily, he'd come up with the idea of a complimentary candy dish. He'd paid for the candies himself—not just cheap peppermints, either— and borrowed the bowl from his best friend, Julia, his just-friend, Julia, who said she loved him like a brother, and, well, sure, maybe that would change someday, but no, she didn't really think so. Julia wasn't saved, at least not yet. Still, she liked the desk clerk's new circle of Bible-reading friends so much better than she'd liked his old circle of pot-smoking redneck friends that she'd said, okay, fine, you can take it, but remember it's my mom's and she'd freak if it was missing, so just make sure I get it back, all right?

He glanced down at the small white button he wore, at all times, on his belt. It read: *W.W.J.D.?*

What Would Jesus Do?

Little did he know that, as he contemplated the boy and girl, wondering whether he should confront them (Jesus in the temple) or else turn the other cheek (Jesus crucified), as he tried to decide which Jesus of all the Jesuses in the Bible he was supposed to be, the boy and girl were contemplating him with an equally fierce intensity. Stanley and Lacey needed their coats to make the dash back to the Lodge and suite thirty-three, for the outside temperature was gritting its teeth somewhere in the teens. And their coats had been checked by the desk clerk, who would certainly want to know where they were going, and what they were doing, and wouldn't it be better to wait for an adult to accompany them?

It was Lacey's idea to set the fire. Unlike Mickey's fires, which were random acts of impulse, Lacey's fire-to-be had a strong and linear sense of plot, which Stanley admired. She'd ignite something, say, a pencil, and carry it into the ladies'. She'd fill a toilet with rolls of paper, set the whole thing ablaze. Then, calmly, she'd retreat to the lobby, approach the desk clerk, and in her best Southern belle, say, "Ex*cuse* me, *suh*? Ah just went to use the ladies' room an' hit's awl filled up with *smoke*." Her face would be so troubled, so filled with deep concern, that the desk clerk would suspect nothing. At least, he would not suspect her. He'd run off to investigate, leaving them plenty of time to slip around the counter and into the back office for their coats.

At this point Stanley would have agreed to much worse. He had met a girl he liked who actually liked him back. He'd imbibed two disgusting cups of beery froth without embarrassing himself. He'd managed to pocket a handful of condoms, scrambling around on his knees in the bridal suite, and he had those moist little pleasures to look forward to later, at home, in the privacy of his bedroom. And, then—who could have predicted this?—just before the dance got under way, Aunt Libby and a man she introduced as her *friend* had given them, like, fifty quarters, held together in a large, linen napkin. "I hear there's a game room downstairs," she said. "Consider this your baby-sitting fee. Remember, they'll behave themselves better if you bribe them."

"A game room?" Mickey said, all innocence. "There is?"

So they'd trooped back through the lobby and down the steps to the game room, Sam and Jenny running behind them, mewling for quarters. Even Margo was drawn by the promise of all the pinball she could play, though she still wouldn't speak to Stanley and made certain to keep Lacey between them at all times. Barney Lohr had been there, too, playing pool with someone Stanley didn't know. "Hey, Stan-the-man!" he'd called. "Is that your girlfriend?" Stanley ignored him, the way he ignored the assistant bartender, who wanted to know—ha-ha—were they all twenty-one. Stanley had never liked

Barney. He'd never liked being called Stan-the-man, or having his hair messed up, or being asked stupid questions about girls, all of which he'd endured during the years that Barney and April had been dating. However, he soon forgot all about Barney, and suite thirty-three as well, seduced by the ringing of the pinball machine, the blinking lights, the *thunk* of the balls against the bumpers.

But Lacey said it was important that they all put in an appearance at the dance. That way, no one would get worried if they disappeared for a while later on. And so, over Mickey's protests, they'd abandoned the remaining quarters to the younger kids and returned to the ballroom, where they discovered Mickey's mother dancing—waltzing, actually—with her *friend* in a way that was, well, awfully *friendly*. Mickey stared at his mother. Then he stared at his father, who was also waltzing, and not with Sara. Sara was sitting alone by the wall, and she didn't look any happier than Mickey. She'd kicked off her shoes and propped up her feet, which looked like monstrous wedges of cantaloupe.

At that point Mickey lost all interest whatsoever in suite thirty-three. "I wanna play pinball," he told the others in a strange flat voice. "You guys are just gonna get in trouble anyway. There's nothing out there but somebody's stupid room."

To Stanley's surprise, Anderson agreed. "I've had enough hide-and-seek with you babies," he said, and Mickey said, "Yeah, maybe the two of them want to be *alone*," and Anderson said, "Yeah, maybe they want to play hide-and-seek all by *themselves*," and Mickey said, "Hide the salami, you mean."

"Eat scum," Lacey said, but Anderson and Mickey were already walking away, laughing the theatrical laughs of boys destined for popularity, for vice-presidencies and weekend houses in the country. Stanley and Lacey watched them go. The phrase *hide the salami* hung awkwardly between them.

"Do *you* want to do this?" Stanley had asked. He'd been thinking better of it, too. They would open the door and find—what? An empty room. The faces of strangers. Some nice couple asking, Was there a problem?

"I don't know," Lacey said.

"We could just walk over and see," he said. "You know, check it out."

"We could always say we got mixed up and thought it was our room."

"The desk must have given us the wrong key," Stanley said, practicing.

"Excellent," Lacey said.

But first, there would have to be a fire, and starting one was harder than Stanley would have thought. They spotted a wood chip on the fireplace floor, coaxed it onto the hearth, but whenever they tried to pick it up, the fragile ember winked out. At last, it caught. Flared. Lacey held it by her hip like a cigarette as she crossed the lobby toward the ladies' room. Stanley wondered what would happen if someone was already in there. He wondered what would happen if she got caught. He wondered what would happen if they opened the door to suite thirty-three and there really were prostitutes inside, big-breasted and fishnetted, wearing hip boots and leather vests. He imagined them speaking to each other in the polite but stilted language of *Ouch!*

"Would you like to beat me now?"

"Yes, please."

Or what if they found a gang of drug dealers with guns, a suitcase filled with cash? These and other possibilities strummed the tight piano wire of his spine until Lacey reappeared—without the ember. Stanley had to admire the way she didn't even glance in his direction. Half a minute later the desk clerk was flying down the hall, an enormous fire extinguisher banging painfully against one hip. They rushed behind the desk and into the back office, where they discovered a walk-in closet hung with rack after swinging rack of coats. But how would they ever find their own? How were they all organized?

There was no time to crack the desk clerk's code. They began to claw through the coats, which tumbled free of their hangers. Gloves flew. Change rattled from pockets. Here were some car keys. Here were a couple of lipsticks—Lacey pocketed one for herself. Panicking, Stanley embraced the coats, pulling them down by the armful. "Just grab anything," Lacey said, slipping into a floor-length fur. Stanley rooted around until he found a stiff navy-blue broadcloth, and they charged back into the lobby, through the entryway, and onto the porch. From behind them came the scouring sound of the fire extinguisher, a few final whoops from the dancers, notes like pieces of crystal tossed into the air.

Then silence. The sledgehammer weight of the cold. A path had been trampled down the front steps, blurred by the snow which continued to fall even as they followed it toward the pale light over the entrance to the Lodge. The key to suite thirty-three was the faintest of jingles, a lone sleigh bell in Stanley's pocket.

"I've never seen this much snow in my life," Lacey said, reverently.

THE woman from suite thirty-three watched them go. She watched the man, back in their suite, pacing to and fro before the stone-cold bed. She watched Barney Lohr come up from the game room and make his way through the ballroom toward the relative quiet of the dining room. In the far corner, nests of infants and toddlers slept in collapsible playpens and cribs; beside them, a few older children dozed on a makeshift pallet of coats. Mothers and grandmothers played cards by candlelight, and when Barney sat down at a nearby table, they studied him briefly before returning to their conversations, endless cycling stories of illness and birth and death.

The In-Laws announced their break, and the woman from suite thirty-three watched them lower their instruments into velvet-lined cases. She watched the guests migrating toward the lobby bathrooms, toward the front porch for a smoke, toward the front desk to retrieve their coats, for the air was chilly against sweat-soaked skin. Outside, the snow was tapering off. There were reports that the plows were making progress, that the interstate could open by midnight. A general optimism had started to spread, and many people switched from wine to soda pop, daring to hope they might be able to make the drive home. Surely, Elmer Liesgang's buddies would manage to detour at least one plow toward the Chapel!

The woman from suite thirty-three was finding it hard to pay attention. She was thinking about the woman in the red dress: her peculiar smell, her shining rage. She was thinking of the body she'd seen on the bed. Her body. She wasn't certain what it meant. It was one of those small, meaningless details that keeps coming back into your head. She patted her skirt, making sure that the zipper was straight. She licked her upper lip, tasting to see if she needed more lipstick; she tousled her hair with her fingers. Everything seemed to check out okay. Briefly, she sat down beside Barney Lohr, understanding the comfort he took from the presence of the sleeping children. She knew his secret wish was to be a child again, snuggled into his bed by his mother's soothing hand.

Another little girl was settled onto the pallet of coats. A few more grandmothers seated themselves to play cards. The woman watched the smallest of the infants, his delicate red nostrils; she watched the oldest child, who was sucking her sister's thumb. She watched one of the grandmothers cheating. She watched Hilda Liesgang, who saw the woman cheating but said nothing, out of rage and helpless despair. There were pennies all around her, stacked up in little piles, for the grandmothers were betting.

And all of these things, the woman understood, had something to do with love: the children walking through the snow, the man and his endless sorrowful pacing, Barney and his despair, the grand-mother cheating for pennies. Was this what her father had been trying to tell her, on her own wedding day, during the father-daughter dance? Was this what the woman in the red dress had meant?

Anything that sticks to you, you wind up calling it love.

Anything familiar. It doesn't matter, good or bad.

And now she could feel the mattress, firm beneath her hips. The pillow smelled of detergent, and dust, no heavier than a house cat. She knew that somebody entering the room might draw the wrong conclusions. They might think there was something wrong. They might wonder how she could breathe that way, under that pillow, lying so still. A thought occurred to her then that was so outrageous, so ludicrous, she knew it had to be true. The thought was this: he's killed me. This time, he's actually killed me. He's finally gone and done it. She experienced a strange satisfaction. No one could accuse her of overreacting now. It reminded her of something she'd read about one time, an epitaph that was actually carved on someone's tombstone: I TOLD YOU I WAS SICK.

It wasn't funny, but she started to laugh anyway. How she wished that her husband would stop his endless pacing. She wished he would come over and lie down with her on the bed.

She wanted to tell him the joke. She wanted to take his hand.

She wanted to tell him that it was okay, she wasn't mad at him anymore.

BOUQUET TOSS

HE last time April had seen Barney Lohr, they'd met briefly at her apartment in Madison to return each other's things. His class ring. Her engagement ring. A camera. Items of clothing, CDs. Barney had been crying. April had cried, too. By then, the bruise on her stomach had shrunk to the size of a fist, though her ribs still hurt her, especially at night, when it was hard to find a comfortable sleeping position. Two broken ribs. She'd told the doctor at the health center she'd fallen. Friends thought she had the flu, brought her soup and orange juice. Looking back, it all seemed like something that had happened to someone else. Or, at least, it had until now.

She'd watched Barney not-watching her through the rest of the sit-down supper, through the tapping of forks and silly, forced kisses, through the cutting of the cake. Then, just before the dance began, just as she was bracing herself for his approach, he'd suddenly disappeared. Perhaps he'd made his point, whatever it was, and headed on home—though with the snow, that didn't seem likely. Or perhaps he was still not-watching her, concealed now in one of the service hallways spindling off toward the kitchen. He might be standing behind the floor-length curtains in the windows. He might be moving in and out of the crowd so that, wherever she glanced, it was where he'd just been.

But she couldn't worry about that now. It was almost time to toss the bouquet, and she still couldn't figure out where the hell she'd left it. At first, she'd thought one of her single friends had swiped it as a prank, but all of them shook their heads: no, not me. Most had already assembled in the center of the ballroom like beautiful blossoms in a wide, clear bowl. Earlier, the ladies' room off the lobby—lit by an assortment of flashlights—had been a happy hive of wisecracking, powdering, fluffing, spritzing, the constant flush of the toilet like a cheer. Someone had propped the door open with a trash can; still, the almost-pleasant odor of smoke hung thickly in the air, and there was animated speculation about the fire, gestures at the evidence: one barred stall. But all of that sloppy camaraderie had given way to a new, brittle edginess. It didn't help that bachelors had started to gather on the sidelines, scuffling around, slapping shoulders, hassling those who had steady girlfriends:

She's lookin' determined, there, Mark. Your days are numbered.

Watch out, Ricky—she's got the legs of a quarterback.

Among the women themselves, a few unhappy discussions were under way. Some of the thirty-somethings felt that no girl younger than twenty should be allowed to try for the bouquet. Some of the women who'd never been married felt that anyone who was divorced should do the right thing and sit down and give the rest of them their chance. Everyone talked about a recent wedding in which a girl—a really homely, unlikable girl—had caught the bouquet, had actually snatched it out of the hands of a more deserving girl, and now this homely girl was a happily married woman. In fact, some of the women had heard she was already expecting her first child.

"You mean Betsy Colby?" April asked, and Lanna Yoderman, hands on her white-sequined hips, said, "Yeah, can you believe it?"

"I always liked Betsy," April said, and Lanna said harshly, "Oh, April, you like everybody," and April's friend Paula—they'd been best friends in high school—muttered, loud enough for everyone to hear, "A serious personality flaw, clearly."

Paula didn't care about getting married. She wanted to catch the bouquet out of spite. So did several of the other women. Nobody wanted Lanna to have it.

"Look," Lanna said, and that white dress sparkled angrily. "I'm older than most of you, and if I want a family, something damn well better happen soon."

"How old is that?" Paula asked.

Stop it, April wanted to say. It's just a stupid game, a superstition. Like spilling salt or knocking on wood. And yet, hadn't she herself once believed in the luck of the bouquet? There were always stories like the Betsy Colby story. There were always debates about whether or not the underage girls should be allowed to compete. It was depressing, petty, ridiculous. "Maybe I left it in the ladies' room," she said, already half running toward the lobby door.

She'd been only thirteen when Mary Fran had pushed her forward into the circle of older girls at a neighbor's wedding, ignoring their grumblings, the sounds they made as they sucked their teeth in disgust. "Like *she* needs a bouquet," April heard one of them say. "Like she needs a *bra*, for Chrissakes," another said, and then they'd all laughed, April's face flushing crimson. She could still remember the dress she'd worn, some god-awful thing Mary Fran had found at a yard sale, pale blue with a childish, quilted bodice. It wouldn't have occurred to her, then, to refuse to wear it. A white satin ribbon hung from the waist, so irresistibly smooth that she'd kept stroking it until she'd discolored it with her fingers.

And then, her senior year in high school. Her cousin Mercy's wedding. She was going steady with Barney then, so the older girls couldn't complain. On the sidelines, her uncles were razzing Barney good, saying April might look puny but she was strong, a scrapper, she could jump like a cricket, and a fellah was never too young to get started. When Barney saw April watching, he grinned and mouthed *good luck*. He meant it. He really did want to marry her— not this summer, but the next. She'd visit him at the Magic Carpet on weekends, and he'd be wearing a suit coat and tie, like his dad, speaking knowledgeably about fibers and Scotchgard: grown-up, levelheaded, always proud to introduce her as his girlfriend. So different from the other boys his age.

"April's an artist," he'd tell anybody. "She's amazing." He was the only one, back then, who thought of her that way. Certainly, her parents didn't. In fact, they wondered what Barney saw in her. Kids at school wondered, too. They figured she must be really wild in bed. She must be one of those girls who wouldn't just sleep with a guy but would do, you know, *that*. Boys sucked their fingers in the hallways as she passed. Somebody drew a penis in permanent marker on her locker. At first Barney said he would kill the mother-fucker who did it. Then he wanted to know how come there were so many rumors about her if it was true she was still a virgin, the way she said.

She wondered if she'd ever feel for Barney even half of what he seemed to feel for her. Mary Fran said love happened over time, and she shouldn't make any hasty decisions. Barney was a nice guy with a solid future, and nice-enough looking to boot, what more could April want? With Barney, she'd never have to hold up both ends of a conversation. With Barney, she'd always have a social life, and while April couldn't imagine what it was like to be without friends now, Mary Fran could assure her from personal experience that it wasn't any picnic living with a man who never wanted to go anywhere, never wanted to do anything but watch TV and mess around with bicycles.

You can't imagine, Mary Fran had said, what it's like to be this lonely. You just don't know how good you've got it, how lucky you are.

Sometimes, as April and Barney were driving home from, say, a movie, and he'd be talking and talking and talking about the plot and the characters and what the director should have done, she'd think about dying—not of killing herself, not like that, but about just *not being*. Someday, it would happen. She would get through her life, and then she'd be gone. And nothingness had to be better than this feeling of disconnectedness, always pretending to be grateful because she had everything she could want: food and clothes and medical care, a family who loved her, a boyfriend who loved her and said he understood all about disconnectedness, too. In fact, he said he felt the same way. He said that if April would only sleep with him—*make love with him,* was how he always said it—that feeling would go away because it would be something that connected them, always, no matter what. Circling her cousin Mercy amidst the cries of "Just toss it!" and "C'mon!" she wondered if she *should* sleep with Barney and get the whole awful burden of her virginity over with. Maybe then everything else would fall into place. Because, clearly, something was wrong with her, and it was only a matter of time before people found out. The truth was that she didn't want to *make love* with anybody. She wanted to be left alone. She wanted to paint, to read, to think. And she didn't need Elmer's constant nagging to remind her that these were not practical desires. She had to get serious. She had to grow up.

With that, Mercy's bouquet exploded against her chest.

She clutched it to her—an automatic reflex—as girls shrieked and petals fluttered all around them, like ash. How many times in anyone's life does clarity strike with such precision? She'd run across the dance floor then, thrown her arms around Barney's neck, whispered, *All right, all right then,* and he'd known exactly what she'd meant.

The line for the ladies' room extended halfway through the lobby; April excused and pardoned her way toward the stalls. The smell of smoke lingered. "Anybody seen my bouquet?" she called.

Nobody had.

Someone suggested she check with the front desk but, back in the lobby, she saw that a line had formed there as well. Ralph Bamberger was talking angrily to the desk clerk; idly, April wondered if somebody's coat was missing. She returned to the ballroom just as Caleb walked through the dining-room archway, carrying a plate of candles, affixed by their own wax. The flames were round and dark as buttons.

"You find it?" he called.

"Nope."

"Me neither. I checked under all the tables."

She said, "Well, I have to toss something."

"How about your grandmother's corsage?"

"Shh," she said, laughing, and then she thought of something. "I wonder if I left it upstairs?"

They both squinted up at the nuptial balcony. The scarf which had concealed the heirloom crucifix had slipped. Beneath a halo of Christmas-tree lights, Christ's agonized face was torqued with shadow.

"Doesn't that thing give you the creeps?" Caleb said.

April shrugged. "It's hung in my grandmother's dining room for as long as I can remember."

"And y'all *ate* in front of it and everything?"

"And your daddy gets the spirit and speaks in tongues?"

They grinned at each other.

"Come upstairs with me," April said.

They stopped when they reached the balcony, the spot where they'd stood to be married. Below, guests milled about, waiting for the band to return. "I don't see Barney anywhere," April said, her voice thick with relief. "I really think he must have gone home." Caleb had just seen Barney in the dining room, but he didn't tell her that. And when he put his arm around her, she leaned into him, content.

"I'm so glad we did this," she said.

"The ceremony?" Caleb was surprised. "You are?"

"Well, the supper, anyway. And the dance. My dad was right— I'd have regretted it if we'd just sneaked off somewhere."

"Well, I hope you'll feel just as glad about"—he lowered his voice—"the Fellowship wedding."

"Can you believe I'm starting to look forward to it?"

He was pleased. "There's always a potluck, after. It'll be kind of like this. Lots of bland food, kids running wild, everybody talking."

"No alcohol, though."

"Mama can always get hold of some."

She gave him a sly look. "No air hockey."

"There's a pool table, actually."

They kissed, Caleb holding the plate of candles away from her dress. Somebody whistled shrilly, and Paula hollered up at them, "Save it for the honeymoon!"

April flipped her the bird.

"Manners, girl," Caleb said.

"I'll show you manners," April said, her hands beneath his tuxedo jacket.

"Hey!" he shouted, juggling the candles. "Unfair!"

The women on the ballroom floor cheered as he fled down the hall toward the dressing rooms. April raised her hands like a wrestling champ. Then she hurried after his retreating light.

The air in the hall was strangely sweet-smelling. The door to the dressing room stood ajar. He reached it first and then stood there, the candles flickering wildly, until April pushed past. "Oh," she said in a soft, ruined voice, but it took another moment before he understood what they were seeing: the shattered mirror in which their images appeared to be scribbled out, as if by a vindictive pen; the dress April was to have worn the next day—they'd chosen it together, his wedding gift to her—flung upon the daybed, facedown, as if it, too, were an anguished victim. The upended suitcases. The carry-on bag wrenched clean of its intimacies. A frail light quivered in the adjoining bath, the white toilet bowl and sink standing aghast, onlookers who, later, will refuse to testify, glowing with the importance of all that they have seen. Here was the source of that sweet, sweet smell. The air was choked, swollen with the odor of perfume.

"The bastard," Caleb said.

April glanced at him, said nothing. She crossed the room and bent to retrieve the flattened bouquet. With surprising matter-of-factness, she shook it out, fluffed it like a hat. "It's still good enough to throw," she said. Kneeling clumsily beside the carry-on bag, she began to pat the floor around it, locating combs, credit cards, lipsticks. Caleb stared at her for a moment before squatting beside her, setting the plate of candles between them. They found their plane tickets, passports, her coin purse.

"The bastard," Caleb said again. He wanted April to say something, and when she didn't, he was confused. "It *was* Barney, wasn't it? It had to be him."

"Just let it go."

He thought he'd misheard her. "What?" When she rose, she

stepped on the hem of her dress, and she would have fallen into the candles if he hadn't grabbed her arm. "What do you mean, *let it go?*"

"Nothing's been stolen. It's no big deal." She picked her way over to the dressing table, righted the chair, and sat in it.

"Why not let your Uncle Frank decide what's a big deal and what isn't," Caleb said. "Jesus, April, we've got to report this."

She'd already begun to tidy the dressing table, arranging the hair spray, the hand lotion, the mascara, the moisturizer. "He's just trying to get my attention." She'd dropped something, a hard little bottle. "He was always doing stuff like this. I'd be busy, you know, I'd be thinking about something else, someone else, and he'd just—freak out."

He watched as she felt around with her feet, then bent to pick the bottle up.

"That was when he—hit you," he said.

She shrugged. "More often he'd break stuff, kick things around."

"So it happened more than once," he said. He'd meant to shape the sentence as a question. The darkness extended the silence between them.

He said, "You didn't tell me the truth."

"When you talk about stuff like this," she finally said, "it takes on a life of its own. It isn't just something that happened and now it's over and you can forget it. It keeps coming back. And each time, it gets bigger. The way it's doing now."

He set the plate on the dressing table. Her mouth was set in a thin, hard line. The top of the dressing table was immaculate, the candlelight liquid between them.

"How long was all this going on?" he asked.

"It wasn't just him," she said. "*I* broke things, too, if you want to know the truth. This one time he shoved me and I jumped back up and broke every goddamn plate in the kitchen. *My* kitchen, *my* plates. It was crazy. He was yelling, *I'm sorry, I'm sorry,* and I ran out of my apartment and drove all the way back to Holly's Field. I sat in my parents' driveway until five in the morning and then I drove back, can you believe it? Because I didn't want them to know. They liked him so much, my mom especially. And when I got back, he'd cleaned everything up. It was like nothing had happened. Except I didn't have any plates." She laughed, a small, disbelieving sound. "He bought me a whole new set. It had a creamer and a gravy boat and this hopeful yellow floral pattern, these little bunches of daisies—"

"So you stayed with him because he replaced your dishes."

She stood up, gave him a strange, stunned look. "I broke up with him, Caleb."

"But after how long?"

"What difference does it make?"

"It makes a difference."

"Why?"

He said, "How could you let somebody do that to you?"

"But I *didn't.*"

"You did."

"I left him—"

"You stayed with him. You put up with that kind of shit. I don't get it, April."

He was imagining it now, her breaking those plates. Running from the apartment. Coming back, and coming back. He wanted to scrub the images from his mind, but it was too late, they were part of him now. Part of the way he would see her. If there'd been a reason, some kind of excuse—but no. She and Barney hadn't been married. They weren't even sharing an apartment. There were no children to consider.

"Fine," April said. "I stayed because I'm stupid, is that what you want to hear? Or maybe I just enjoyed it. Yeah, that last year in Madison was a great time, it was fucking Christmas morning every day because I was just so happy getting knocked around—"

"Look," he said, "let's not fight, okay? We've got the rest of the wedding to get through," though what he was thinking was, *We've got the rest of our lives to get through,* something which, only minutes earlier, had seemed like such a gift.

Downstairs, a single accordion began its warm-up: those loose, watery scales, a drowning swimmer fluttering up, again and again, for air. The skirt of April's dress answered it—*shush-shush*—as she crossed the room and sat down on the bed. The bodice itched, the long, tight sleeves. She scratched and scratched, her finger-nails raking over furrows that the seams had plowed into her skin.

"I wish you'd told me, that's all," Caleb finally said.

"You won't respect me now."

"That's not true," he said, although it was. Or, at least, it had been for a moment.

"God, if my parents ever found out," she said. "Or my friends—"

He felt terrible. Ashamed. He got up, pulled her to her feet, rubbed his hands over her rigid shoulders as if she were only cold.

"I can't explain it," she said. "It was like living underwater. Every-thing was heavy and blurred and *loud.* I just sort of—hung there. I thought there was something wrong with me. I kept thinking that if I waited long enough, things would work out somehow."

They stood that way for a long time, leaning hard against each other. The candles flickered out, one by one. Guests had gathered in the ballroom below, the murmur of their voices like a slow, rising tide, and now deliberate footsteps were coming down the hall. A woman's voice called, "Uh, you guys?" Paula's voice.

"I'm okay," April said, her voice muffled against his chest.

"I know," Caleb said. And he let her go.

Paula was calling, "I've been sent by the masses to inform you that married sex doesn't last more than five minutes, and the band's been waiting for ten."

"Don't you see that the thing about dealing with this," April said, gesturing at the room, "is that I'll have to deal with *him*? I'll have to accuse him. And he'll have to deny it. His parents will get involved, mine will get involved, and this will just go on and on and everybody's going to know about it." She ran her hands through her hair. "Besides, maybe it wasn't him. He isn't even here anymore."

"He's in the dining room," Caleb said. "I didn't want to tell you."

"Christ," April said, and then the beam of Paula's flashlight shot into the room, lighting up any corners the candles had missed. Paula followed, grinning, but her smile vanished as she looked around. "What the hell happened here?" she said.

"Somebody trashed the room," April said.

"Why? Some kind of prank?"

There was a pause, and then Paula said, "Barney wouldn't do something like this, would he?"

Caleb shifted his feet, but said nothing.

"I don't know," April finally said. "Nothing's missing, just rearranged."

"What's he even doing here?" Paula said. "You didn't invite him, did you?"

"My mom invited his parents," April said. "I guess he thought he was invited, too."

"Do *you* think he did this?" Caleb suddenly asked Paula, who glanced at April, then looked away.

"There's some other stuff going on, too," she said. "Somebody got behind the front desk, messed everything up, and stole a couple of coats. And then there was that fire in the ladies'. Your uncle is looking into it, April. You want me to tell him about this, too?"

"You'll miss the bouquet toss," April said.

"Yeah, and the disappointment might kill me."

April looked at Caleb. She looked at their shattered reflections in the mirror. Then she turned back to Paula. "Thanks," she said. "But tell him—maybe we can handle it quietly? Maybe he wouldn't have to report it to anybody else?"

"I'll tell him," Paula said. "Hey, is that the bouquet?"

April held it up for her to see: misshapen, ragged as a dead hen. Paula laughed. "Lanna can have it," she said.

IN the ballroom, the guests waited restlessly, nervously. Ten inches of snow had fallen, according to Ralph Bamberger's battery-powered radio. There still was no word on when and if the power would return. Rumors of a mysterious fire in the ladies' room had spread, and now there was this strange trouble behind the front desk: coats knocked off their hangers, the room left in disarray. Must be a poltergeist, somebody said, and someone else said, You go on and laugh, but the house I grew up in had a ghost, a little girl who'd died of influenza or diphtheria or something, and she'd do things like set fires in the kitchen sink.

Yeah, and if that's what a little girl would do, think of what ol' Gretel Fame has in store for all of us.

I'm not joking.

Who says I'm joking?

Hush, a woman said. Here they are.

April and Caleb were hurrying down the stairs. They ducked their heads, looking decidedly sheepish. What were they doing up there! But no matter. Already, the single women were forming an eager circle around them. When the In-Laws began a slow waltz, exaggerating the beat—*one*-two-three, *one*-two-three—Caleb covered April's eyes. The crowd clapped time as he spun her in place; the single women walked counterclockwise, calling, "April, over here!" and "C'mon!" At last, April raised the bouquet, but even before she'd released it, even before she had set it loose like a colorful bird, ungainly as love itself, petals falling from it like droppings, ribbons dangling like a falcon's tack, even before it had left her hands, the circle collapsed as women rushed forward, fighting to intercept its clumsy flight. Several managed to capture it for a second or two, but by the time Caleb dropped his hands from April's eyes, Lanna Yoderman had wrenched it away.

The applause which followed was stingy, seasoned with grumbles. Lanna didn't seem to care. Briefly, she raised her prize above her head: a victory salute, perhaps, or maybe a terse *fuck you*. And that was it. After all that waiting, it had taken less than a minute. The In-Laws began a lively polka, something intended to clear the room of any lingering tension.

In the dining room, Barney Lohr heard the music resume and knew the bouquet toss was over. He hadn't bothered to watch it. All he wanted now was to find a ride home, though there was little chance of that happening until after the midnight toast. Even then, it was possible that he might be stranded for the night. The storm was blowing out over the lake, but that didn't guarantee it wouldn't boomerang. And what if the plows didn't come this far east of the interstate? What if nobody offered him a ride, not wanting to risk driving out of their way on such a bad night? His head ached; his tongue was swollen, sore. How he wished he hadn't drunk that last glass of Asti Spumante. How he wished that he'd never met the stranger, and listened to things he wasn't meant to know about, and spoken of things he'd promised himself he'd never tell anybody. How he wished he'd taken Coot's advice and gone straight home in the first place.

One by one, the grandmothers were returning to their card games, relighting their candles. A few more mothers led fussy children toward the makeshift nursery. Mary Fran passed by with Margo, whose scowling, chipmunk face looked almost deliberately comical; earlier, Mary Fran had settled Libby's daughter, Jenny, on the bed of coats. Once, these little girls had been almost like sisters to Barney. He'd bought them Christmas presents, sung "Happy Birthday" at their parties. Now they acted as if they didn't recognize him. Maybe they truly didn't. Mary Fran flashed him a quick, apologetic smile, and he tried to smile back. He'd hoped they'd get a chance to talk, maybe even dance a little. He'd loved Mary Fran. He'd always called her *Mum*, pretending to tease her, but both of them had believed it would mean something someday. What was he supposed to do with all these feelings now?

This was a question he had asked that doctor, but the doctor hadn't answered him, not exactly. Instead, he'd asked Barney what *he* thought he should do with those feelings. Sometimes it seemed to Barney that the doctor didn't know any more than he or anybody else did. He'd think about that microchip, the one he'd always half believed he was missing, and wonder if maybe there were other people who'd been born without one, too. Or maybe it was just that there weren't any answers for some questions. Maybe you just had to learn to live with that. But this seemed unbearable to Barney. It seemed to him that, one way or another, if you were smart enough, and diligent enough, and waited long enough, everything would resolve. He wondered if that was what the stranger had been trying to tell him. *Get back on the horse*, he'd said. The expression on his face made it clear that he'd wanted nothing more to do with Barney. If there were such a thing as that microchip, the stranger probably had two. He was a good man, with a wife waiting for him, and he hadn't understood a thing that Barney'd said to him. He probably couldn't imagine hurting anyone the way that Barney had done.

Corrine and Hilda settled themselves at a nearby table, away from the larger groups of cardplayers. They called, in voices dripping with sympathy, if he didn't want to join them in a nice game of rummy?

"No, thanks," he said. "Maybe later." How he wanted to go home! He stared at the candle in front of him, fingering the dribbles of cooling wax, going over that last fight with April in his bedroom. Gradually—as he'd done many times before—he reworked it, revised it, reshaped it. Why not? In this version, April (tearfully) told the truth: she wanted to leave early because there was somebody else. And they sat down together on his bed to have what his mother called *an adult conversation*. In his daydream, Barney listened calmly to everything she said, and then he accepted the return of his engagement ring. Not to worry, he told her. He absolutely understood. Distance, he said, was hard on any relationship. She was free to see other people if that was what she wanted to do. But he wanted her to know that his love for her wouldn't change. "This ring will be waiting for you," he said, "whenever you're ready to wear it again." He started to put it in his dresser drawer, but then April stopped him. She said she'd made a mistake. She said she wanted to get married right away, she didn't want to put it off any longer.

When he looked up, he was unable to reconcile the April he saw in his mind with the April standing across from him. She looked tired, her eyes glassy, her mouth drawn tight. Caleb stood beside her; Frank Liesgang and Ralph Bamberger were there, too. Barney knew Bamberger. He'd sold him wall-to-wall carpeting for three newly renovated suites. Bamberger had quibbled over every detail, then taken his sweet time paying off the bill.

"April," Barney said, staring into her strange, familiar face.

"How's it going, son?" Frank said.

Barney stood up. "All right." He thought about how he'd planned to shake Caleb's hand. He didn't think he could do that anymore.

"I'm Barney Lohr," he said stiffly.

Caleb said, "I know who you are." Up close, Caleb was, well, funny looking. He had deep-set dimples and pale blue eyes, an odd reddish tint to his blond hair. The bridge of his nose was freckled. His lips were thin and chapped looking, like a child's. Barney imagined those lips moving over April's body, the two of them together in her Madison apartment, naked on the futon bed that doubled as a couch.

"I guess I should say congratulations." Barney didn't look at either of them when he said it.

"I thought we could all sit down for a minute," Frank said. He pointed to a dark table in the corner. "Try and straighten out a few things."

"What things?" Barney said. He glanced at April. Her face was without expression. Maybe the stranger had gone and told Caleb what Barney had done. It crossed his mind that he was about to be arrested.

"Maybe over there at that corner table," Frank said in his easy way. "Give ourselves a little privacy."

Frank Liesgang had never been one to jump to conclusions, and he wasn't about to start now. For one, he remembered the fire that Mickey and Stanley had set at the Liesgangs' last summer. For another, he found it peculiar that the only things missing from behind the front desk were two coats, one of them his own, plus a single duplicate key. And while Barney was a fool to have come to the wedding in the first place, Frank couldn't believe he'd be stupid enough to walk up the balcony stairs, in full view of all the guests—most of whom knew him—in order to commit an act of childish vandalism he was certain to be blamed for. But Bamberger, on the other hand, had his mind made up. He'd spoken to the bride's friend Paula, and heard her opinions on the subject. He'd spoken to the groom. He'd seen the mess behind the front desk, sniffed the smoky air in the ladies', viewed the destruction in the bride's dressing room.

"Where've you been for the past hour?" he asked.

"What's it to you?" Barney said.

"Hold your horses," Frank told Bamberger. "I'm warning you."

The grandmothers were watching them now, the cards pale and motionless in their hands. From the pallet of coats, Mary Fran watched, too. Even Margo understood that something was about to happen. Hilda called, "Frank? Is there a problem, Frank?"

Frank said to Barney, gently, "I missed you at the dance. Seems like you always used to be the first one out on the floor."

Barney said, "I was downstairs shooting pool with—" He paused. It hadn't seemed awkward, at the time, that the stranger hadn't volunteered his name. "He said he was an old friend of your family's," he told Caleb.

"*My* family?" Caleb said. "That's not possible."

"Well, that's what he said. We got talking at supper."

"So what's this fellah's name?" Frank said.

"I didn't ask." Barney turned back to Caleb. "Good-looking guy, maybe thirty. He's staying at the Lodge with his wife. He said that his family and yours go way back."

"There's nobody here like that. Just my mother. And my niece and nephew."

"Then I guess I've been shooting pool with Nobody all this time," Barney said, folding his arms.

Bamberger said to Frank, "It don't take the FBI to figure this one out."

"One more word," Frank warned him.

"Frank?" Hilda Liesgang had abandoned her card game; Corrine Shannon followed, walked around the table to stand beside her son. "What's the matter?" she asked him, and Caleb said, without taking his eyes off Barney, "Mama, do we have any guests at the wedding? Aside from you and me and the children?"

"No, of course not," Corrine said, bewildered by the question.

By now, Mary Fran had joined them, too, Margo clinging to her hand. Several more grandmothers approached the table. People were watching from the ballroom archway, squinting into the comparative darkness of the dining room.

Christ, Frank thought. We got dry timber, all we need is a spark.

"You're a liar," April told Barney Lohr.

And there it was. "Now, kids," Frank said.

Barney said, "You should talk."

"What the hell is that supposed to mean?"

"You're the one who was two-timing me up in Madison. With *him*. His friend told me all about everything."

"I've never even *been* to Madison," Caleb said.

Barney said to April, "Now who's a liar?"

"There's no need for name-calling," Hilda said, and Corrine said, "It's an emotional time for everybody."

Everyone ignored them.

"Tell the truth," April said. "You went upstairs to my dressing room and trashed it." Her voice was like a recording of a voice, stripped of its color and tone, and Barney remembered how she could speak to him like this for days. How she could look at him and be looking right through him, as if he wasn't even there. How could he be invisible to her, when she was everything to him? He loved her so much, and he hated her, too. He would have done anything to make her see him. He wanted to put his hands around her throat and squeeze. He must have leaned forward, because she took a step back, and then he felt Frank's hard hand on his shoulder. Jesus, it was happening again. And all he'd wanted was to wish her well. All he'd wanted to do was to envision, together, that time in the future when they could sit calmly at a cookout or a baseball game, chatting about their spouses, complimenting each other's children, leaning into each other with the easy intimacy of old friends, of a brother and sister who've survived a senseless childhood to emerge, happy and whole, on the other side of it all. For the first time he realized they'd never have a conversation like that. After today, he'd probably never see her again. Abruptly, he sat down, put his head in his hands. "I didn't do it, April," he said, his voice muffled. "I didn't do anything like that."

"Maybe you just flew off the handle for a minute?" Frank said. That calm, reasonable tone. "Understandable, if you found out something that upset you."

"I shot some pool and then I came in here."

"He's been sitting here at least an hour," one of the grandmothers volunteered. "Since before the band took its break."

Mary Fran said, "I saw him when I brought Jenny in, oh, about a quarter to ten."

"But what about before that?" Bamberger asked. "Anybody see him playing pool with the invisible man?"

Before Frank could object to that, Margo said scornfully, "The man wasn't *invisible*."

Everybody looked at her. She was sucking on her index finger.

"You saw him, sweetheart?" Frank said.

Margo nodded. Mary Fran pulled the finger out of her mouth.

"What were you doing?"

"Pinball."

"What was Barney doing?"

"Pool."

"Speak nicely," Mary Fran said.

"Who was with him?"

"I *told* you. A man."

"Can you tell us what he looked like?"

Margo thought about it. "He had brown hair," she said.

"He said he was staying in the Western Suite," Barney said desperately.

"Suite thirty-three?" Bamberger said, suddenly alert. The missing duplicate key had belonged to suite thirty-three. And he was not unaware of the rumors surrounding that suite, rumors which, despite his best efforts, he'd been unable to extinguish. Every now and then, some nice-enough-looking fellah would mention suite thirty-three as he checked in, half-joking, but also half-serious. Bamberger never smiled. "I run a clean, family business," he'd say.

"He didn't tell me the number," Barney said. "We ate supper together. He was sitting right across from me. Big guy." He was pleading now. "Good-looking. He said his wife was sleeping."

"He was wearing a ski sweater," Hilda said. "He didn't have a suit."

"*Yes*," Barney said. He tried to think of some other detail.

"I noticed him, too," Mary Fran said. "He came in late. He was wearing khaki pants."

"Yes!"

"Well, he's no friend of our family," Corrine said. "I've never seen him before in my life."

"I'm sure I haven't either," Hilda said. "But it would be easy enough for anybody to stroll in here and pretend to be one of us."

For a moment no one said anything. They were in the middle of nowhere, isolated by a winter storm. The power was out. There'd been several unexplained disturbances. There was somebody walking among them who was not the person he claimed to be. April and Barney looked at each other, then looked away. Even this, then, would be left unresolved. Even now, there was nothing to say.

Unless, Barney thought, we can find the guy.

IN suite thirty-three, the man was weeping. He wept softly, patiently, steadily. He wept the way that the snow had been falling for the past six hours. He wept with the self-absorbed concentration of someone deep in prayer. As he wept, he paced, and as he paced, Stanley and Lacey followed his movements with their eyes. They sat side by side on a leather love seat. They held plastic cups of tap water on their knees. The man's plastic cup was filled with brandy. The dulled lamp on the nightstand flickered slightly, fluttering shadows over the dark walls of the room.

Nobody looked at the woman on the bed.

Of course, they recognized the man. He'd been playing pool in the game room; he hadn't paid any attention to them, then. But when they'd arrived at suite thirty-three, the door was standing open, as if he'd been expecting them. "Come in, come in," he'd said, almost happily, when he'd first seen them peering inside: Lacey in her grown-up fur, Stanley in his broadcloth. He offered them something to drink, as if this were a social call. Perhaps he'd mistaken them for somebody else. They clutched their glasses uneasily as he told them all about the suite, gesturing like a museum tour guide at the hot tub, the wagon-wheel headboard, the framed paintings of cowboys. They smiled at everything politely, even though there was a waterlogged towel floating in the hot tub, bits of broken glass on the floor. A broken lamp lay in the center of the room, its shade crushed, its cord ripped from the wall. Stanley had been relieved to see that there weren't any guns or cash-filled briefcases. No naked women, either. Just the man's wife, who was lying on the bed. All you could see of her was her hair. Her face was covered by a pillow. The rest of her was covered up with blankets, one spread over the other, and the man had even laid his overcoat across the top of them.

"She's cold," the man had explained. "With the brownout and all. It's awfully cold in here, don't you think? Are you kids cold?" That was when he'd started to cry. He hadn't seemed to notice, so they'd pretended not to notice. But the tears kept rolling down his cheeks as he asked them how old they were and where they went to school, the sort of small talk adults make when they're not used to speaking with children. After a while he'd run out of questions. He'd tipped the tap water out of his own cup onto the floor, right onto the carpet like it didn't even matter, and excused himself to the kitchenette, where, he explained, he had some brandy. He supposed they were a little young for brandy. Lacey looked like she might protest, but Stanley said, "We're fine, thanks." After the man had gone into the kitchenette, he whispered, "How can she be cold under all those blankets?"

"Anderson sleeps that way," Lacey whispered back. "All covered up. Mama says he's going to smother—"

She didn't finish. They could hear the man moving around, clearing his throat.

Stanley said, "What if he killed her?"

"He wouldn't be crying if he killed her." Lacey was clearly pleased to have worked this out.

"We should tell somebody, anyway," Stanley said.

"Who would believe us? Besides, what if she's just sleeping—"

She stopped because the man had returned.

But Stanley had seen a dead person before—two, in fact. The first was Hilda's sister, his own great-aunt Suzie. He'd been ten years old and, after much discussion, his parents had permitted him to attend the wake. Great-aunt Suzie had died of many things, all of which amounted to old age. Her body looked wrong against all that white satin, like a stain, like a dried-up leaf that had settled there by accident. He was careful to do what everybody else did: he knelt for a moment in front of the body, hands folded, eyes down. But the whole time, he kept sneaking peeks. He wondered what it was like to be dead. He couldn't understand how he could be this close to a dead person, and not know anything more than he had when he'd first awakened that morning. He would have been content to kneel there hour after hour, studying her wrinkled face and hands as if they were a map, but then he'd felt Mary Fran's hand on his shoulder and understood his time was up, that he should have understood by now, and it was time for him to move along.

The other dead person he'd seen was a kid, a boy who'd lived two doors down from Stanley. He was Margo's age and he'd been killed in a car accident. He and his brother and mother and father had been going to the mall in Sheboygan, the same way Stanley and Margo and Elmer and Mary Fran sometimes went to the mall, only something had gone wrong. This seemed quite different than Great-Aunt Suzie, and Stanley was expecting more from the wake, some insight or revelation. But to his surprise, his throat got painful and tight, and when he saw the body, he didn't kneel down. He walked right past it, as if he hadn't seen, kept on walking, in fact, right out of the funeral parlor and across the street to the municipal playground, where Mary Fran found him after the service had ended.

Stanley knew the woman on the bed was a dead person. He knew Lacey knew it, too. You didn't have to be a doctor to figure it out. The man paced and wept, and each time he faced away from them, Stanley looked at Lacey like, *Let's get out of here,* and Lacey looked at Stanley like, *Let's get out of here.* But neither of them moved. They couldn't just stand up and leave. They hadn't finished their tap water. They hadn't even taken off their coats. And, besides, the man was so very unhappy. It seemed wrong to leave him alone. They waited for him to do something or say something that would let them know what to do next.

After a while the man excused himself again. He was going back into the kitchenette for another brandy—could he get them anything? He had some chocolates, he'd just remembered that. Would either of them like some chocolates?

"No, thank you," they both said politely.

"You're going to leave, aren't you?" he said. "Please don't leave." The tears made his face shine like a doll's.

"We won't leave," Stanley said.

As soon as he'd gone, he and Lacey stood up, but then they quickly sat down again. There were footsteps in the hall, the sound of men's hushed voices; they turned to see Frank Liesgang in the doorway. "What the hell," he said, stepping into the room a little bit hesitantly. Stanley, relieved, chirped, "Hi, Uncle Frank." Behind him was Barney Lohr, followed by the owner of the Chapel. Bamberger narrowed his eyes at Stanley, and Stanley tried not to flinch. This was the man who'd yelled at him and Mickey for eating all the trout pâté at the reception. How were they supposed to know that the one little plate was meant for everybody? The coat Frank wore was camel-colored; he'd left it open, for it was too tight around the middle, a little too short in the sleeves. It looked particularly odd against the dark blue of his uniform.

"Hey," Frank said, as if he couldn't believe it. "*There's* my coat! Stan, you've got my coat."

But Barney Lohr was looking at the bed. "Christ," he said. "Oh, Christ."

By now, Frank and Bamberger were also looking at the bed, unconsciously shifting their bodies to form a wall between the children and what they saw. Nobody moved until Frank stepped forward, groped for the woman's hand. His fingers settled on her marbled wrist. Released it. He glanced back at the children and then—

"We'll need an ambulance," he said, shoving Bamberger toward the phone. "Take it into the bathroom. These kids have heard enough—" He didn't finish his sentence. As Bamberger closed the bathroom door, leaving a crack for the phone cord, Frank knelt down beside the bed. The children leaned forward hopefully, but Barney turned toward them, blocking their view. He was breathing hard. He could smell April's perfume. It confused him, flooded him with self-loathing and hopelessness and despair. He wanted to turn and walk out of the room, down the hall and out into the snow toward the lake, where he'd plunge through the ice and drown. He wanted to hang himself from one of the gaunt, black trees. Had Frank Liesgang asked if he'd murdered this woman, Barney would have confessed. Barney would have claimed the crimes of the whole wide world. It was the way that Barney had felt on that day he'd walked out into the snow. And it seemed to him now that it must show on his face, that he must appear every bit as monstrous as he felt inside. But when Frank stood up again, he didn't even seem to notice Barney. His face was haggard, still. "Stay with the kids," was all he said, and then he opened the bathroom door, stepped inside.

"What are you doing here?" Barney said. Earlier, in the game room, he'd observed the sweet awkwardness of their brushing shoulders, their cautious, curious hands. Now, in the dim light, decked out in her furs, Lacey could have passed for a grown woman; beside her, Stanley looked like a bright-eyed, shrunken old man. Barney wanted to tell them everything, but he wanted to protect them, too. He wanted to take their hands and clasp them together like a tender promise, some kind of guarantee.

"The man invited us in," Stanley said defensively.

"What man?"

"That man you were playing pool with," Lacey said. "He's in the kitchen."

Slowly, Barney turned to look at the saloon-style doors. He forced himself to keep his mouth slightly open, relaxed, the way he did on stage when he was acting.

"He's crying," Stanley warned him.

"He offered us chocolates," Lacey said.

"Don't move," Barney said, calmly, and he went over to the bathroom, stuck his head inside the door. Bamberger had passed the phone to Frank, who was propped against the sink. Bamberger himself sat on the closed seat of the toilet. When he looked up, Barney could see the Chapel's reputation, present and past, flashing before his eyes.

Frank said, "I got an ambulance and a squad car on the way, but they'll have to wait for a plow once they leave the interstate—yeah." He rolled his eyes. "They transferred me, the son of a—" he muttered, then spoke into the receiver again. "Yeah, this is Frank Liesgang. I'm gonna need a plow at Bittner's exit ASAP." Barney beckoned to Bamberger, who squeezed past Frank and followed him back into the main room of the suite.

"What now?" he said flatly.

"The guy's hiding in the kitchen," Barney whispered.

"Christ."

"Get the kids out of here."

Bamberger seemed more than happy to do just that. He pointed to the children, jerked his thumb at the door. "There's a lounge down the hall," he said.

As soon as they'd gone, Barney edged up to the swinging doors, peeked into the kitchenette. It appeared to be empty. Overhead, a fluorescent light hummed, spat out a faint, grainy light. He could make out a bottle of liquor on the counter, a box of candy, a plastic cup. Below, one of the cupboard doors was slightly open. "Hello?" Barney called. He stepped into the room, squatted down in front of the cupboard. He could hear the man's breathing: choked, harsh, thick. The air smelled of brandy. "It's Barney Lohr," he said. He wasn't uncertain or afraid. He felt as if he were the older man now, speaking to a younger man, perhaps a younger brother. "We shot some pool, remember?"

The cupboard door opened and the man's legs spilled out onto the floor. How had he managed to fit into such a tiny space? His handsome face was swollen, as if he'd been trying to hold his breath. "My wife," he said. His lips were bitten, purple. He squinted as if the light hurt his eyes.

"An ambulance is coming," Barney said, as if he were answering a question. He stood up, and the man stood, too. "So she's all right, then?" the man said, but then he stared past Barney at Frank, who was peering over the swinging doors. The man studied Frank's uniform. He rubbed his eyes, hard, as if he were very tired. He said, "I made this reservation, I don't know, three, four months ago? So she waits until we get here, and then she says she's leaving me." He reached for the half-filled plastic cup. Then he pulled his hand back and, instead, dug around in the pocket of his trousers. This made Frank tense up a little—behind the swinging door, his hand was on the revolver he always carried—but all the man did was pull out a penny. "See this? See what I found?" He chanted, *"Find a penny, pick it up, that means seven years good luck.* You ever hear that?"

Barney nodded. The man tucked the penny back in his pocket. "Well, it's not true. We been at it like cats and dogs. I'm about to throw in the towel." He reached for the cup of brandy again, paused, seemed to think better of it. "Listen," he said. He put his face close to Barney's. He was speaking in the same confidential tones that Barney had used in the game room. "She's always going on about counseling, you know. Did you ever try that? You and that bride?"

"She wanted me to," Barney said. He glanced at Frank. Frank didn't say anything. He was staring at the brandy bottle. The smell of the brandy hung, golden, between them.

"I'll tell you what," the man said, "I'm about to try anything. Once all this gets straightened out, I'm thinking I ought to give it a whirl. Maybe her and me both."

"Sure," Barney said uneasily.

"She didn't say anything to either of you, did she?"

"Not a word," Frank said. It was the first time he'd spoken.

"Tell her I'm sorry, okay?" the man said. "I didn't mean to hurt her or anything."

Frank didn't reply.

The man smiled at him anyway. Then he touched Barney's shoulder. He seemed to be regaining some of his confidence. "I shouldn't have told you those things about the groom," he said. "Christ, I can't tell you how he met that girl. I never laid eyes on either of them before in my whole life."

"It's okay," Barney said, just to say something—it would be a while yet before the squad car came. He was grateful that he hadn't let the children see the woman's face, grateful that he hadn't seen it either. He could not have guessed that what he'd seen or not seen wouldn't matter, that the woman's face would appear to him anyway: in the faces of women he dated; in the face of the woman who'd choose him for her own; in the sleeping faces of their children. He'd see her unexpectedly as he opened the Magic Carpet, shining in the glass like an imperfect reflection, a not-quite-identical twin. He'd see her in the face of the counselor he was seeing, this one and the next one and the one after that. He'd see her in the face

of the new, young priest at Saint Michael's and, once, in the face
of a woman who sat beside him on a plane, tears falling into her
lap. For the rest of his life he'd see that face and wonder where the
woman would be if she were a living person. What she might be
doing. What she might be thinking about. But the man's face, which
he'd actually seen, he would not be able to remember. By the end
of this day, it would have vanished. He'd have to look at newspaper
clippings to bring it back.

"Those kids leave?" the man said. "That boy and girl?"

Barney nodded. How would they remember all this? And April.
She was certain to hear about it, too. Her wedding was ruined and
he was responsible. All of this was his fault. He felt himself tumbling down and down the endless mountain of his shame and despair, but then a thought appeared out of all that whiteness, dark
and solid as a branch. *You've done nothing wrong.* He grasped at it,
clung to it, steadied himself against it. And by distinguishing between what he'd done, then, and what had just happened, now, he
brought his terrible thoughts to a stop. What he felt, in their silent
aftermath, was something like a prayer. It was wordless, and full
of hope. It was shining with every good thing he could wish for
April, and also for Caleb, who loved her, and would know how to
comfort her.

"Nice kids," the man said. "I been thinking I might like a kid
someday." He reached again for the plastic cup, and this time, he
picked it up. Neither Frank nor Barney made a move to stop him.

"He's got kids," Barney said, gesturing at Frank. How much longer
could that squad car be? "Grandkids, too." But Frank wasn't listening. Frank's eyes were on that drink, rising and falling with the
motion of the man's trembling hand.

Down the hall in the lounge, sitting across from the children,
hands clasped loosely between his knees, Bamberger was kind of

wishing for a drink himself. Indirect light spilled in from the hall; the long row of candy machines gleamed in a sinister way. Somewhere outside, a branch scraped the wall. The children had confessed to the mess in the back office, but they insisted it was an accident. They'd just been trying to find their own coats, when they'd all come tumbling down. And as to the vandalism of the bride's dressing room?

Stanley interrupted before Lacey could speak. He'd been up in his sister's room when the power went out, and he'd knocked down a few things trying to find his way out in the dark. He might have fallen against the mirror, he didn't know, it had been too dark to see.

So what had he been doing up there in the first place?

Well, there hadn't been a sign saying PRIVATE or anything. He knew April wouldn't mind.

And what were the two of them doing over here?

Stanley pulled the key out of his pocket. "We found this when we were looking for our coats," he said, handing it over. "We were going to return it."

"That's when we saw the lady in there," Lacey added.

It was the first time either child had mentioned the body. Bamberger sure as hell hadn't wanted to bring it up. He was hoping that, somehow, they'd forgotten all about it. He was thinking about how they'd run back to the Chapel and tell everybody in the ballroom what they'd seen. He was imagining the lawsuit that their parents would file, demanding compensation for psychological damages, future psychiatric bills. He was recalling all the other Lodge deaths, the scandals and newsworthy events: the suicides and accidental overdoses; the people who had simply up and died out of spite; that incident with the senator, unconscious behind his Batman mask. A woman who'd lost her memory had checked into the Parisian Suite and lived there, happily, for nearly a week, while her family searched the fields and dredged the rivers. A man had died after eating a jar of apple seeds he'd saved for months, not realizing each seed contained organic arsenic. Last summer, a drowned swimmer had washed up on the Hideaway Lodge's private beach. Of all the goddamn places! Hundreds of miles of lakefront—

The power came on with a *pop*, no warning, a flash of jolting light.

"Jesus!" Bamberger said, leaping to his feet. Lights buzzed, heat pumps hummed. What was left of the ice in the ice machine came thundering down into the bin.

Stanley stared at Lacey, stunned by the new, brilliant light. Black-and-purple spots floated before his eyes. He rubbed them, blinked at the candy and soda machines. After so much time in darkness, the lines where the walls met the ceiling and floor seemed too sharp, too exact. Had they always looked that way? Bamberger was grumbling at them to hurry up and button their coats. He wasn't waiting around any longer! He had work to do and their parents, irresponsible as they might be, were probably looking for them. He acted as if *they'd* delayed *him,* as if they hadn't been longing to go back to the dance all this time.

Nothing was said, or had been said, about suite thirty-three, or the man and his brandy. Nothing had been said about the woman on the bed.

Stanley wondered if Lacey had been right, and the woman had only been sleeping. After all, hadn't Uncle Frank said to call an ambulance? Why would you need an ambulance if somebody was dead? He was beginning to doubt everything he'd seen. Maybe he'd imagined about the ambulance. Maybe he'd imagined that a total stranger had invited them into his room, and offered them drinks as if they were grown-ups, and paced and wept before them.

"Let's go," Ralph Bamberger said, but in the hallway they met Barney, who'd come to tell them that the plow had arrived. The ambulance, he said, was only waiting for the parking lot to clear.

So the ambulance, anyway, was real.

"Is that lady—all right?" Stanley asked, interrupting them. Both men stared at him as if he'd said something very strange.

"Uh, we don't know yet," Barney said, and then Ralph Bamberger jumped in and told Stanley that he should apologize to Barney for his mischief up in the balcony, because April had blamed Barney for it, and Barney could have wound up going to jail. Stanley opened his mouth to speak, but his throat ached with everything he wanted to ask, and couldn't ask, or maybe he just didn't want to ask, and then a single glistening tear rolled down his cheek into the corner of his mouth. Lacey was sniffling, too. Barney gave Ralph Bamberger the sort of look you give a crazy person, or a murderer. Then he told Stanley not to worry about it. He told him to tell April not to worry about it, either. "Tell her I would have thought the same thing in her place—will you do that for me?" he said. "Don't forget. I don't want her feeling bad. It's her wedding day." And he smiled at Stanley then—a big, handsome leading-man kind of smile—and said he and Lacey should go back to the dance, forget about it, enjoy themselves.

"Come back yourself," Ralph Bamberger said abruptly, and now he was smiling, too. "No hard feelings, right? Have a drink on the house. It's been quite an evening for us all."

But Barney said no, he'd be riding back to town with the squad car. That way, if anything else went wrong, Bamberger wouldn't be able to accuse him of doing it. His smile disappeared when he said that.

All the way back to the Chapel, Bamberger muttered beneath his breath, thrashing through the knee-high drifts as if they'd been put there just to aggravate him. Stanley and Lacey walked behind him, gradually dropping back. Soon they were alone. They could hear the gnash and grind of the plow; its clear cold light slashed between the trees. Stanley wondered if he should take Lacey's hand. He could hear that she was still sniffling. Or maybe he was still sniffling.

"You okay?" he asked.

"Sure," she said. She wiped her nose on the sleeve of the fur. He caught her hand just as it was diving back into her pocket. It trembled, stilled, and he was amazed by its simple, comforting warmth.

"You really think she's going to be all right?" she asked.

"Sure," Stanley said, and as soon as he'd said so, he could almost believe it was true. He imagined how she'd be taken to the hospital, how the doctors would attach an IV to her arm, and soon—maybe even in as little as a week—she'd be able to go home. One day, maybe in spring, Stanley would be riding his bike, or picking up something for Mary Fran at the store, and he'd see her, and know it was her—who could say how?—and the lady would know him, too. She'd invite him to come over for a cool drink. She'd show him into her living room, where she'd sit on the couch. (He'd ease himself, shyly, into a parlor chair.) It would be a nice house, with a dog and cat, and clean smells of apricot and sunshine. There, the woman would tell him she was sorry if he'd been frightened, and Stanley would say that it was okay. She'd ask, not teasing in the least, if Lacey was his girlfriend, and he'd say he didn't know, he wasn't sure. Then the woman would confirm what Stanley was beginning to suspect: that nobody was ever really sure where love was concerned. She'd say there was always something more to learn, and that's why people fell in and out of love, sometimes with different people, sometimes with the same person over and over again. And each time it happened, it was like entering another country. Things you thought you understood didn't make sense anymore. Sometimes it was wonderful, and sometimes it was terrible, but either way, you never could go back to what you'd been. Like dying? Stanley would say, and she'd say, A little. Another kind of letting go.

MIDNIGHT
CHAMPAGNE

WHEN the lights came on in the ballroom, the old photographer didn't waste any time. Aiming his camcorder this way and that, he was the first to notice Elmer Liesgang conducting the band from the balcony. Elmer's hair stood up every which way. His suit coat had ripped out beneath one arm. The old photographer zoomed in, attracting the attention of the dancers. As soon as the In-Laws realized what was going on, they faced the balcony, bowed to Elmer in formal unison, then bent their knees and rocked their shoulders and swung their instruments in exaggerated time. Somebody called, "Hey, Elmo! Feeling awful merry tonight, aren't ya?" Somebody else said, "Yeah, see how merry he feels in the morning."

Mary Fran hurried toward the balcony stairs; Hilda, emerging from the dining hall with Corrine, maneuvered her friend so that her back was facing the awful spectacle. But Elmer wasn't thinking of his mother, or his wife, or anything beyond his own exhilaration. The anxiety he'd carried with him since the engagement had fallen from his shoulders like a massive, gray stone, smashing into sawdust as it hit the dance floor far below. This was his daughter's wedding, and these were his honored guests, and he, Elmer Otto

Liesgang, was the architect of their happiness. Without him, there
would not have been a wedding in the first place, much less a wallet
to finance it! And hadn't he made certain that everything was first-
rate? A meat dish instead of spaghetti. A sit-down supper instead
of a buffet. A live band instead of a DJ. And—for the midnight
toast—bottles of *real* champagne at eighty-five dollars a pop. Already, servers were rolling carts into position along the sidelines.
Each cart was draped in white linen, decorated with pink rose petals. Each bore a silvery champagne bucket, an arrangement of delicate, fluted glasses. How grateful he was that the lights had come
up in time for the guests to see it all.

Eighty-five dollars a *pop*. Elmer laughed at his own joke.

"Have we had a bit to drink?"

Mary Fran stood on the landing, hands on her hips. Elmer knew
she was running through her options: coax him down quietly? Run
up and snatch him? Ha! Let her try. No doubt she'd dismiss his
euphoria—this new, raw state of grace—on all those vodka and
tonics. People had been treating him, toasting him, ever since the
father-daughter dance, telling him he needed to relax, live a little,
lighten up because nothin' in the world was worth a heart attack.
And wasn't that God's truth! Elmer hadn't ever drunk vodka before,
hadn't really seen the point of drinking anything that smelled like
antiseptic, but now, at last, he understood. This wasn't some fuzzy
beer buzz. This wasn't a sleepy-eyed buttered rum. Hallelujah! He
had seen the light!

He noticed that the band wasn't playing anymore. The band was,
in fact, applauding. So was everybody else. Elmer stopped conducting and applauded right along with them until he realized they were
applauding—could it be—for him? Guests were pouring in from the
dining hall, from the lobby, from the whole wide world. All those
dear, upturned faces! Elmer accepted their adoration as his due. He

executed a bow so deep he nearly toppled from the balcony. Then Mary Fran's steel arm had him by the waist and they were coming down the stairs together.

"On behalf of everybody," Jackie Vogel shouted from the stage, "I want to thank the father of the bride for helping us through that last polka!"

"Did you see me?" Elmer panted, and Mary Fran said, "Oh, I certainly did."

"We hate to stop," Jackie Vogel called, "but it's almost midnight and there's champagne chilling and we've only got time for one more tune." He tugged at his drooping lederhosen, waiting for the crowd to settle down. "So listen, all you shy fellahs out there? I'll tell you what. This here is your last chance. Time flies and the future is a mystery. If you don't ask that pretty gal to dance right now—"

He paused, as if he were about to say something meaningful.

"—the next time you see her, she could be old and fat!"

Without waiting for the varied reactions of the guests, the In-Laws—smiling their most innocent, boyish smiles—began the "Too Fat Polka."

> I don't want her, you can have her
> She's too fat for me
> Too too fat for me
> Doggone fat for me

"Sexist bastards," Mary Fran said, grunting under Elmer's relaxed weight. Ralph Bamberger was waiting at the foot of the stairs, and he wasn't smiling, either. His mouth, in fact, was bolted into a frown. Poor fellah, Elmer thought. He could sympathize with that kind of emotional paralysis. He'd felt the same way himself until the father-daughter dance, when April had told him she was having a wonderful time, that everybody was having a wonderful time, and it was all because of him, her father, who had talked her into having this wedding—

"I love you," Elmer had interrupted, blushing helplessly, horribly; April had blushed, too. "Huh?" she'd said, but then she'd said, "Oh," and then she'd said, "Well, I know that, Dad," and then she'd said, "I mean, I love you, too."

Staring into Bamberger's nickel-colored eyes, Elmer wanted to tell him everything he'd learned about happiness during the past few hours. But then he heard Mary Fran say, "Oh, no," and he realized that Bamberger held Stanley by the shoulder, as if the boy might suddenly dash away. Stanley! Elmer lurched forward, wrapped his arms around the slender shoulders, kissed the smooth, dark cap of hair. "I love you, Stanley," he said.

Stan said, "Get a grip, Dad."

Mary Fran said, "Elmer, *please*."

Obligingly, Elmer straightened up, giving Stanley a just-between-us-men kind of wink. Then he crossed his arms over his chest, prepared himself to hear whatever it was that Bamberger had to say. But Bamberger spoke to Mary Fran alone as he explained that it had been Stanley—not Barney Lohr, and not the man posing as the Shannon's family friend—who was responsible for the damages in the bride's dressing room. A large mirror had been broken. A bill would be sent to the Liesgang household.

"I *knew* Barney wouldn't do a thing like that," Mary Fran said, flushing at the memory of Barney in the dining room, his head in his hands. "Did you find out who that other man was?"

"He wasn't involved in the vandalism," Bamberger said, and neither his voice nor expression betrayed anything. "I haven't informed the bride about this. I felt it was a family matter." Then he excused himself, saying he had a few announcements to prepare.

"You bet it's a family matter," Mary Fran said, turning on Stanley. "*Stanley* will inform the bride. *Stanley* will take responsibility for his actions for once in his life! Why did you do it?" She thought of Barney again, didn't wait for an answer. "You're going to apologize to Barney. You're going to get a paper route. You're going to pay this out of your own pocket—"

Stanley suspected that Lacey was watching from somewhere in the ballroom, and he was determined to make up for his earlier tears by taking this like a soldier. Just as he felt his lower lip start to tremble, April swooped between him and his mother. "Stanley!" she cried, grabbing his hand. "I've been looking for you everywhere! I've been saving the last dance!"

He blinked at her. "Okay."

"Are you all right?" She looked at him, then at Mary Fran, then at Elmer, who was weaving slightly. "What's wrong?"

"I broke the mirror in your dressing room," Stanley said, without giving himself time to lose nerve.

April looked at him. "Oh," she said.

"Don't just tell her you're sorry," Mary Fran said. "Tell her how you plan to repair all the damage you've caused, and I'm not just talking about some broken glass."

April was still holding his hand. Slowly, she walked into the middle of the dance floor, pulling him behind her, unresisting, a balloon on a string. Couples spun around them, brushed their shoulders, bumped their hips.

"What happened?" she said, turning to face him. The In-Laws were building toward the final refrain, and she had to raise her voice to be heard. "The truth, okay? Not whatever you told Mom."

He was relieved to get it off his chest. "Me and some other kids? We were goofing off up in your dressing room during supper, and I—threw this bag at Mickey and it hit the mirror." He glanced at

April's face, hurried on. "I'm sorry. It was an accident. Lacey sprayed me with perfume, and then Anderson—"

He realized that much would be lost in translation.

"I'll pay for everything," he said. "It's easier if everybody thinks it was just me."

"But we all thought Barney did it," she said, her eyes brightening. "We accused him. I accused him."

"He said I should tell you he isn't mad," Stanley said. "Honest. He said I should say he'd have thought the same thing if he were you."

"Where did you see him?" She was looking around, as if she expected he'd be somewhere on the dance floor.

"Over at the Lodge," Stanley said. "In suite thirty-three, with Uncle Frank."

"What were you doing over there?"

"The man staying there asked us in for drink," he said. He couldn't help but enjoy the adult sound of those words.

"You and Uncle Frank?"

"Me and Lacey."

April stared at him. "What *haven't* the two of you gotten into tonight?"

The jaunty polka modulated, without pause or warning, into "Auld Lang Syne." Guests sang along, arms around each other, swaying side to side. To Stanley's relief, April put her arm around him, and he knew she'd decided to forgive him. "We never really got to dance," she said, and Stanley said, "It's okay." He caught a glimpse of Lacey, swaying between Caleb and Corrine. Caleb saw him with April; he grinned, gave him a thumbs-up.

"That man in suite thirty-three," April said, "did they find out who he was?"

"I don't know," Stanley said. "Mr. Bamberger made us leave."

"The man was—all right, wasn't he? Asking you in like that. He wasn't creepy or anything?"

He almost told her about the woman on the bed, but then he stopped, remembering what Barney had said. *I don't want her to feel bad. It's her wedding day.* He thought of the broken lamp on the floor, the way that the man had been crying.

"I think he'd had a fight with his wife," he finally said.

"A bad fight?" April said.

"Yeah," Stanley said. He couldn't resist adding, "They had to call an ambulance."

He felt her arm tighten around him; he tightened his arm around her.

"I hope she's okay," April said, and Stanley said, "Me, too."

"Auld Lang Syne" ended with a flourish, and the In-Laws put down their instruments, took their bows. The applause which followed intensified until everybody clapped in time. The dance was over. The electricity was back on. The storm had eased and the roads were being cleared and the world seemed merciful and good. At the back of the ballroom, people had gathered to watch the plow complete its last, slow revolution around the parking lot. Several were already complaining about the drift it was leaving behind the cars. There'd be plenty of shoveling left to do, no question about that. And what were those other lights out on the highway? Emergency vehicles of some kind?

"Maybe they're gonna help shovel us out."

"Fat chance."

"Maybe they're setting up a checkpoint. Gonna Breathalyze us on our way out."

Only Hilda Liesgang did not smile at the joke. She had her face to the window, hands cupped against the glare. There was a ringing in her ears, a heaviness in her chest, for she'd recognized the shape that she'd been looking for. One of the vehicles was an ambulance. Here it is, she thought. Dear Lord, here is it. Around her, the applause was finally breaking apart, absorbed by the rising roar of conversation. The In-Laws scattered into the crowd, and Ralph Bamberger, mounting the stage, called for everyone's attention. "I have a few announcements—" he began.

"If I might ask—"

Nobody listened.

And Melissa Liesgang, waiting at the edge of the stage, was grateful for the delay. She examined, again, the widemouthed pewter bowl she'd found in the game room downstairs. Sure, you can borrow it, the assistant bartender had said. I don't know where it came from, you can even keep it if you want. Melissa still didn't know what she was going to *say*, but at least she'd figured out what she was going to *do*.

"You ready?" Brian had come up behind her.

"Sure."

"Lying to me, aren't you."

"Yup."

"Ladies and gentlemen," Bamberger cried, "if I could have your attention for a few brief announcements!"

Shouting to be heard above persistent conversations, he spoke about the plow's arrival as if he'd personally arranged for it. He announced that the interstate would, indeed, reopen at midnight. He reminded people that the roads remained treacherous; fortunately, a few army cots were still available at the desk, and for only a ten-dollar linen fee. He thanked everyone for their patience during the power outage. "Last but not least," he said, "I'd like to congratulate the Shannon and Liesgang families"—he bowed to April and Caleb—"and to wish the bride and groom every happiness in their new life together. Our toastmaster . . . er, mistress . . . for the evening has a few more words on the subject, and so it is with great pleasure that I turn the floor over to her."

Servers were already rolling the champagne carts between the guests; Melissa hurried onto the stage. "Could we wait the champagne for just a minute?" she called.

Well, that got everyone's full attention. In the sudden quiet, she heard the groan of the plow fading off toward the highway. Scanning the faces of the guests, she saw curiosity, expectation, amusement. And, yes, there was that Midwestern reserve, the fear that she might ask them to do something unexpected.

"I'd like everybody to write down one anonymous piece of advice for Caleb and April," she said. "You don't have to be in a relationship, or even have a sweetheart. Kids can do this, too."

People looked at her, looked at each other. Was *this* a toast?

A gloomy-looking man called, "What are we supposed to write on?"

"A cocktail napkin will work," Melissa said, pointing to a stack on one of the champagne carts. "But you could also use a fifty-dollar bill."

This got a laugh. Encouraged, she held up the pewter bowl. "C'mon, let's be creative here. Look around, check your pockets. I'll be coming around to collect your advice as soon as I've written mine down."

"But what are we supposed to *write* with?" the man said.

"I must have a dozen pens at the bottom of my purse," Mary Fran called, and this was the straw which shifted the general mood from uncertain reluctance to enthusiasm. Change jingled as people dug through their pockets. Others hurried to the sidelines for purses, handbags, diaper bags, excavating pens and scraps of paper: shopping lists, coupons, receipts. Somebody hollered, "Bonanza!" and everyone turned to look. Libby Schrunk was holding a big box of

crayons in the air. Her youngest son stood beside her, blushing with
pride and embarrassment. "Sam says he's happy to share as long as
he gets them all back—" Libby stopped, bent her head to listen.
"But he says not to use the green one because it's worn down pretty
far."

Now everybody was laughing, talking, passing the box of crayons
from hand to hand. Someone distributed cocktail napkins from
the carts. Someone tore sheets of lined paper from a pocket-size
notebook. People turned and wrote against each other's upright
backs, like schoolgirls, and Melissa had a sudden memory of her
elementary-school playground, the perpetually vandalized swings,
the jungle gym made out of old tires where high school kids came
to smoke cigarettes. Each summer, battered hollyhocks grew up
along the snow fence; in September, during recess, she and her
friends picked the white-skirted flowers, leaving a stem like a sturdy
neck, to which they attached a hard green bud. Making brides, they
called this. While the boys played kickball, baseball, soccer, they
crouched on the sidelines in the matted grass, arranging their brides
in a row. They gave their brides beautiful names—Natasha, Alana,
Marie. When the bell rang, they weighted their dresses with sticks
and stones. Regardless, the wind always blew them away, like so
many youthful ideas.

And with that thought, Melissa knew exactly what she was going
to say.

She circled the ballroom once, twice, collecting everybody's advice. By the time she gave the pewter bowl to April, it was brimming
with crayoned cocktail napkins, receipts, grocery lists, even a candy
wrapper. Melissa kissed her, kissed Caleb, too—this drew a few
whistles from the people nearby as she hurried back to the stage.
Once again, the servers were distributing champagne, and she
accepted the glass that was handed to her.

"Oscar Wilde said," she began, "that men marry because they are tired, and women because they are curious, and that both are disappointed." Primed, the crowd laughed agreeably. "He was right about the disappointment. You will be disappointed." She was speaking directly to April and Caleb now. "Not just in each other, but in yourselves. It's inevitable that you'll each fall short of your own expectations." Nobody moved. Once again, there was the sound of tires spinning, a vehicle rocking forward and back. "But you will also exceed those expectations, again and again, and in ways you can't possibly imagine. And my wish for you both is that there will come a time when you'll look back on this day and realize that—in spite of the disappointments—even the best of your old expectations seem pale in the face of the actual life you have lived together." She paused, then raised her glass. "To your happiness," she said.

"Here, here," people said, and everybody drank.

Everybody, that is, except Hilda Liesgang. She'd remained where she was at the back of the ballroom. She alone had seen the ambulance back up to the path leading to the Hideaway Lodge, watched the attendants carry an empty stretcher through the snow. Now they had reappeared with their burden. The stretcher was lifted into the ambulance, the door shut behind it, and then—what was this?—Frank and another officer emerged from the trees. A third man walked between them, and it seemed to Hilda that he was looking straight at her.

Abruptly, she stepped back from the window. She couldn't have been more frightened if the man had been pointing a gun. Remorse seized her, a convulsion so fierce that she nearly cried out with the physical pain. If only she'd managed to find that penny. If only she'd persevered, looked a little longer, a little harder. If only she were less critical of heart, more generous in her nature. If only she'd been a better wife, a better mother to her sons.

A hard, red light flooded the ballroom as the ambulance rolled forward. Other guests joined Hilda at the window in time to see it pass out of the parking lot, a squad car just behind it. What had happened? Even before the champagne was finished, there were rumors, speculations. Someone had heard something about a stranger posing as a wedding guest. Someone else had heard that he'd stolen a computer from behind the front desk. There was talk about Barney Lohr, something about him snooping through April's dressing room upstairs, murmurs of a recent suicide attempt, but no—that sort of talk was quickly put to rest. Barney was a helluva nice guy, and he'd been a good sport about all this, his usual chipper self. Still, hadn't he been seen leaving the Chapel with Frank Liesgang and the manager? Come to think of it, where the hell was ol' Frank, anyway?

Another story was circulating, too, and this story no one believed. It was a story that the Tennessee girl had told her grandmother, a story that was surely a misunderstanding, an exaggeration. Girls that age, people said, shaking their heads. Who could say what she'd really seen? By the following afternoon, of course, these very same people would be speaking quite differently. Some would insist they'd known all along that things weren't right at the Hideaway Lodge. Others would claim they'd felt, well, *something* as they'd passed by the room where the dead woman lay. Who could doubt, after so many tragedies, that the Chapel and Lodge wasn't—well, if not *haunted*, then *unlucky*, shadowed by misfortune too great to be contained within the past. And, as always, several men—those nursing the most vicious hangovers—would swear they'd been approached in the ballroom by a woman in a cherry-red dress.

"Dance?" she had asked them. "Dance?"

*   *   *

BY twelve-thirty, Bamberger had turned off the ballroom lights. Only the chandelier sparkled faintly, like a hovering spacecraft, an otherworldly sign. In the lobby, two women in open-toed shoes waited for their husbands to drive up to the door, but the rest of the guests had already departed, some toward their homes, others toward the Budgetel, others trampling a wide path toward their rooms at the Hideaway Lodge. Bamberger tucked the cashbox into the safe, locked the back office and planning parlor. The fire in the fireplace had burned down to coals. The desk clerk had gone home. Dimmer and Jeffery were in the parking lot, shoveling out the last few cars, one of which was their own.

Bamberger went to the kitchen, where Emily was attacking the mess of dishes set aside during the power outage. Steam rose over the sink as she wrestled a cavernous pan. One dishwasher was already running; another stood open, half-loaded.

"You want help?" he asked from the doorway, and she flashed him her dead mother's smile: light, sweet, indifferent. "No, Daddy, I'm fine," she said, as he had known she would.

"I'm heading to bed, then," he said.

When he returned to the lobby, it was empty. He switched off all the lamps but the one, then headed up the steps to his apartment. The front door of the Chapel was never locked; anybody who needed assistance during the night simply walked in, rang a buzzer that sounded upstairs. In his bedroom, he undressed quickly, crawled beneath the down-filled comforter, and shook until his body conquered the chill of the sheets. Even now, so many years after his wife's death, lying down alone was the most difficult part of the day. Now he saw the face of the woman in suite thirty-three. He saw the face of the man who'd died from eating all those apple seeds, swollen and content. He saw the face of his wife, who had choked on a chicken bone at his table: her outrage, her absolute denial of what was happening. He wondered what expression his own face would wear, and who would be there to see it.

His shivering had subsided; he rolled over onto his side. Sometimes he thought about selling the Chapel, moving to a warmer climate. Someplace with a seashore—Florida, perhaps. There were plenty of tourists in Florida. No state income taxes, either. He imagined a pink stucco chapel at the edge of the ocean, the yelp of seagulls on the beach. The Sunshine Chapel, he'd call it. He let it take shape in his mind, dimpled as an orange, and just as sweet. He could hear the hush of the waves. He could feel that tropical sunshine, warm as love, upon his forehead.

Out in the Lodge, the guests were also settling in for the night. Doors slammed as relatives dashed back and forth between the rooms. Some lingered in the snack lounge, lifting the lid of the empty ice bin, gulping at cans of juice. The younger people walked the length of the hallway, restless, looking for evidence of whatever had happened earlier. There was none. And so they wound up at the honeymoon suite, standing in the open doorway for a moment before finding a seat—on the edge of the hot tub, on the floor, on the arms of the crowded love seats—or sprawling across the heart-shaped bed where April and Caleb sat propped against the red satin headboard, drawing slips of advice from the pewter bowl. There was a pyramid of leftover wedding cake on the dresser, each piece individually boxed, and people helped themselves and ate with their fingers and passed around the bottles of champagne—who bothered with cups?—that someone from the gallery had brought. Caleb still wore his tuxedo pants; his white shirt was untucked. April wore sweatpants and one of his cotton shirts. The guests had mostly changed into jeans, though a few still wore their dresses and suits, and one of Caleb's friends from Minneapolis was already in his bathrobe, his legs bare beneath it.

Caleb unfolded a yellow piece of paper that turned out to be a receipt from a traffic violation. It took him a moment to decipher the red, crayoned scrawl: *Don't be afraid to break the rules.* The name on the ticket had been scribbled out; people studied it, held it up to the light, but no one could figure out who it had belonged to.

April drew the next slip. Groaned. "Guess what it says?" she said, and everyone yelled in unison, "Don't go to bed mad at each other!"

She put the slip on a separate pile, counted through the slips already there. "That's the seventh one," she said. There were other piles scattered around them for religious advice (*Say the rosary together every night*) and sexual advice (*A dirty movie once in a while never hurt*) and practical advice (*Take turns cooking*).

"Well, there's only one left," Caleb said, peering into the bowl. It was a grocery receipt; he turned it over, grinned at what he saw, then handed it to April. "I haven't learned anything," she read. "Hope you do better."

Everybody laughed so hard that, at first, they didn't hear the knock on the open door, where a man was standing—a stranger in pajamas and sheepskin slippers, his thinning hair every which way—who asked if they wouldn't mind keeping it down, or at least closing the door, because their children were having trouble sleeping.

"We're leaving now anyway," Paula assured him. "It wouldn't be much of a honeymoon night if we stayed."

So the party broke up. People said their good-byes. Doors closed up and down the hall; water rumbled through the pipes. And then, silence spread, room to room, through the Hideaway Lodge.

In the Frank Sinatra Memorial Suite, the retired couple—awakened by the commotion—fell back into sleep with their arms around each other, the woman's head cradled in the silky hollow of the old man's chest. Next door, Hilda Liesgang knelt back down beside her king-size bed and, rolling her rosary beads between her fingers, began the Third Sorrowful Mystery. Two doors down and across the hall, Frank Liesgang stood in the bathroom, naked to the waist, splashing icy water on his face. The door was open. His wife, Francie, watched from the bed, her wide, pale face still flushed from dancing. Frank had already told her everything about the woman in suite thirty-three, and the man in the kitchen, and the brandy on the counter. He'd told her how the smell of that brandy had been warm as a living thing. He'd told her how its color had crept into his head. Now, try as he might, he could not stop thinking about it. A shower would have helped, but there wasn't any hot water, an after-effect of the brownout. He splashed his face and neck one last time, dried himself roughly, unsympathetically. Then he started toward the bed where she waited with the pillows stacked behind her, the blankets in a ruffle around her waist.

"Francis," she said softly, using his given name.

"Frances," he replied, using her own. If only he could unwind a little. If only he could just lie down and sleep. He thought of the dead woman, her youthful face. He thought of her murderer, her husband, who'd loved her. He thought of his own life, the blur of lost years. And now, the new hard edges of his sobriety. He put one hand to the high, hard belly left over from his drinking days. For the first time in twenty years he weighed less than Francie, who'd always been what his dad had called *a big ol' gal*.

"It's not like we didn't have our rows," he said, studying himself in the floor-length mirror: feathers of gray around each nipple, navel slack as a crying mouth. Who was this aging man? How could it be that so much of his life was over and past already?

"We had a few," Francie said.

"I never once laid a hand on you, though."

"Never once," Francie said.

"No matter how messed up I was."

"It's true."

"Busted up the place a couple of times."

"Not enough to dwell on," Francie said, and he turned to her then, so grateful for her lie that he wanted to fall to his knees and weep. Instead, he got into bed beside her, rolled himself into the sweet, scarred comfort of her body. Her breasts were loose and full beneath her nightgown, the undersides rough with gooseflesh. He pushed his face between them, breathing in her familiar almond smell, and now he wept, there was no help for it. "My angel," he whispered against her, and she said, "My baby. My darling boy."

Mary Fran and Libby were settling the children into their beds, ignoring the sound of Elmer's aggravated snores, which drifted in from the connecting suite. "How are we supposed to sleep listening to *that*?" Mickey said. He sat on the dresser, wearing red-and-white striped pajamas.

"Shh," Libby said, pointing to the girls' bed, where Jenny and Margo were already zonked. In the boys' bed, Sam's eyelids fluttered. Stanley's eyes closed, too. But Libby could tell he was faking. His lip twitched. His cheeks had a strange, high color. "You feel okay, Stan?" Libby asked, and Mary Fran, who'd been hanging up the children's discarded trousers and jackets and dresses, came over to look.

"I feel fine," Stanley said, without opening his eyes.

"I'm not sleeping with him if he's sick," Mickey said.

"He's not sick," Libby said. "Get in bed."

"How come we can't sleep in our room?"

"Because it's my room tonight," Libby said.

"Why?"

"Because I need a little vacation."

"But *why*?"

"I just need some time alone to think about some things."

"What things?"

"For heaven's sake," Mary Fran broke in. "A person would think you'd never spent the night away from your mother before."

Humiliated, Mickey divided a long, hateful look between his mother and his aunt. Abruptly, he flung himself into the bed. "Move over, butt-munch," he told Sam, jamming his legs under the covers.

"Bite me," Sam cooed, half-conscious.

Libby bent over the edge of the bed. "We'll have a nice breakfast in the morning," she said. "McDonald's, Burger King—anything you want."

Mickey didn't answer.

Mary Fran had already turned out the light; now she led Libby into the adjoining suite, where Elmer sprawled, fully clothed, in the center of the bed.

"I feel terrible," Libby whispered, glancing back at the children's room.

"That's just how he wants you to feel."

"I know."

"Here. You're going to need these." Mary Fran held out her hand.

"What—?" Libby began. "Where—?" Gingerly, she accepted the condoms, handling them as if they were rare coins.

"When I picked up Stanley's trousers, they fell out of the pocket."

Libby shook her head. "I guess I have no reason to back out of this now."

"Why would you want to back out?" Mary Fran said. "Or maybe you'd want to trade places?" She indicated the bed. Elmer choked, cleared his throat, snored on. Suddenly, surprising them both, Mary Fran kissed Libby on the mouth. "Now hurry up," she said, "before he thinks you've changed your mind."

In the children's room, Stanley heard her go, heard the door close too quietly behind her. He kept his breathing steady, but Mickey nudged him anyway. "Where do you think she's going?" he said.

Stanley held perfectly still. He didn't feel like talking to Mickey.

"So did you and Spacey, you know, see anything? Over at suite thirty-three?"

Silence.

"How come you guys won't tell us anything?"

Stanley made a sleepy little sound in his throat.

" 'Cuz you didn't see anything," Mickey said. "I bet you didn't even go over there. I bet you were too busy sucking face."

Silence.

"Not that you'd know how."

Stanley listened to the sounds his mother made as she moved around in the adjoining suite. He listened to the soft, wet sound of Sam's breathing. He listened to Mickey's breathing gradually even out, become regular, childlike, serene. Lacey had given him her address. She had said maybe sometime he could come to Nashville with Caleb and April, and he'd said that he would like that.

"Thanks for not telling about the other wedding," she'd said—it was the very last thing she'd said to him—and Stanley had made another invisible X across his chest.

He wasn't sleepy. He couldn't keep still. He slipped out of bed, stood shivering in the chill air. Through the partially open door, he saw his mother sitting on the edge of the covered hot tub. She wore a long, blue nightgown he'd never seen before. Her legs were folded under her. She was staring at the window's flat, empty face. A single light burned somewhere in the room. Stanley wondered what she'd say if he told her about the woman in suite thirty-three. He decided not to risk it.

A slight sound made him glance over at the girls' bed; Margo was

sitting up, looking at him steadily. She didn't seem to be mad anymore. He walked around to her side of the bed, and she lifted the
covers so that he could slip in beside her. When they lay down, she
cupped his cold feet with her warm ones, just like he did for her
when she climbed into his bed at home.

"Did you go to suite thirty-three?" she whispered. Her breath was
sour, familiar, comforting. A wisp of hair tickled his cheek.

"Yeah."

"With Lacey?"

"Yeah."

Margo made room for his head on her pillow.

"There was a woman," Stanley began. Margo waited. "I think she
was dead."

She sniffed, thinking. "Then she's in heaven now," she said.

Stanley tried to imagine the woman in heaven, but all he could
see was the shape in the bed, the shattered lamp, the man and his
tears. He didn't think the woman was in heaven. But that seemed
like a mean thing to say to Margo—even meaner, somehow, than
what he'd said to her during the ceremony—and then Mary Fran's
face appeared at the door. "Shh!" she hissed, without really looking
in. After she'd gone, Margo rolled over, wriggling the sharp points
of her spine into Stanley's stomach.

" 'Night," he whispered after a while, but Margo was already
asleep.

Mary Fran turned out her light, though she didn't get into the
bed. Instead, she returned to the lip of the hot tub, stared at that
dark, empty window. And for the first time in many days she permitted herself to think about the man she'd met at the Knights of
Columbus Halloween fund-raiser, the man she'd been meeting for
coffee ever since—not often, not at first, but more frequently since
the new year. The last time, he'd walked her out to her car, and as

she'd reached for the handle to open the door, he'd placed his hand over hers, a question she did not answer. A question he did not retract. A question she considered now, again, for a long time.

Gradually, as her eyes adjusted, she realized it was snowing once more. How beautiful and wild it was out there. She felt as if she might step through the glass as effortlessly as through clear water, float away into the snow, into a world behind the snow, and never be seen again. But Elmer's snores were tugging at her shoulders, her waist; she felt like a boat, a little dinghy, being reeled in toward a bleak and rocky shore. Direction, she supposed, was better than drift. After a while she yielded to the pull and lay down beside him to wait for sleep.

THE ceiling of Darien Cole's suite was covered by a latticework of jungle greenery, punctuated by hanging clusters of plastic grapes and other, less recognizable fruit. Artificial stones lined the edge of the hot tub, and on the opposite wall, there was a childish mural of an apple tree: brown stick trunk, round wheel of foliage, and in its midst, a single red apple.

"It's supposed to be the Garden of Eden," Darien explained as Libby stepped inside.

"Before or after the Fall?"

They smiled at each other uneasily. When they kissed, their teeth knocked together.

"Sorry," Darien said. He wore new flannel pajamas, the creases still intact, the sort of thing she and the kids might have given Aaron for Father's Day. The top button was unbuttoned, and there was something about the way his hand kept straying there that made her suspect he'd unbuttoned and rebuttoned it, trying to decide which way looked best. He looked different than he had in his well-cut suit, in the ballroom's forgiving light. Smaller, somehow. His hair had less pepper, more salt. She felt ridiculous. He was so much older. They had only just met. Sex was the furthest thing from her mind.

"Your kids give you a bad time?" he asked, sitting down on the bed. It was a king-size bed. You could sleep all night in a bed like that and never bump into the person sleeping with you.

"The oldest sulked a bit." She sat down on the opposite side. The air in the room was scented, damp. She noticed the bathroom mirror was steamed and she realized, with dismay, that he'd taken a shower. Maybe she ought to take one. Only what would she wear when she came out of the bathroom? It would be prudish to put her dress back on. And if the towels were like the ones in her room, they'd be too small to be effective. She wished she'd thought to run back to her room, grab her nightgown—though, considering its condition, she was just as glad she hadn't. And Lord, which pair of underpants was she wearing?

Darien said, "It was a lovely wedding."

"It was fun."

"They looked really happy together."

"They've only known each other three months."

"It's strange, though," Darien said. "What works out and what doesn't. You really can't predict."

"I suppose."

Darien lay down.

Libby lay down.

They listened to each other's unhappy breathing. The grapes loomed above them like small, purple thunderheads. The red apple gleamed in the tree. Who could say how long they might have lain there, motionless, miserable, had they not glanced at each other?

"The Garden of Eden," Darien whispered.

Laughter broke over them both without warning, wave upon wave, fierce as grief. But when the last aftershocks had subsided, they'd managed to land, as if by accident, warm and joyful against each other in the center of the bed.